THE ENDLANDS

VINCENT HOBBES

PRESENTS

THE ENDLANDS

With an Introduction by Nathan Palmer

INCLUDES STORIES BY

Jordan Benoit • Jennifer Chapman • Christina Estabrook • Janelle Garcia

Patrick Greene • Cristin Martin • Nathan Palmer • Jairus Reddy

David Stubblefield • Craig Wessel • Tamara Wilhite

Hobbes End Publishing, LLC

Vincent Hobbes Presents: The Endlands
Published by Hobbes End Publishing, LLC, a division of Hobbes End Entertainment, LLC

1st Printing
Hobbes End Publishing: trade paperback, 2010
Printed in the United States of America

Vincent Hobbes Presents: The Endlands
All rights reserved.
Copyright 2010, Hobbes End Entertainment, LLC

ISBN:
978-0-9763510-4-7

Cover design and internal design: Jordan Benoit

The sale of this book without its cover is unauthorized. If you purchased this book without a cover, you should be aware that it was reported to the publisher as "unsold and destroyed." Neither the author nor the publisher has received payment for the sale of the "stripped book."

This product is a work of fiction. Names, characters, places and incidents are either the product of the authors' imagination or used fictitiously. Any resemblance to actual events or locales or persons, living or dead, is entirely coincidental.

Without limiting the rights under copyright reserved above, no part of this publication may be reproduced, stored in or introduced into a retrieval system, or transmitted, in any form, or by any means (electronic, mechanical, photocopying, recording, or otherwise), without written, express permission from Hobbes End Entertainment, LLC. The scanning, uploading, and distribution of this book via the Internet or via any other means without the permission of the publisher is illegal and punishable by law. Please purchase only authorized electronic editions, and do not participate in or encourage electronic piracy of copyrighted materials. Your support of the authors' rights is appreciated.

Vincent Hobbes Presents: The Endlands is the sole property of Hobbes End. All artwork, cover, and characters are exclusively owned and licensed by Hobbes End Entertainment, LLC and Hobbes End Publishing, LLC accordingly. All rights reserved to Hobbes End Entertainment, LLC. This includes the right o reproduce this book or portions thereof in any form whatsoever.

For information, contact:
Hobbes End Entertainment, LLC
PO Box 193
Aubrey, TX 76227
www.hobbesendpublishing.com

Table of Contents

	Introduction	Nathan Palmer	11
1	Room 422	Patrick Greene	25
2	A Night in Polidoria	Cristin Martin	43
3	Flying Fish	David Stubblefield	61
4	Limbo, Population 458	Vincent Hobbes	75
5	Finders Keepers	Janelle Garcia	89
6	Loose Ends	Craig Wessel	95
7	To Read or Not to Read	Vincent Hobbes	101
8	Phases of Normal	Tamara Wilhite	123
9	Propaganda	Nathan Palmer	143
10	King of the Jungle	Jordan Benoit	153
11	The Hour of the Time	Vincent Hobbes	173
12	Thanksgiving	Jairus Reddy	189
13	Into the Small Hours	Patrick Greene	207
14	The Dragon of Delinar	Vincent Hobbes	217
15	The Best BBQ on the Interstate	Jennifer Chapman	235
16	Glass Prison	Christina Estabrook	265
17	THEY	Vincent Hobbes	293

I would like to thank the following:

My family and friends for their continued support—especially my Mother, who always encouraged me to be creative.

Jordan Benoit for his wonderful design work and late night editorial madness.

My publisher, Jairus Reddy. Without him, my work would remain unpublished. I am eternally grateful.

Nathan Palmer, for sticking by my side, and for making my writing better.

I'd also like to thank my best friend, Chad—because being friends with him is always an adventure.

I would especially like to thank the writers who made this project possible. I am honored to be published alongside them.

And finally, to my beautiful wife, for so delicately handling my insanity. Thank you for everything.

– Vincent

This book is dedicated to Rod Serling

Introduction

Dear Reader,

Over the course of human history, short stories have always been told. Even cave drawings of our earliest ancestors show signs of ancient tales. The Vikings told sagas, speaking of mythical creatures that lurk in the unknown. Ancient mythology gave us stories of heroes and villains, and great tragedies. Over time, as human imagination progressed, tales and fables, myths and legends became more common, and were recorded, recounted over generations. Every culture has its own version of a story, and anything that can breed imagination is susceptible to becoming one. And that tale *must* be told.

The unknown pulls at our innermost thoughts and feelings. Without the unknown, these tales, these sagas, would never have come to light. People fear the unknown, and yet it is a place of endless possibilities. It is a place deep within us all; it speaks to us at night, and although you may not be able to hear the words, it is always there—creeping, crawling, slithering. The unknown lets us know just how small we are, and we remain far from the shadows

Vincent Hobbes Presents

because of it. It causes us to fear what could be around the corner, or down in the basement. Without these feelings, we would be void of emotion, because fear is learned, and if we had never heard stories that scared us, we wouldn't know what fear is.

Once upon a time long since forgotten, the world knew true fear. It was a genre known as horror, and for a long time it captivated us. Great literary works came from this genre. Yet, as time went on, and as society changed, the human mind became numb to the shriek in the night—the classic short story.

We crave more. We yearn for the most shocking things we can find. The more bodies, the better. The more blood, the better. Sadly, this is where we've arrived.

In this project, the short story reigns. There is no map, there is no way out. *The Endlands* is not just a book, but also a place within us all. A place that brings us back to our childhood fears. It's the clicking in the night and the scratching at your door. It's the unknown, and although we think we know it all as we grow older, truth is, we know nothing. We still try to ignore those sounds we cannot explain. We still tuck our heads under the sheets for safety. We're trapped here, lost in another dimension. So embrace your fear, and hope you will be allowed to return.

I know for a fact, that Mr. Hobbes' greatest influence for this project is the late Rod Serling. He's told me many times he hopes to pay homage to one of the greatest creative minds of modern fiction. The imagination of Mr. Serling, and the creativity of *The Twilight Zone*, should be an inspiration to us all. Mr. Serling could have gone a different way, but didn't. He didn't count on gore or high body counts. He realized that is not true horror. Not true fear. Not reality.

This book reminds me of *The Twilight Zone*, and it has been a great honor working alongside Mr. Hobbes for this project. Personally, I see the same qualities in Vincent as Rod Serling possessed. He is dedicated to the 'strange tale', and he has an odd humor about him that I enjoy. I have had the honor of reading other works of his, some which perhaps will never see the light of day. That said, I can say without a doubt, Mr. Hobbes has a love for storytelling—a love for fear—and he has turned it into something to which we can all relate, and embrace.

I am beyond happy to be part of this project, and I'm proud of all the authors included. Each story has its own twist and turn, all weird and kooky in their own right.

Dear reader, embrace these short stories, because each is a piece of that author's imagination—a piece of the fear they have each embraced—all with their own place in *The Endlands*.

– Nathan Palmer

DO YOU BELIEVE
IN THE
UNBELIEVABLE?

ARE YOU READY TO FACE THE DARKEST CORNERS OF YOUR IMAGINATION?

Then turn on a light, just enough to see.

AND . . .

Welcome to the Endlands

Room 422

BY
PATRICK GREENE

National Finance, the magazine Phillip Troyer held, might as well have been written in Ancient Hebrew.

Upon learning of his wife's pregnancy, Phillip had made a resolution to become more financially savvy. Sitting in the hospital waiting room, alone but for his regrets and ponderings, Phillip reached the conclusion that he had neither the patience nor intelligence to venture into that mundane territory. He dropped the magazine on the table beside him and perused the other choices. *Sports Illustrated, U.S. News & World Report, Reader's Digest, Craft Showcase*. S.I. featured pitifully little coverage of boxing these days, and the others promised only boredom.

Four nurses wearing expressions of the same incapacitating boredom joked among themselves in the nurse's station nearby.

He checked his watch: 2:14 A.M. The impetus to pay an obligatory visit to Charlotte in the delivery room weighed upon him, but the presence of his mother-in-law, Regina, surely listing his shortcomings even at this moment, gave him a reason to put it off a while longer.

On the muted television that hung from the wall nearby, a news network continued its unending broadcast vigil. The prim and pretty Asian reporter recited a story about a series of high school murders in Virginia.

An odd rhythm, like someone walking in fishing waders, caught his attention. It belonged to a well-dressed, balding man, forty or so, who approached the waiting area at a brisk pace. The man walked with an awkward gait, allowing his smooth-soled shoes to drag on the carpet. He wore a distant, blissful expression, which Phillip suddenly felt obliged to wear as well. The man turned into the waiting area and deposited himself across from Phillip, but quickly rose again, extending his hand.

"Name's Conagher."

Though Conagher was a little too close to his personal space, Phillip shook the man's hand and returned the greeting.

"You gonna be a daddy?" Conagher asked.

"Yeah."

"Same here! Congratulations!"

This apparently called for another lively handshake. Phillip's hand, still sore from working the heavy bag earlier, felt small within the folds of Conagher's long-fingered, spidery grasp.

"Thanks, same to you."

Conagher rocked back on his heels comically. "Yep. Just waiting on Doctor Borland. Who's your doc, Phillip?"

"Pope. Doctor Pope."

"Good man, I hear." Conagher plopped into the chair once more. "You look nervous if you don't mind me saying so."

"Yeah, a little. This was kind of a surprise. We . . . thought we were, you know, covered."

Conagher waved a dismissive hand. "You'll love it. Got another one at home." Conagher could have been talking about a jet ski or foosball table.

"Sure. It's just . . ." Phillip laughed uncomfortably before finishing, ". . . money's a little tight."

"Oh? What do you do?"

Phillip always hated that simple question. "I'm a boxer. But I work part-time in a print shop."

"Boxer, huh? Like a fighter? You good?"

"I do all right." Phillip hoped he had ridden the wispy line between modest and confident. But there was none of the expected judgment in Conagher's eyes.

"*Hm.* I'm in accounting. Do pretty good, if I say so myself. You go to church, Phillip?"

"No. Not in years."

"The wife and I, we coach young couples in our church. Maybe you can come out sometime."

Phillip offered no response, though he was sure that Conagher would not allow any awkward silence in the conversation. The loud man was indeed about to speak again, when Doctor Pope appeared, regarding Phillip with earnest, alert eyes set within youthful features. Phillip rose to shake hands.

"Phillip," Doctor Pope nodded to Conagher but deftly returned his attention to Phillip before Conagher could initiate a conversation. "I'm on my way in. You joining us?"

"No, I don't think so," Phillip responded, a bit miffed that Pope had brought it up. He had made his feelings clear repeatedly.

Conagher interjected. "Not gonna watch? Why not?"

"I just don't think I could handle seeing Charlotte go through that."

Conagher found this eminently amusing. "Squeamish, huh? I was like that the first time. Everything will be fine. I was hearing on the news the other day that the percentage of pregnancies successfully reaching full term has come way up in the last few months. The baby will be just fine."

Doctor Pope turned to Phillip with trademark earnestness. "Your friend is right. You sure you don't want to be there? It's quite a moment."

Phillip wasn't sure he was comfortable having Conagher referred to as his friend.

"I'm just not good with blood and stuff."

Conagher could not resist an observation: "Hey, that's something. A boxer who's squeamish."

Pope nodded. "Tell the nurse if you change your mind."

"I will."

Doctor Pope's pretty nurse, known to Phillip only as Jeanette, turned the corner and offered a polite smile. A pang of guilt surfaced, as Phillip remembered the intense sexual attraction he had felt toward her when they first met at Doctor Pope's office. Jeanette touched Doctor Pope's arm in a way that made Phillip feel a bit jealous, or at least envious.

Turning to Phillip, she said, "Mister Troyer, I thought I'd let you know, your wife has decided to go with an epidural."

"Oh . . . I thought she wanted to go natural."

"She's changed her mind."

Phillip was not surprised to see Conagher staring directly at Jeanette's ass with no attempt at discretion whatsoever.

"Well, alright. Thanks."

Doctor Pope said goodbye and walked away with Jeanette, leaving Phillip uncomfortable in the presence of Conagher.

"You look worried," Conagher offered.

Phillip rubbed his stubbly chin, deciding whether to share any more of his personal life. "The expenses just keep adding up."

"Better get used to it. Doesn't get any cheaper, buddy."

For the next few minutes, Phillip listened intermittently as Conagher discoursed about tax deductions, annuities, savings bonds and the like, all of which sounded something like static to Phillip. Catching Conagher between breaths, Phillip excused himself to check on Charlotte.

The hallway was a never ending circle. Each door varied from the others only by its decorations; a variety of balloons and cards taped around the entrance. Phillip walked through the open door to Room 422.

Charlotte breathed deeply, wearing a determined expression. Charlotte's mother, Regina, held her left hand. Charlotte offered Phillip an optimistic smile in sharp contrast to Regina's judgmental and disappointed glower. Charlotte was also attended by the fine Nurse Jeanette and another, neither of which appeared to have been converted to anti-Phillipism by Regina.

"Hi Cutie," Phillip said, avoiding eye contact with the elder woman.

"Hey Baby."

"How ya feeling?"

"Ready to have a baby. Contractions are coming every

two minutes now. You?"

"Guess I'm nervous... So you decided to take the drug?" he ventured.

Not surprisingly, it was Regina who answered. "I felt it was for the best. Surely you don't want her to suffer needlessly."

Phillip studied her. Every bit of the accusation and contempt he heard in her voice was evident in her face. "Sure, that's good, yeah." Turning back to Charlotte: "I just wanted to make sure you're okay."

Charlotte smiled again. "You're sweet, as always." Phillip knew that this statement was primarily aimed at her mother, and that was just fine. Regina wasn't going to become president of his fan club any time soon, but his stock would surely rise, once she saw what a good father and husband he became. And while he told himself he held little regard for how Regina felt about him, it would be nice to have her let up just a little.

"Not to be rude, Phillip dear. If you're not going to stay for the birth, perhaps you should leave now." Regina sang politely, letting her intended condescension show in her expression.

Charlotte turned to her, face flushed with embarrassment.

"Mother!"

"It's disruptive. You need... stability now."

Phillip felt tense. "She's probably right, Charlotte. I'll check back in a while."

"Okay. Love you."

"Love you back."

The Endlands

In the hall, Phillip slowed to listen a moment, wondering if they would talk about him. Regina did not disappoint. "Have you spoken to him about getting a better job?" She asked, to which Charlotte replied, "We'll be fine, Mom. Please don't do this right now."

Regina pressed on. "This prize fighting thing is fine for twenty year-olds. He's thirty-three. It's time to move on."

"No more Mother, please. This is what's disruptive."

"I'm sorry. You'd like it better if I didn't care, I suppose."

Phillip didn't stay to hear more.

The package of crackers created a thunderous echo as it fell to the vending machine's paid zone. Phillip removed it and strained against the plastic. It was not giving up its protective duties easily, but Phillip would not use his teeth to rip the package. For him, this was a point of pride. He would grapple with the packaging and beat it cleanly.

The wrapper held firm. Phillip searched it for a weak spot, a place where his fingers could penetrate. No, he would not use his teeth. He would succeed the hard way. He had once hoped this philosophy would bring him the World's Cruiserweight Championship, but that aspiration was becoming vaguer by the day, and the tiny package represented a vestige of that dream.

Absently continuing his steady assault on the plastic, he turned his attention to the emergency room next to the vending area. There, sat several small pockets of misery. Bleeding, bandaged, or suffering in some way not visible to Phillip, they all shared a certain resignation, disturbing in its uniformity.

Vincent Hobbes Presents

The sound of a diesel engine and a steady beeping caught Phillip's notice. He looked out the window to see an ambulance backing toward the ER's receiving area. The rubbernecker in him demanded an investigation, so he found himself walking outside to see just what would emerge.

Phillip fiddled overtly with the package, painting himself as just a guy taking a snack break in the fresh air that was, in fact, not so fresh, thanks to the heavy diesel fumes. The back doors swung open, and several EMTs and a policeman gathered around, as the gurney wheels dropped. Its passenger was a young woman, around twenty though it was difficult to tell, what with all the heavy bruises and contusions. Her right eye was swollen nearly shut; a tennis ball-sized knot had grown all around it. Her lips were similarly bloated, with a fresh black scab caked around a split near the center of her upper lip.

As her good eye found Phillip's gaze, a tear streamed down the side of her face, disappearing into her black hair. Suddenly feeling like a voyeur, Phillip turned away and took a seat at the scarred bench against the wall. The gurney and its entourage disappeared into the swinging doors, and Phillip regarded the cracker package for a while, absolved for the moment, of his hunger.

Soon, one of the EMTs reappeared, accompanied by the cop. The tech lit a cigarette while the cop sloshed coffee from a Styrofoam cup as they stood at the edge of the walkway some ten feet from Phillip, staring at the city before them.

"She said she fell off a ladder trying to change a light bulb. Her boyfriend just stood there, kind of smirking while we loaded her. Even chuckled at her clumsiness. We get in the ambulance, and right away Pam starts pushing her to tell the truth about what happened. The woman finally comes clean, says her boyfriend roughed her up for taking some of his money," the EMT explained.

With a nod, the cop replied, "That explains why she didn't want to talk to me. She's damn sure not going to press charges."

"Of course not. Hell, he's her dealer. It was his profits she stole!"

The cop raised his coffee cup in a mock toast. "White trash soap opera."

"You know what makes it worse?" continued the EMT. "She's three months pregnant."

Phillip felt a surge of righteous anger, not only toward the unseen battering boyfriend, but also toward the girl, and the calloused civil servants as well. The cop tossed out a final remark. "No shit. That'll be another little low-life to make my job harder one day. If the dad doesn't kill him first."

The cop returned to the hospital, having never sipped from his coffee. After a final drag, the EMT joined him. Now alone, but for the traffic just yards away, Phillip tore open the plastic wrapper with a feral snap.

Phillip polished off the last of the crackers and sat alone in the February chill for a while, trying to push back the gnawing feeling that he was trapped, missing his prime, and getting broker by the day. He rose and made for the elevator, again passing through the holding area of the ER. On the television that presided over the room, the eternal newscast continued. A field reporter spoke through a garbled satellite connection, while images of turbaned soldiers doing battle in a desert city street flashed. The caption underneath read: *"Treaty Violations Lead To Unrest"*.

The elevator ride would be the last shred of solitude for Phillip. The doors slid open to a far different atmosphere than when he had left some twenty minutes ago.

A harried orderly ran by, nearly colliding with him en route to the stairwell. At the nurse's station, two nurses stood close together, sharing a look of bewildered horror, speaking in hushed tones.

Seeing Phillip, they averted their eyes.

An uneasy feeling washed over him, pushing him faster toward Charlotte and Room 422. Rounding and rounding the unending corner, he passed through clusters of urgency and confusion. Nurses, doctors, and security personnel jockeyed and shuffled, jostling him without so much as a glance. This was a good sign, wasn't it? That something was wrong besides . . .

From Room 422, Nurse Jeanette appeared and looked down the hall with wild eyes. She saw Phillip and quickly withdrew. A rangy security guard stepped out and met Phillip's panicked gaze, setting himself authoritatively. Phillip's brisk stride had become a run, just as the security guard met him head-on, catching him by the arms.

"Hold on, buddy," said the guard.

Then Charlotte uttered a shrill scream that shook Phillip to his soul.

Phillip pushed forward. "What are you doing? What's wrong with my wife?"

"Just a minute." The guard's tone was more menacing than soothing. Phillip was becoming quite strident, ready in fact, to misuse his pugilistic skills, when Doctor Pope appeared in the doorway, looking stunned.

"It's alright. Let him come in."

Phillip didn't like the breathless sound of Pope's voice. He shoved past the guard and entered Room 422.

Charlotte was crying, her face squinched in a brand of distress that could only be maternal. Jeanette held her right hand, Regina the left. Phillip rushed to Charlotte, searching her contorted face, fearing and anticipating a miscarriage. He also felt a deep and selfish little part of him hoping for it—and quickly squashed that.

"What is it? What's wrong, honey?"

"The baby..." Charlotte began, crying fresh tears, before covering her mouth with trembling hands.

"Something's wrong with the baby? What is it?"

They remained maddeningly silent, offering only sorrow and fear in their countenances. Doctor Pope took Phillip aside to the far corner, where he searched for articulation.

"I'm sorry."

"The baby's... dead?"

"... No. No, not that."

"Well?"

"It's... not normal."

"What do you mean? You said everything was fine..."

Pope seemed to be suppressing a shiver. His professional veneer was showing cracks. "I know, and it was. I thought. I don't know what happened." He stared into Phillip's chest.

"Has... Charlotte been exposed to anything unusual in the last few days?"

Phillip drew a blank. "Like what? What are you getting

at?"

"I DON'T KNOW! It's just not normal. That's all I can tell you. We've had it and the others removed to an isolated room for examination. I've put in a call to a colleague of mine."

"Wait a minute... What do you mean, 'it'? What others? What the hell is going on?"

Phillip had gotten past any fear of a stillbirth. It was fear of the unknown that now held reign. Pope continued to avoid Phillip's gaze.

"Please bring back my baby," Interjected Charlotte softly. "I just want my baby."

Regina stroked her daughter's hair. "Don't do this to yourself, dear."

Pope just looked at her, helpless. "I'm sorry, Mrs. Troyer..."

"I WANT MY BABEEEE!!"

The outburst, so unlike Charlotte, startled everyone in the room. Phillip turned Pope around and stood close, staring into the smaller man's eyes.

"Just bring the baby. I want to see it."

"I'm afraid I can't do that."

Phillip's patience was spent. Grabbing Pope by the collar of his surgical gown, he shook him.

"BRING OUR BABY IN HERE, NOW!"

Pope, still wearing the stunned expression, seemed to be only mildly frightened by Phillip's gruff insistence. Something else had shaken him far worse.

"Alright. Alright. You'd best prepare yourself. Jeanette. Bring the... child."

Phillip released Pope and went to Charlotte, his mind racing with dreadful possibilities. "Are you in pain?"

"I just don't understand. I did everything right. How could this . . . ?" She hitched with a sudden sob.

"Tell me what's wrong with it?" Phillip ventured again.

"What's wrong with it!" Regina broke in. "It's not human. I don't know WHAT it is. This is God's punishment, Phillip. For the way you live your life."

"Mother. Shut! UP!" Charlotte startled the room again, nearly lunging off the bed in her sudden rage.

Pope stepped forward. "Stop it, please!" he pleaded.

He turned to the door, drawing everyone's attention to Jeanette. She stood in the doorway with the tiny bundled figure, holding it away from her a few inches.

"Come on in, Jeanette."

She walked to Charlotte and handed her the bundle. Charlotte's look of terror and confusion had vanished, replaced by a loving smile and the bliss of new motherhood. Regina looked at the baby a moment, and then broke into desperate weeping as she slowly backed away from it. Charlotte did not acknowledge this, instead turning the tiny being toward Phillip for his first look.

Phillip had returned to the waiting room, staring in stupefied silence at the floor while countless doctors, nurses, and orderlies trotted past him. He was for the moment oblivious to the rush, the madness that was overtaking the hospital moment by moment.

Whatever perception Phillip held of reality had been washed clean. He had entered room 422 with a set of values

Vincent Hobbes Presents

and beliefs, and had left with only a vague memory of those absurdities. Another world had slipped in over the one he knew, and was quickly erasing the original, familiar planet Earth, and with it, all sense of order.

Yet, Phillip sensed there was a greater order taking shape.

Hearing a familiar clumsy shuffle, he raised his head to see Conagher ambling down the hall. This was not the garrulous capitalist who had engaged him in awkward small talk an hour ago. Conagher now wore the shell-shocked expression that was becoming the order of the day and was talking to himself in low tones. Phillip stood and intercepted him gently.

"Conagher. How's your wife?"

Conagher seemed to be staring through him, struggling to focus. "My wife?"

"Did she deliver?" Phillip asked.

"Deliver? Yeah. She delivered. But not a baby."

Phillip felt the numb terror again.

"I . . . I don't know what it is. I've never seen anything like it." Conagher's voice sounded odd, detached.

"You too," Phillip stated.

Phillip let go of Conagher's arm, and the gangly accountant continued his aimless trek, like a wind-up robot. Phillip watched his progress for a moment before his attention was drawn to the sudden drone of the Asian newscaster on television. One of the nurses had turned up the volume. Two, and soon four of her co-workers joined her in front of the set, folding their arms in front of them as if to be protected from the report that frightened and fascinated them.

". . . Number of reports are surfacing from hundreds of

sources around the world that newborn babies appear to be radically abnormal. Since these reports initially broke, not one of several thousand new babies has come out of the womb without these, quote, bizarre-yet-symmetrical deformities, to use the words of one doctor. No photos or images of the children are being released at this time, and few details have surfaced. However, an Arizona doctor has reportedly stated, "It's like an all new species." We hope to have more on this astonishing story in a few minutes."

Phillip stared at the image of the Asian woman, feeling anything but relief that he shared this circumstance with apparently every other new parent in the known world. The nurses chattered in confusion among themselves.

From down the hall, a female voice cried out. Phillip swallowed, tasting a vague, acrid mix of crackers and bile. As he started back toward Room 422, he found Doctor Pope standing at the nurse's station, alone, rubbing his left temple.

"What's this mean, Doctor? Tell me why this is happening," Phillip asked.

Pope squinted at Phillip, saying nothing for a long moment. He looked down at a chart, then back to Phillip. "I can't tell you, exactly. You'll find out for yourself soon enough."

"Are you hiding something?" Phillip asked.

"No."

"Why not say it?"

Pope pondered a moment. "I have an associate who's a psychologist. He's had several patients who were mothers-to-be. They came to him independently of each other, worried about dreams they'd had." Pope aimed the remote at the mounted television and turned it off. Phillip noticed his hands were shaking, despite his calm and measured voice. "Sweeping, vivid dreams, that humanity was being pushed aside by some growing, unseen force. They all felt vaguely complicit somehow. Traitorous, yet just as doomed as everyone else."

Pope finally looked directly at Phillip. "How's Charlotte been sleeping?"

Phillip knew his voice would come out strained and desperate. "This is crazy."

"Crazy. What's crazy is that we've lasted this long. God, or whatever, has finally come up with a better idea."

Phillip wanted to believe that Pope had just cracked under the strain. But a growing part of him knew that he hadn't.

"We've run out of time," Pope finished.

Phillip had a sudden and profound need to return his world to normal, at any cost. He started down the hall at a quick pace, turning long enough to say, "I'm going to stop this."

"Oh really? How?" Pope asked with resigned sarcasm.

Phillip did not answer.

"It's pointless, Phillip. There's no stopping it now. Face it. We've had our shot."

Phillip turned and fired a baleful stare at the doctor, who offered nothing further.

In Room 422, Phillip found Charlotte still holding their progeny amid an unnatural quiet. Regina was standing back from the bed as though she was an attending servant, a role Phillip could not have imagined her playing. Her expression was serene, another incongruity. Jeanette quietly crossed the room in her practiced task of tidying.

Charlotte looked up from the baby for a second to cast a contented smile at Phillip. "It's beautiful," she said.

They're still saying 'it', Phillip thought, as he searched the room for an improvised noose.

His gaze fell on a cloth surgical mask. Taking it, he wrapped it once around his fist and pulled it taut with the other hand, holding it low as he advanced on the child he knew he must murder. Regina continued to stare into space, while Charlotte calmly turned the child to face Phillip.

Phillip stopped in his tracks. The surgical mask slipped from his hand.

He clamped hands against his temples, feeling movement inside his skull, as though a skittering but purposed rodent had just burrowed inside. The initial shock was painful, but after a moment, it seemed natural. Phillip's secret sins were found and examined, much to his embarrassment.

Under his child's influence, these transgressions were reduced to simple evidence of flawed conditioning. Phillip was allowed to draw the same conclusion that Pope, Charlotte, Regina, Jeanette and doubtlessly many others had reached.

He allowed the intrusion, feeling he no longer had a right to fight it.

The baby's large black eyes, analytical pools of obsidian capable, Phillip sensed, of seeing far beyond the normal human spectrum, made Phillip feel like *he* was the child, amusing in his deluded self-importance. Its pointed, bat-like ears cocked minutely toward every tiny noise in the room, and seemingly beyond. Its tiny fingers flexed and fisted; more dexterous and nimble than Phillip could ever hope to be.

Vincent Hobbes Presents

Other than these features, the child might have been human. Its 'mutations' were actually vast improvements.

It raised itself from Charlotte to lean toward Phillip; apparently fascinated by his dysfunction, his weakness disguised behind the parody of strength.

Regina walked out of the room as Phillip took several slow steps toward the baby, seeing it now as not something alien, or ugly, or beautiful, but just superior.

Phillip felt very tired, very drained, and quite obsolete. The baby's gaze followed Phillip as he sat down at the chair beside the window and took a long final look at a polluted world of blaring sirens, abused drug addicts, religious assassins and flaming trash barrels.

A Night in Polidoria

By Cristin Martin

The city of Polidoria was different from most cities. The houses there consisted of windows with silver bars melded into the shape of a cross. The nails used to construct these homes weren't made of steel like most nails; Polidoria was unique for manufacturing nails of pure silver. There was a silversmith on every block. Lampposts were all over; the brightness spilling from them was blinding. Of course, every light was switched on the moment the sun set. No one ever slept with the lights off—they didn't dare. A crucifix hung in every room of every house. Bottles of holy water were stored in the cupboards and sharp wooden stakes hid underneath seat cushions. Meals were eaten with cloves of garlic, the food always blessed by a priest. And every night, at five o'clock, when the sirens went off, the people automatically evacuated the streets and took refuge.

Diana Nedderman had grown familiar with the rules of her city and accepted them like everyone else. In her seventeen years, Diana had never been allowed to leave the house at night.

She was an ordinary girl, realistically average, and so was her boyfriend. His name was Lowell, and he was new in town. Had Diana been brought up in any other city, the teenage couple would have gone to the movies or dances. But Diana knew the rules. She hated them because they isolated her from truly living, but she knew they existed for her own safety. Better an isolated life than no life.

But Lowell was an amateur to the Polidorian way of life. He did not understand. They had dated for only a few months. During those months, Lowell often attempted to coax Diana out of the house at night, and more than once told her how silly it was to believe in such hocus pocus.

"You can't spend your entire life being afraid," Lowell would whisper as he kissed her. "You have nothing to fear. I'll protect you." He would kiss her again, always harder the second time.

But Diana would only smile and blush, then wisely shake her head 'no'.

Tonight was like every night. When the sirens rang, Diana threw a final glance at the sun. She had to go indoors. Diana made her way toward the house and was about to shut the door when she stopped suddenly. Mr. Walpole, another neighbor of hers, was still in his yard, whistling. It was as if he was oblivious of the darkening sky. Behavior like that wasn't right. It wasn't normal. Diana lingered at the door, curiously watching him. Her fingers involuntarily flew up to her neck as she felt the heavy silver locket given to her at birth. As a baby, it had dangled protectively above the cradle. Now, she always wore it around her neck. Tonight, as she eyed Mr. Walpole, she was grateful she owned such a powerful talisman.

Mr. Walpole's appearance was rough, the type of look she expected one of *them* to have. Tall and powerfully built for

The Endlands

his age, Mr. Walpole's features were craggy, his hair disheveled with bulging, wild eyes. She hung back long enough for Mr. Walpole to notice her. He returned her gaze with a demented smile. With an unpleasant jolt, Diana slammed the door and bolted it.

Diana was alone. She was unaccustomed to being home without her parents. Mr. and Mrs. Nedderman had gone to visit an old friend of the family. Poor Mrs. Lycan. The old widow had turned reclusive after her husband's grisly slaughter. Visits always gave the poor woman a little bit of cheer. *Mom and Dad must have lost track of time*, Diana told herself with a childish stubbornness, refusing to think otherwise. No matter. They were safe, and so was she. The rules of safety had been drilled into her for so long that they were second nature.

"For God's sake, let me in!" The cry was followed by a frenzy of knocks against the front door. "For the love of God, let me in!"

Diana peered through the peephole. It was Lowell Chaney, standing on the front porch. She opened the door at once; he stumbled through the doorway.

"What are you doing here?" she scolded, shutting the door behind her and bolting it again. "You're lucky it's still light out, you stupid jerk!"

"I know, I know!" said Lowell. "I got a flat tire, and my folks are gone. I couldn't get in—I lost my key. I had no where else to go."

"Oh?" said Diana, grinning wryly. "Not so brave now, are you?" She realized that she was making light of the situation and added quickly, "What you did was stupid, forgetting your key. You should always be on your guard—otherwise you'd be *dead*!"

"I don't mind being by myself," he retorted irritably. "But I heard something—"

"Strange noises are nothing to be alarmed at." Diana interrupted.

"But it was close by."

"What was it?"

"Dunno. But it sounded freaky, like a cat getting its tail stepped on, only worse." He gulped. "Didn't you hear it?"

"No, but you should be grateful that weird sounds are the least of your troubles. Don't you ever check out the lunar calendar? There's a full moon tonight!"

"I didn't know that."

Lowell—poor, naïve, unsuspecting Lowell—looked terribly pale, and his blonde hair was drenched with sweat. He was twitchy; whatever he heard must have given him a good scare. Lowell went out of his way to avoid walking past the barred window, as if afraid someone outside was glimpsing in. He also edged nervously away from the walls before collapsing onto the sofa. Diana had to suppress a sneering laugh—*this* was her mighty protector sitting here. But truthfully, she was relieved to see him. It gave her some comfort to know that Lowell was safe inside her home, and she was grateful that she was no longer alone. She eyed Lowell, and her amusement softened into a genuine concern. He looked sickly, clammy, and unstable.

Diana's hand dipped in her pocket.

"Here," she muttered, placing a small clove inside his open palm as she kissed him. "Eat some of this. It will protect you."

Lowell didn't bother looking at what she had given him. He swallowed it and made a face. "What the hell was that?"

"Garlic."

"It's disgusting!"

Diana grinned. "It's an acquired taste."

She ambled towards the fireplace mantel where the family trinkets were kept and found a silver-plated chain that had belonged to her grandfather. "You should wear this, too, you know. Everyone wears them." Diana reached up and lifted her own pendant, turning it this way and that so it could catch the light. She flaunted her wrist; the charm bracelet she wore gave a jingle.

Lowell sneered. "Dammit! It's bad enough you had me eating garlic. Now you want me to wear a necklace?"

"It's simply a precaution," Diana tried to explain.

"Precaution, my ass! I don't believe in these fairytales, and you people are stupid for accepting them." Diana's fierce anger must have shown because Lowell said quickly, "Look, these rules and traditions . . . It's so much . . ."

"I know," she said reluctantly. "But it's all true."

"If it's true, then why do you still live here?" Lowell questioned. He suddenly began to choke violently.

"Do you need anything to drink?" Diana asked, her anger softening into concern. "Soda? Juice? A glass of water?"

"Water, thanks."

"What about a snack? Do you want anything to eat?"

"Later, but not now."

"Okay."

Diana disappeared into the kitchen to get them drinks.

Vincent Hobbes Presents

Moments later, she returned holding a glass of ice water in one hand and a can of soda in the other. She handed Lowell his drink before settling once again on the couch.

"So why do you live here?" Lowell choked out after he had taken a long swig.

Diana shrugged her shoulders, "Why do people continue to live in places that have earthquakes? Why do people live where tornados are common?"

She frowned. Lowell was wheezing rather loudly now. "Are you sure you're alright?" Diana saw that hives had erupted over Lowell's face and arms. "Lowell? Are you alright?"

"Fresh air," he gasped. "I need fresh air. Now."

"But, it's almost dark out . . ." Diana said. There was now a pleading tone in her voice, and she wrung her hands together, slowly regressing into a frightened child. She did not know which unnerved her more: Lowell's worsening illness or the idea of venturing outside.

"Diana, please."

She looked at his peaked face. The red spots stood out vividly, like droplets of wine soiling a piece of linen. She nodded, putting fear aside for the first time in seventeen years.

Diana helped him out of his seat, slinging his arm around her neck and supporting him as best she could as she guided him outside. The evening air did wonders. At once, Lowell recovered from all ailments. Color returned to his face; the hives went away, leaving behind only a small trace of the rash on his skin. Lowell straightened up, beaming at her. In return Diana breathed a sigh of relief.

"So I finally got you out at last," he said brightly, moving forward and clasping her waist. "I've been trying to find a way to lure you out of your sanctuary," he added and kissed her.

"Very funny," Diana said with mock annoyance while she playfully removed herself from his grasp. "Now that you've miraculously healed, let's go back inside. I have a bad feeling about being out like this, Lowell. It's our neighbor, Mr. Walpole. I fear that he might be one of *them*."

"Walpole? That old asshole is nothing to be scared of."

"You don't know him like I do," said Diana, her smile fading a little. "We really shouldn't be out here, especially tonight. Look," she pointed to the sky. "The sun is setting."

He grinned. "It's too late now."

"Come on, let's go," she pleaded, tugging at Lowell's arm. "We can stay in the kitchen. I'll unlatch the window and open it a bit for you."

Lowell didn't budge.

"I've been watching you for some time now," he said. "My parents—and I must say that I agree with them—said you'd make a tasty dish with your tender, young flesh. Enough to fulfill any appetite. They've been saying that since we moved here."

"Stop it!"

"This place is great. It's a perfect place for my parents and I to be with more of our own kind. The only hassle is those damn superstitions of people like you. No matter. It just takes some brains to overcome those obstacles."

"You're making fun of me again," she said angrily. "It's just a joke to you, isn't it?"

"Not at all. I take it seriously."

"I'm warning you," said Diana. "Keep it up, and I will go

Vincent Hobbes Presents

back inside without you and lock the door behind me!"

"Why do you think I was so sick inside your house?" He did not wait for an answer. "It's that damn silver you people have inside your walls. I couldn't have my meal with those toxins contaminating me. You know my yarn about the flat tire, losing the house key, hearing strange noises—? All a bluff."

Lowell glanced at the sky.

"Any minute now," he said. "Doesn't happen until it is fully dark."

"SHUT UP!" Diana screamed. "Just keep your stupid mouth shut!" She brushed past Lowell angrily and tried to open the door. It didn't open. She pulled, harder this time. The door was locked.

Diana involuntarily lifted her hands to her neck. Her amulet, the silver locket, was missing. Slowly, she turned and faced Lowell.

"Noticed at last, huh?" he jeered. "How do you think this happened?" He presented a raw and blistered hand.

Diana blanched. "What are you saying?"

"I unclasped your little good luck charm as you were helping me outside," Lowell said simply, studying his burnt hand. "The touch of silver has that effect on me when I'm in my human form, and would have killed me once I transformed into my *other* state, *my true form*. We can't have that, now can we? It will spoil the feast I've been looking forward to. You know," he said as an afterthought. "Every time I kissed you, my mouth watered."

As he spoke, the sun disappeared over the horizon.

No, Diana prayed. *Not this. Not Lowell. Don't let him be one of them...*

Her insides wrenched violently as she watched blonde hair sprout from Lowell's skin. His normal, human fingernails changed into gruesome talons. Worse than that were the elongating fangs. Those fangs, if they should bite into her, could lead to her death or force her to become a monster herself.

Diana shut her eyes with hopes that this was all a dream. When she opened them again, instead of being safe inside her bedroom, Diana found herself standing before a fully transfigured werewolf with fur as yellow as Lowell's hair had been.

She bolted.

The monster galloped after her.

A single swipe of his claws took her down. The slashes were deep; blood spurted out. Diana hastily unclasped the bracelet that Lowell had forgotten to remove and hurled it at the werewolf. The creature leapt aside, snarling. The bracelet barely hit the target. However, it was enough for the silver to work its magic; there was a blistering welt precisely where the bracelet had struck. The odor of burnt hair drifted to her nostrils. The werewolf was down, but still alive.

Diana scrambled up. She was still bleeding, but it was okay—claw wounds would have no effect on her. They would heal over time.

"Miss Nedderman!" A rasping voice shouted out. "What the hell are you doing out here! You should be inside!"

Diana—breathless, heart pounding rapidly—turned to see Mr. Walpole's form framed against a backdrop of light that poured from his windows.

Vincent Hobbes Presents

"Help me!" she cried, forgetting the suspicious attitude she held towards her neighbor only moments ago. "Mr. Walpole, help me!"

The monster was back on its feet. Diana saw it hurtling in her direction.

She screamed.

"Miss Nedderman!"

Mr. Walpole sprinted forward; there was a deadly looking knife glinting inside his clenched hand. He reached Diana when the werewolf did. The knife slashed open Lowell's side, but the monster did his share of damage as well, for it had lunged forward and tore at Mr. Walpole's throat. He hollered, brandished his knife, and became silent as he fell dead.

Shock and loss of blood left Diana disorientated. She shook her head with confusion as though she did not understand what she just witnessed. The girl fumbled about in a dreamlike state, tripped over an exposed tree root, and collided into what she at first thought was the tree. But it was no tree—it was soft, like flesh.

Mumbling incoherently to herself, Diana raised her face toward a shadowy figure very human in shape. She smiled with relief, believing the figure to be one of her parents returning.

"Mom? Dad?" There was no answer. "Please, I want to go home . . . I am so tired . . ." She began to whimper like a scared little girl. "I don't like this place anymore. It's a bad place. I feel all funny. Mom? Dad? Do you hear me?"

"Your parents are no longer here, my dear child," a voice said.

Yes, that's right, my parents are away from home, she

thought.

So who was talking to her? For a wild instant, Diana believed it was Mr. Walpole speaking. Then she remembered that he had been killed. Her mind replayed the scene, and she was jolted back into reality. Diana was revived to some extent, though not by much.

"I could not help but watch the struggle," the voice said. "I regret to say that your friend died in vain. The wolf still lives." Whoever was speaking to her sighed as if the werewolf's survival was a disappointment.

"Werewolves are such loathsome creatures," the voice went on. "They give the rest of us nocturnal beings a bad name."

"Nocturnal beings?" Diana dully repeated.

"Yes, vampires and werewolf filth such as he."

Vampires! So it was a vampire addressing her! Wide-eyed, Diana searched her pockets and realized that she had given her clove of garlic to Lowell. On the ground, there was no wood, nothing she could drive into the vampire's heart. All her weapons were back inside her home.

Diana received another unpleasant jolt when a marble-white face emerged from the shadow, illuminated by the moonlight. Slowly, soundlessly, the face materialized into a full-bodied figure wearing a long trench coat. Diana stared, yet did not run away, even as the vampire circled her, toying with her the way a predator toys with its prey.

"I can help you, child," said the vampire. "The attack has made you weak. You cannot escape. The werewolf is alive, and he will attack you again. You are doomed. If I don't bite you, he will." The vampire nodded to the werewolf. His lip curled in disgust at the sight of the monster struggling to get up.

"Are you going to bite me?" Diana whispered. "Are you going to drink my blood?"

"Not without your permission," said the vampire. "Though I must say you do not have enough left in you to make a satisfactory meal," he added, indicating her blood-soaked shirt.

"Could you bite the werewolf instead of me?" Diana asked desperately.

"No," he replied.

Diana took the answer and accepted it.

"You are doomed either way," the vampire continued. "Bare in mind that I will not kill you. You have my word, and I have every intention of keeping it. I have *some* dignity, you know."

"Can a vampire kill?"

"Certainly," he said, shrugging his shoulders casually.

"THEN I WANT TO BE KILLED!" Diana shouted out vehemently.

The vampire took a nonchalant step towards her. "Is that truly how you feel? It can be arranged."

Diana opened her mouth to speak, hesitated, and then shook her head 'no'.

The vampire looked as though the change of mind was expected.

"I promise you, child, that you shall not be killed tonight," he said with what might have been a smile. "The cursed beast does not have enough strength to kill. But he has strength enough to ensure the creation of another like himself, because—"

"Because vampire bites are like werewolf bites." Diana finished the sentence for him.

"Precisely. If I bite you, you become a vampire. If *he* bites you, you become a werewolf. If no one bites you, you will bleed to death. So you see, my dear, you have a decision to make."

Diana trembled all over, covering her face with her hands. "I don't want to become a monster!"

"A monster?" The vampire echoed silkily, raising his eyebrows. He ran his deathly, white hand along his jaw. "I am a monster, yes, but I must say that, between him and me, I am the lesser monster. We vampires choose whom we do and do not attack. Werewolves do not have that option, even in their human state. They lack the ability to reason and possess the atrocious instinct to kill anything in sight. That is all they can think of—killing and eating. We vampires are noble creatures, elegant in both appearance and mannerism. Have you ever seen an elegant werewolf? I should say not. Vile creatures, werewolves. Bloodthirsty brutes, if you ask me."

Diana began to cry.

"If your conscious is bothering you, you needn't fear. A vampire does not have to prey on humans. The blood of any animal will suffice."

Diana's hands lowered slightly, exposing only a pair of wet eyes. "Do vampire bites hurt?"

"There is a small amount of pain, yes," he answered. "However, they are nowhere near as painful as a werewolf's bite. I only hope that your parents did not suffer too badly—"

"My parents?" Diana inquired urgently. "What happened to them?"

"Poor child, if only you knew."

"Tell me!" Diana shouted. "My parents! What happened to them?"

"It was a trap, child," the vampire continued. "The old woman, the one your parents were visiting, is also a werewolf."

"Mrs. Lycan?" Diana gasped. "No! It's not possible!"

"Anything is possible," the vampire answered. "She has been a werewolf for many months now. I believe that her husband was killed by one while she had managed to survive the bite."

"But Mrs. Lycan was never bitten!" Diana shouted, shaking her head wildly. "She was only scratched! She told us so!"

"The old woman was lying."

"No! I don't believe it! My parents trusted her!"

"The way you trusted him?" The vampire asked dryly, nodding towards Lowell, who was struggling in the grass. He went on, "The old woman and her fellow band of wolves had it all planned out. It was her duty to get your parents out of the house. It is amazing what werewolves are capable of when they put their minds together. Of course, they have to join forces. A single werewolf simply does not have the brain capability to hatch out such a plan. Like regular wolves, werewolves work as a pack. They would starve to death otherwise."

In her mind's eye, Diana saw her mother and father being bitten. Her stomach wrenched. "My parents," she murmured fearfully. "Are they alive?"

"No."

More tears flowed from Diana's eyes.

"That's enough," the vampire said shortly. "You have to choose!"

Diana gulped and struggled to compose herself. She contemplated the options given to her. Either a werewolf or a vampire—but which? Her fingers brushed against her side. She lifted her hand at eyelevel, seeing the blood, remembering that she had been wounded. She recalled how she fussed over Lowell inside her home, bringing him a drink, giving the last of her garlic to him and helping him outside, when all along he was plotting to kill her while others like him killed her parents.

She did not want to be like them.

Lowell was now getting to his feet. Diana scowled at the sight of him. The vampire was right; werewolves were miserable beasts, sneaky, evil beasts with no morals or decency. At least the vampire gave her a choice. Diana felt a grudging respect toward the vampire, who no longer seemed so monstrous.

"Hurry!" the vampire hissed. "The werewolf is approaching!"

Lowell had risen to his feet and was moving forward at a quick pace.

Diana gathered together her hair and tilted her head to expose her neck. The silent gesture gave the vampire permission to do what he had to do.

A pain shot through her body when the vampire's teeth sunk into her flesh. Her blood was being drained; the pain turned into any icy sensation, as if her blood was becoming frozen. The world spun like being on a roller coaster. Her

Vincent Hobbes Presents

eyes rolled back inside her head.

And then it stopped.

The two puncture marks on her neck healed, as did the slashes caused by the werewolf. Diana felt alive again, healthy and stronger than ever before. Her pupils dilated, like a cat's eyes in the dark. The world came into focus. More than that, her sight changed. The nighttime sky was different. It was just as dark, but to Diana's modified vision, everything was as clear as it was during the day.

New instincts overcame her. When intuition told her to concentrate, she concentrated. She closed her eyes, envisioning herself flying over the treetops. A pair of leathery wings sprouted between her shoulder blades.

She smiled at her newfound ability.

The vampire took Diana by the hand and she saw that he too possessed similar bat-like wings. They lifted, wings flapping in the sky. For the first time in her life, Diana's skin was exposed to the night air. She never before realized how beautiful the dark hours were with their velvety blackness. And the stars . . . she had never seen stars before because the lights from the homes had always hidden them from her. Diana knew that she would never see the sun again, but that was all right. The moon, the beautiful silvery orb, was just as beautiful as the golden sphere that was the sun. From now on, the moonlight would be her sunlight.

As she soared over the city, Diana enjoyed the sensation of flying. She twirled in the sky, performing aerial feats, laughing joyfully. It was a bizarre, unearthly sound, similar to the wind during a storm, so different than her old, human chuckle.

The Endlands

Inside their homes built with silver nails, with their bottles of holy water in their cupboards and their gardens of garlic cloves, the citizens of Polidoria heard her. They knew what the sound was and shuddered as they made the sign of the cross. A merry vampire was never a good thing.

There was nothing more frightening than the sound of vampire laughter.

Flying Fish

By
David Stubblefield

Fer Wilkins tugged hard at the thick nylon rope. Another wave slapped at the side of his wooden boat, soaking the aged fisherman with frigid seawater. He really didn't want to lose another anchor, but if he couldn't get this one up, he'd have to cut it loose—one of the hazards of the area. The fish loved the wrecks and debris that littered the deep water, but the same wrecks loved to eat anchors. Over the years, Fer had lost a half dozen or so anchors, wedged under a rusting hull or dropped neatly through an open hatch. He pulled again, swore to himself, then sat on the side and reached for a rag to wipe his face.

Hard to believe I could work up a sweat in this cold.

He'd give it another shot—pull and release and try to jar the cheap metal hook loose—then cut the line and move on if he couldn't free it. It was really more about the rope than the anchor. He could make an anchor out of scrap sheet metal—he'd once used a two-foot length of railroad—but half an anchor rope was no use at all.

"One more time." Fer pulled.

Nothing.

He stretched for his tackle box and found his thick-bladed utility knife and turned to look over the edge and reach as far into the water as possible to salvage a few feet of rope. Something caught the light in the featureless deep—something big. The boat began to lift as if a huge swell had passed under, then it began to creak and tilt, rising higher but still held by the anchor line.

"Whales." Fer muttered under his breath.

The wake from one of the huge animals could tip a boat if it got too close, but they usually passed in seconds just making the deck unsteady. But the boat kept straining upward and the nylon rope grew taut as piano wire. Fer shot a glance at the life preserver hanging on a peg next to the helm, but before he could move the boat heaved upward.

It's coming up directly underneath me!

For a moment, the Lucky Leena rose bow upward, then began to slide aft first toward the sea on the back of the whale. The crash sent spray flying in a fan shaped arc from the rear of the boat, and backwash poured in as the boat righted itself, still swirling and twisting around the anchor line. Fer landed on his back in the middle of the open deck.

Fer rolled over to his stomach, grabbed a rail for stability, and rose to one knee. A quick glance told him the boat wasn't sinking. The engine had stalled, probably water in it. He could get it going, but . . . there! The huge whale that had risen up under his keel was breaking the surface. But something was not right. The whale didn't perform the graceful roll so characteristic of its mammoth gasp for air. It rose slowly, but didn't drop back down. First the broad head came completely out, then Fer saw the lateral fins emerge, and last of all there was a huge wave as the tail propelled the animal slowly but completely out of the water. And it continued to rise at a forty-five degree angle. It looked as if someone had fired a tractor out of the ocean in slow motion.

Fer watched open mouthed as the massive whale cleared the surface, water still pouring off its sides and tail. It waved its fluke three or four times in the air picking up speed, and Fer felt the wind blow against his face. About a hundred yards out, it dipped once, picking up more speed in the dive, and leveled out cruising just above the tops of the swells. Finally, it fanned its tail, maybe a dozen times, each time the fluke tips splashing gently against the surface. Accelerating, then gracefully arching and coasting upward, the whale silently fled until it became a dot in the distant sky.

Fer slumped down to the deck of the boat. "Holy Mackerel!"

"Sheriff. We got another call."

Sheriff Art Nettles stood at his desk and looked up from a stack of messages. "What does this one say?" he asked.

"Says the whales are terrorizing Warner's Bluff Elementary."

Warner's Bluff was near the coast, and the school was just close enough to see the ocean from the windows, but it was far enough away that the children had no chance of wandering off the precipice.

"Parents are calling in, too. Asking if we know anything."

Nettles had finished leafing through the notes. They all said the same thing—flying whales. Some from panicked parents. Some from fishermen. Seems like half his job was investigating false alarms, and even though he didn't believe in UFOs, Chupacapra, or Elvis sightings, he still had to investigate. He came in on his Monday off because his newbie deputy had called him, unsure how to proceed.

"Let's go see."

When they arrived, a crowd had gathered near the small elementary school. Some parents were already pulling their kids out of school. Others were just arriving. Cars filled every parking spot and some were pulled up on the grass. A news truck from a TV station in nearby Dowt was parked in the fire lane in front of the main door.

"Doug, go threaten anyone in the fire lane with being ticketed and towed. If we had a real situation there's no way an emergency vehicle could get in here."

Doug headed off for the fire lane and Sheriff Nettles walked around the side of the school where he saw a crowd in the playground facing the bluffs. "Art! Come to see the show?" Art turned to see Nancy Graig. She taught biology at Newkirk Junior College.

Nettles rolled his eyes. He was sure it would be some kind of prank. "Oh, yeah, nothing gets me perked up like swimming weather balloons."

Graig's eyes danced with mischievousness. She knew something. "C'mon. I think even you will be impressed."

As they rounded the back of the building, there was a mix of adults and children. Inside the back windows there were more children with their faces next to the glass. Before he could ask Nancy for details, someone yelled, "Here they come!" Nettles turned toward the ocean expecting to strain to see some distant, obscure mirage, but instead he stumbled backwards and fell surprised by the sight of a gigantic California Grey Whale rising over the edge of the cliff and headed straight up. It soared up, then paused as it lost momentum, then began speeding downward at an angle and curving in a path that would take it right in front of the school windows. As it neared the ground it leveled off and cruised just above the playground fence and left a wake of wind as it passed.

"There are the others!" Again a shout came from across the playground.

Not just the one, but also a pod of three more whales rose above the edge of the bluff, peaked, and tilted over to race past the school. The first one had risen gently at the end of its pass and shot back down the cliff out of sight toward the ocean. Then, the others passed, each one leaving the parents and children awash in awe. As the last of the three dropped over the edge, the crowd broke into applause.

Art was stunned. He looked questioningly at Nancy who grinned and shrugged her shoulders. "I don't have a clue," she said. "But isn't it cool?"

By late afternoon all the networks arrived. Someone had posted cell phone video on the Internet. The local Dowt station had sent good quality video to national affiliates. There were reports of soaring whales all over, but for now, Warner's Bluff seemed to be the only place they kept appearing to ride the cliffs like hang gliders.

Someone from CNN had telephoned Sheriff Nettles to ask about an official statement, but he had nothing to offer. The big animals weren't breaking any law. So far there was no health hazard. The children would have to play inside—no one wanted to see little tykes crushed by a clumsy whale—but otherwise it was a spectacular show.

That night the media was completely preoccupied with the event. Scientists bluffed their way through interviews, late night talk shows were full of whale jokes, and talking head politicos offered an amazing variety of wild, self-serving guesses.

One said, "global warming" was the cause for this radical behavior change. Others suggested oceanic pollution, alien invasions, government genetic experiments, Al Qaida, hoaxes, Republicans, and overfishing.

"What do you think?" Art took a bite of his grilled cheese as he sat at a corner seat at the counter of Aunt B's Diner with Nancy.

Nancy shrugged. "Don't know. Nobody can know. There's nothing like this in all biology. They're not flying, they're floating. It must be genetic somehow, but no telling what caused it. It's either environmental, in which case something made them change, or it's inherent in their DNA and something just triggered it." She looked down at her salad. It was clear Art wasn't following. "Could be that something in the water, in their environment, affected their DNA. In that case it's scary, because whatever caused that," she motioned to the TV over the counter showing one of the Greys doing what looked like an Immelman, "might be damaging the DNA of every fish in the ocean. We may be seeing only one version of change. But the odds of something on that scale, that dramatic, are astronomically small. I think it's something already in the whales' DNA that has just been triggered."

"Already in the DNA? You mean that Moby Dick up there has always had the ability to fly, but something just made him turn it on?"

"Something like that. Or some mixture of genetic strains

produced just the right combination. You know, there are gazillions of parts to your DNA that don't seem to have any purpose, but they're there. Maybe you already carry some hidden talent, and your children will manifest an ability that has been dormant for hundreds of generations." There was a hint of flirtation in Nancy's face.

"Okay, what triggered it?"

"Again, no clue. Could be something environmental. Could be solar flares or survival instinct responding to falling population numbers or something else entirely. Could just be automatic at a certain level of development."

"Why multiple animals at once? You'd think one might change, but not groups."

"You got me." She smiled at him, "Maybe change is infectious."

Art stared at the grilled cheese. "What if what triggered the whales to fly triggers something else?"

Nancy grinned. "Everything we love would be up for grabs."

It took about a week, but eventually, classes at Warner's Bluff Elementary were temporarily turned into whale watching parties. The students flooded the windows to catch the passing whales. The crowds, mostly gawkers and news people, overran the place making any hope of classroom decorum impractical. Tuesday of the second week, a crew from National Geographic set up a camera on the playground directly under the whale's flyover path. A lone cameraman stood with mounted equipment and carefully aimed the lenses at an oncoming pod.

Vincent Hobbes Presents

As the first big whale closed, it twisted its head slightly to give an inquiring look toward the cameraman, then it twisted back sharply just as it passed, turned it's head sideways, opened its jaws and snapped its mouth shut on the cameraman leaving only his wiggling feet hanging out. The whale pulled directly upward, opened its mouth for a moment to bite hard and let gravity drop the meal in deeper, like a gull gulping down a fish. It broke from the usual path and headed directly over the bluff to the sea. A single hiking boot, with a foot still inside, fell on the playground next to the swings.

Children inside the windows screamed. Reporters bolted for cover as the rest of the pod broke ranks and began to swerve over the playground and parking lot chasing reporters like a school of minnows. The whales were big and fast, but they couldn't make sharp turns. The reporters made it to the trucks, and seconds later, the world was hearing that the playground whales had turned to killers.

By nightfall, the mood of the country had turned dark. Maybe they were cute and amazing, but the whale charm had been lost. Reports were coming from around the globe of similar incidents. Other flying whales were buzzing ships, sometimes snapping up deckhands or knocking them into the water. Some were venturing farther inland. At one Northern Californian mall an entire row of cars had been crushed by a whale bashing its fluke on the ground trying to regain altitude after it scooped up three shoppers. Now they were flying at night, especially when it was foggy. When the weather was clear, you could see them coming, but where it was overcast, people just disappeared.

"They appear to like water," Art commented to his deputy. Doug looked confused. "Fog. They like the fog," Art explained.

They had spent the better part of the day answering calls and rushing to sites where whales were unexpectedly showing up and chasing neighbors. Some calls were not just reports; they were complaints that the Sheriff wasn't doing anything practical to help. But what could he do? They were whales. He wasn't Ahab. No one had captured one of the flyers. No one knew what had caused the flight, or attacks, and no one had any idea of how to stop them either. Art was frustrated, feeling responsible to do something.

"I'm going to see what I can see."

The first hour he cruised, sometimes with lights on, then with lights off. He drove slowly with his window down, letting the thick, moist air saturate his clothes and upholstery. He wanted to listen, but the fog dampened all but the loudest noises. "Doug, you getting any new reports in the last few minutes?"

"No, Sheriff." The volume and clarity of the radio startled him in the muffled silence. "Some calls, but mostly tree top sightings. No attacks."

"Keep me posted." Nettles flipped the radio off and stopped the car. There was a streetlight a half a block away. As his eyes adjusted to the dark, he strained to hear anything unusual. He stepped out in the street and slowly closed the door so it quietly clicked shut, then he took a few steps away to the centerline of the empty street and listened. He heard a dog yapping, but it suddenly stopped.

There was nothing.

Just as he turned back, the dim glow from the streetlight

blacked out. He spun and tried to gauge the distance, but couldn't see anything but a growing shadow, lunging toward him. He dropped to the ground and covered his head with his hands just as the huge grey animal passed inches above him, and he could hear what must have been wind whistling over its open jaws. The blast of air was incredible. The fog, thick with moisture, was like a wave at the beach and rolled him over. The whale was back above the trees now, but he didn't know which direction.

Nettles instinctively reached for his holster and lifted the safety strap. With one hand on the grip, he started to stand, and just as he was upright, he heard a ripple in the air. He turned again, straining this time into the darkness away from the distant streetlight, and seconds later heard a fluke smashing the ground as the whale approached from the darkness. Nettles pulled the gun level in front of him. He had to wait. He couldn't just fire off into the darkness. No telling where the rounds might go.

The grey shape was suddenly bearing down on him, water droplets on the massive head reflecting the streetlight behind him. Nettles fired, emptying his nine-shot clip in seconds, and fell backward again just as the beast roared over. He rolled to one side and landed next to his car as the gaping mouth reached for him. The side of the massive jaw grazed his head and he felt the slick skin against his cheek. He crawled up and was back on his feet in time to watch the whale pull up and clear the power lines near the light.

"I gotta get a bigger boat." Looking at his pistol, he holstered it, and stepped around to the rear of the car.

He'd risk the trunk light making him more noticeable; he

had to get more firepower. There was a shotgun, and Nettles started to load shells, but then he paused, and dropped the weapon back in the truck and began digging through the emergency roadside kit. He pulled out a flare gun, loaded a cartridge and lowered the trunk lid. If he could get a flare in the big fish, he could see it coming on the next pass.

The wait wasn't long. The big grey had dipped back into the street in the canyon between the trees and was headed for another pass. Nettles waited as long as he could. He wanted to hit the whale squarely on the snout so it would look like Rudolph.

Wait.

His training overcame his panic as the distance narrowed. He'd need some distance to jump aside or even fire a second round.

"Wait," he told himself.

About fifty yards remained between them, the whale approaching more slowly this time, perhaps remembering the sting of the handgun. *It's huge,* Nettles thought to himself as it decreased speed, warily closing. He wanted to run, but made bait of himself.

At thirty yards, Nettles fired, hitting the whale dead center. It twitched as the shell hit, burrowing into the thick skin. Then, beginning around the flare the entire animal erupted into flames. Over the course of a second, the fire raced down the length of it all the way to the tail, poured around the contours of its mouth inside its open jaws. For a moment, the animal struggled to flee, turning upward and above the trees crackling as it rose. There was a moment when it paused, a hundred feet up, wailing, the fire making the once dark street as bright as a clear noon.

Then, it exploded. A deafening dull thump shook the fog, and great hunks of flaming flesh soared in all directions. Some hit the ground, but most spread across the treetops. Nettles thought for a moment the entire neighborhood would erupt in flames, but even the biggest chunks incinerated into ash in just seconds. Just as suddenly it was dark and quiet again.

The next day brought a fresh round of news reports. Soon, Nettles wasn't the only one to exploit the whales' vulnerability. And although scientists pleaded with the public not to destroy the unique animals, it was just too much temptation for good ol' boys or grieving families with a flare or a bow and arrow. Within days all the sightings stopped. Perhaps some whales still survived far asea, but the coasts were quiet. A week later, school was back to normal at Warner's Bluff. Art and Nancy sat at Aunt B's at the corner of the counter talking over a grilled cheese and salad.

"Turn that off, will ya?" The TV over the counter was still airing stories and video of both graceful dives and horrendous explosions. Art was tired of hearing about it. He had become a kind of celebrity. He was the only living person who had actually touched one of the animals, and he had amassed multiple reputations, ranging from Evil Destroyer of New Species to Brave Rescuer of Children and Dogs. "So, what do ya think, Nance? What turned the Greys into swimming Hindenburgs?"

"I dunno. Same thing that made them fly, I guess. Whatever triggered the flying must have worked by making them lighter and more volatile, like hydrogen. That was probably the same thing that made them more aggressive. If sudden, random evolution sometimes makes a species more advanced, odds are there will be a million bad mutations for every one that proved to be an advantage. You can't choose your mutations. Flying—good. Bursting into flames—bad. If it's a DNA thing, it's just going to happen." She dropped her napkin on the counter and pushed away the half empty plate.

Art pushed down on the counter, shifting his weight to reach for his wallet, but the stool fell away underneath him. Flailing his arms, Art Nettles drifted gently up into the middle of the room.

Limbo, Population 458

By Vincent Hobbes

"I have to pee!" Sara complained for the third time in the past twenty minutes.

Her hands in her lap.

Her legs crossed.

Sara rocked back and forth in the passenger seat, repeating the words over and over as if her husband didn't understand.

"If you want me to pull over, I will. Just go in the woods," he answered.

"No. Someone will see me."

"Sara, there is hardly any traffic on this road. I doubt anyone will see you. And who the hell cares if they do? We're in the middle of nowhere."

His wife thought about it for a few moments. "What if my parents drive by and see me squatting on the side of the road?"

"Ha," he chuckled. "That'd be funny. Won't happen, though. They're at least thirty minutes behind us. Probably longer, considering how slow your dad drives."

"*Hmph.*"

"You should have gone when we left," he added.

"I did. I have to go again."

"Well, honey, your options are simple. You can do one of three things. You can pee on the side of the road, and feel better now. You can hold it, but I doubt we'll find a gas station anytime soon. Or..."

Sara turned her head, a casual smile crossing her face. "Or what?"

"You can just go," he said. A slow grin formed on his face, as well.

The couple burst into laughter.

"Stop," she giggled. "You're going to make me if I keep laughing."

"Okay," he said with a few more chuckles. "So, do you want me to pull over?"

"No," Sara said defiantly. "I can hold it a bit longer."

"You're going to have bladder problems one day."

"I already have bladder problems."

"*Ha*," he grinned. "You should just wear a diaper when we go on road trips."

She giggled again.

Other than the nagging pressure inside her bladder, all was well for Sara McCarthy. She was still married to the same man—thirteen years now—much longer than most of her friends, some who were in their mid-thirties and single, acting as if they loved it. John was good to her, and she tried to be good to him.

They had left Shoshone National Forest about an hour prior. Driving the beautiful roads, followed by Sara's parents—a slow caravan of greasy cheeseburgers, novelty spending, and roadside antique stores. John didn't mind, though. They were buying a new house soon. They would be closer to her family, and that suited him fine. He got along with his in-laws, and knew once he and Sara had a family, they would be very helpful. He also enjoyed this part of the country. The rolling hills and lush landscape was refreshing.

"Have it your way," John finally said. "When you need to stop, just let me know."

And they continued on—Sara with her legs crossed, fidgeting—John with a bit of a smirk on his face.

A few minutes passed.

"*Ah, ha!*" Sara exclaimed. She pointed ahead of them down the long road. "There."

John squinted his eyes. "*Huh?* Are you pointing at *that* sign?"

Sara nodded.

"I can't even read it."

"Just wait a sec."

Moments passed.

"*Ah*, you're right. Looks like a town," said John.

Reading the sign as they neared, Sara's face shined with hope as she read it aloud.

"Limbo. Population four hundred and fifty-eight," she stated.

"Well, I guess they'll probably have a gas station. Maybe I should drive real slow. It's still three miles away."

"I swear if you do, I'll be driving and you'll be riding in this seat," she threatened.

Three miles.

The couple pulled into one of the many open parking spaces in the town square. There were no cars in sight, yet there

Vincent Hobbes Presents

were many people. Dozens laced the streets of Limbo.
 They gathered in small clusters.
 They stood in front of stores.
 They sat on park benches.
 Limbo had that rare, old-town feel to it. It was built in the early 1900's, and was well kept. The nostalgia of Limbo made it appealing. It hosted a traditional town square. A working clock tower. A large, ornate courthouse.
 "I like this place," commented John as he put the car in park. His eyes were wide as he took a deep breath. "I'm sure your parents would, too."
 "I'm sure. Hurry up," his wife replied. "I gotta pee!"
 They exited the car. Closing their doors, they stood a moment, gazing on the town of Limbo.
 "Hardware store. Barbershop. *Oh*, look—it even has one of those spinney things like in the old days," John said. "I swear, it's like living in the fifties. Probably a decent place to raise children."
 "I only care about one thing—the nearest restroom," his wife said frantically.
 "There. A diner." John pointed. "This town is great! That diner looks like it came from an old movie. I bet ya ten bucks there's a man in a white apron behind the counter with slicked back hair," he said, chuckling.
 He held Sara's hand as they crossed the street. She nearly dragged him across. They looked both ways by habit, but no cars were to be seen.
 As they crossed, John waved to a couple seated on a bench.
 They did not wave back.

The Endlands

Sara kept tugging until they reached the diner. She did not wait for him to open the door, instead pulling at it quickly, relieved they were open. A bell chingled as they entered.

The diner was nearly vacant. A man sat in a nearby booth, reading a newspaper. John stole a glimpse his way. The paper the man held was yellowed, and appeared old.

Near the back of the restaurant were three patrons. They looked like farmers. Their backs were to the couple, facing a small television with no picture.

"Strange," muttered John.

He turned, staring at the counter. It stretched a great length down the right side of the diner.

Bar stools.

Marble countertop.

Ice cream.

Forty-two flavors.

Root beer floats and homemade apple pie.

John tugged at his wife's arm, saying, "I was right. See— white apron. Slicked back hair. *Ha!* Talk about living in the days of our grandparents."

John was amused.

But Sara ignored him, saying, "There. Restrooms. I'll be right back."

"I wonder if a Coke is only a nickel," John pondered, staring up at the signs behind the counter.

Sara glanced at him, annoyed. She knew it was merely her bladder pushing against her insides, though, and let go of his hand, scurrying to the restroom.

"Want something to eat?" he asked as she walked away.

"No," she replied.

Vincent Hobbes Presents

"Want something to drink?"

"NO!"

He chuckled as his wife nearly ran. He figured another ten minutes and she would have had to go in the woods. Lucky for her, he thought. He watched as she turned the corner and entered, the door softly closing behind.

John took another look around the room. Everything about this place was epic. A clearly conceived town that remained in the old days, even as modern times passed them by.

John meandered to the counter. He sat on the barstool, a child-like grin on his face.

The man with the white apron and slicked back hair stood farther down the bar. He was bent over, seeming to wash dishes, although John heard no clank of glass. He was in no rush, though, and turned in his seat, looking over the diner in detail. He stared at the man in the booth near the door—the one with the newspaper. John half-waved, but the man was not paying attention.

John peered closer. His eyesight must have been failing him, because he noticed the date on the newspaper. It read, April 7, 1954.

"Impossible," he muttered. He cleared his voice, and with a smile, said to the man, "Anything interesting going on in the world?"

No response.

"Okay," John turned back in his seat. He supposed small town people were not too fond of outsiders. Still, there was no reason to be rude.

He waited.

The Endlands

The television remained silent in the corner.
The fans overhead did not move.
Something smelled different about the diner. Stale. Then, John realized he could not smell anything appropriate of a restaurant. Where were the forty-two flavors overcoming his senses? Where was the sound of running water? The clank of dishes?

"Hi there," John finally said to the man behind the counter. "How's it going today?"

No response again.

"I'd like to order an iced tea... when you get the chance."

Nothing.

"Maybe he's deaf," mumbled John. He sat in silence a few more minutes, carefully eyeing the man.

Finally, the door to the restroom opened.

Sara steadily walked out. She looked relieved. John took a glance her way, but quickly looked back. His eyes now glared at the man behind the counter. Raising his voice, he said, "Excuse me, sir?"

Silence. The man did not move a muscle.

"Hello?" John said. "We'd like to order something to drink."

Sara neared her husband, a faint look of curiosity upon her face.

"What's wrong, hun?" she asked.

"Excuse me, but we're paying customers," he said in a loud voice. "Is there any way we can order something to drink?" John repeated, ignoring his wife's question.

"John," Sara urged. He didn't respond. "John!" she repeated, tugging at his sleeve.

"What?" he said, turning.

Her expression instantly concerned him. "I have a strange feeling. This place . . . it isn't right."

"Tell me about it," said John, growing more annoyed. "The people in this town are rude. That guy won't take my order. He won't even respond. And this guy," he said, pointing over his shoulder with his thumb, "this guy ignored me too."

"No, John. Something is *wrong* with this place."

"I know, honey. Aren't you even listening to me? What restaurant in America completely ignores its patrons?"

"John!" Sara cried out.

He turned again, his full attention now finally on her.

"Those aren't people," she said grimly.

"*Huh*?"

"These aren't people. They're dolls, or something. Mannequins. Fake."

"Mannequins? What the hell are you talking about, Sara?"

Before he could say more, Sara pulled him from his seat. Grasping his hand tightly, she led him down the counter, towards the man in the white apron. He was still bent over, his hands underneath the counter.

They walked directly up to him.

"Hello," said Sara loudly, waving her hand in front of the man's face.

Nothing.

"Hello!" Sara shouted.

Nothing.

John was baffled. The figure looked human enough, but

upon closer inspection, he realized his wife was right. This was no man. It was a dummy, made to look real. The details were awesome. John turned back to his wife, and grinned. He couldn't help himself. "Is this some kind of joke?"

"I don't know, baby. Look at those men in the corner. They're fake, too."

Indeed they were.

Mere statues resembling men.

John turned back to the man behind the counter. He screamed, but got no response. Then, looking to the front of the restaurant, he stared at the man reading the paper. John stormed over, dragging Sara behind him. He tore the newspaper from the man's hands.

He was the same.

Not human.

A joke.

A life-sized doll eternally seated.

"Okay, seriously . . . this *must* be a joke," said John. "Maybe this is a museum or something. If you think about it, it's kinda funny. I mean, they really had us going." He chuckled nervously.

"You think this is a joke?" asked Sara. Her eyes were hopeful. A slight grin formed on her face.

"No doubt it is. Or, like I said, we walked into a museum. Some old diner that the town wanted to show off or something. Come on, let's get out of here. If it is a joke, we'll know soon. People will be laughing at us, and rightfully so."

Sara smiled at this. Looking around one last time, she relaxed. The place was set up perfectly. The dolls were lifelike. Real. In her haste to relieve herself, she had not noticed.

Vincent Hobbes Presents

Hand in hand, the pair walked out.
A chingle-changle of the bell.
Warm sunlight and a busy town.
"See. It was probably a museum. No laughing towns people and no Candid Camera. Looks like we're in the clear. You should have seen the look on your face—" he said, relieved.
"No. Something still isn't right," said Sara glumly.
"What's wrong now, dear?"
"Damn, you are so unobservant. Look at the people. Do you see anything strange?"
He looked around.
Men and women and children.
Standing in front of stores.
Gathered in small clusters.
Seated on park benches.
Only—
"They aren't moving," he finally whispered. "They aren't real, either."
"No. I don't think they are. What is with this town?"
John urged his wife in the direction of the nearest group of people. Two were standing, and two were seated on a bench. They had ignored his wave earlier, and now he knew why. Curiosity drove him as he neared.
"John, I don't think we should—"
"Hold up a second. I just want to see."
Before she could protest more, he approached the seated family. Leaning in close, he observed.
"Yup. They're all fake. Every single goddamn one of them. The whole town. Sara, look around . . . these aren't people."

"There *has* to be someone here. Maybe this is an exhibit or something."

"An entire town?"

"Well, maybe. You have a better idea?"

"Maybe we've entered the *Twilight Zone*."

They walked further down the sidewalk, passing fake human after fake human. They stopped and touched some. John even angrily knocked one over. They entered shops, hollering at the top of their lungs, but it was all the same.

It became a game. They would rush into doors, shouting and making a ruckus. They would touch the mannequins. They would talk to them. Yell obscenities. Laugh and chuckle. It was a simple way to deter their fears.

Still, they were uneasy. After twenty more minutes or so, they stood near their car. John gripped the keys in his hand. The thought of a fast getaway soothed him. He looked to Sara, saying, "Your parents should be coming through soon. We'll wait 'til they stop by."

"I can't comprehend this," she muttered, oblivious to his words. "I don't see any signs saying this is fake. Where the hell are the real people?" A strange feeling overtook Sara. She felt as if she was being watched. "Let's just go. Let's get back on the road and get the hell out of Limbo."

"Yeah, yeah. You're right. What about your parents, though?"

"We can wait on the side of the road. Or, we can just keep going."

"I'm sure your dad will stop."

"That's fine. I still want to leave. Now."

He unlocked the car door.

Vincent Hobbes Presents

She jumped in, closing it behind her.

But John remained standing, motionless. He stared at another mannequin twenty feet away. It was an elderly woman. She wore a blue dress. White hat. Her Sunday best.

His curiosity overcame him once more. He took a few steps closer.

"Let's just leave!" Sara pleaded.

"One second, hun. I just thought—"

"You thought what?"

"I . . . I don't know. Wait here."

John walked over to the elderly woman. Her skin was the same texture as the others. A strange mix—neither real nor man-made. He pressed his fingers against her arm. Her skin was spongy. Her curly, grey hair waved in the breeze.

"What are you doing?" shouted his wife from the car.

"For a second, it looked like she moved," he shouted over his shoulder. "Must have been the wind."

Before he could turn back, he heard something.

A gasp.

A whisper.

Words.

Leaning in close, John listened. His ear was near the woman's face. Then, an awful look crept across his face.

"Hey, Sara," he shouted again. "I swear, I think I hear something. This one . . . it sounds like she's trying to talk."

Sara stayed in the vehicle. Her eyes shifty. Shaking. Insecure.

And John listened intently.

Mumbles.

Words.

Inaudible.
Yet somehow, they made sense.
"Hey, Sara—I think we may have a problem."

Eighteen minutes elapsed. Frank and Suzette Hardy entered the town of Limbo. The same fascination of such an old town drew their interest. They parked in the same space as their daughter. Unaware. John and Sara's car was now gone.
"This sure looks like a pretty town," Suzette exclaimed. "I bet there are some great deals."
Frank immediately saw the mannequin. At first, it appeared real. He even waved. Now, as he neared what looked like an elderly woman, he realized it was fake.
"Get a load of this," he said. "Looks almost real."
His wife had yet to notice. Her attention was on the town, and the various shops.
Frank walked to the next pair of mannequins. He touched them, and whistled aloud.
"Hey, Suzette."
"Yeah?"
"Check these out."
"Yeah, they're mannequins. So what?"
"Don't they look familiar?"
She looked closer. "How so?"
"Well, this one almost looks like . . ." he trailed off.
His wife neared him, but did not seem to recognize the similarities. "I know we're a little behind schedule, but I'd like to look around."
"Sounds good," Frank said, his mind drifting. "Take your time."

And as his wife ventured off, Frank Hardy remained still.

And if his hearing had been a little better, he might have heard it.

But the voice was muffled, and the wind was blowing...

... and Frank Hardy could not hear his son-in-law's screams.

Finders Keepers

By Janelle Garcia

Beth walks to and from work everyday with her keys in her pocket and her vinyl lunch bag clutched underneath her arm. It's yellow, but everything else she wears is black. At work, they call her *the black widow*, which she thinks is childish and uncreative.

Beth works at the Hotel Sunny Days. She's in charge of the lost and found, a job she's had for the past three years. When she first applied, she was surprised a hotel would hire someone for the sole purpose of looking after people's misplaced junk. She imagined a lost and found could only consist of a plastic bin, which probably always held an old sweater and maybe a broken pair of sunglasses. But the hotel is big, huge actually, so the lost and found is correspondingly large, ridiculously in fact—a whole room packed with shelves from floor to ceiling.

This morning, one of the maids is waiting for Beth as she unlocks the door. Beth doesn't know her name although she's seen her often enough. She tries not to learn other people's names in general.

The maid is clutching a plastic baggie, which dangles from her extended fist. Beth has seen dog owners do this after they've scooped up their dog's freshest load, carrying around warm dog shit and chasing after its flea bag as it circles and curlicues around the city looking for the perfect spot to take a piss. Beth has never owned a pet.

Inside the baggie is what appears to be a lump of raw beef. Beth almost tells the maid, in her most sarcastic monotone, to either toss it in the trash or inform the kitchen staff. Once close enough, though, Beth immediately knows what it is—a human heart, complete with four contracting chambers and throbbing sinews. The maid shrugs and mutters how she found it behind a nightstand while vacuuming. When Beth doesn't reach for the bag, the maid sighs and plops it on Beth's desk, apparently unmoved by her find.

Beth is always amazed by the things people are capable of losing. Last month someone forgot a pair of eyes. They just left them by the breakfast bar like they were car keys or a used piece of tissue. A perfectly good set of eyes. Perfect spheres, the irises dark brown, the whites unmarked by the networks of veins and capillaries that make Beth's own eyes burn pale pink on a good day. They reminded her so much of Gabe's—the way the pupils were nearly undetectable. She'd put them in a small plastic tub filled with saline and couldn't help staring at them while nibbling at her tuna sandwich during her lunch break. She tried to picture the face the eyes belonged to—eyeless lids loose and sunken, a face so noticeably blank and incomplete—but she always wound up picturing Gabe. Well, not him exactly, but the B-movie actor everyone always swore he looked exactly like. Lately, trying to picture Gabe had become an impossible feat, yielding incomplete snatches of features that evaporated as soon as she tried to gather all of the images into one composite. As much as she hated it, the actor's face (Matt or Mark something-or-other), which was too angular and symmetrical to be Gabe's, replaced him in her mind.

The eyes didn't last long, which was probably best. Beth had begun to play a little game where she imagined the eyes were actually Gabe's—one small part of him still living and within reach. It was a dangerous game to play. For a while, she toyed with the idea of stealing the eyes and quitting her job (forget her health benefits and accrued vacation days). A freckly lady wearing oversized sunglasses finally claimed the eyes two days later, and Beth relinquished the gaping duo.

But a heart? That takes the freakin' cake. Beth slides it on the body parts shelf in a plastic freezer bag, where it contracts and relaxes silently. She's printed the date and time on the Ziploc bag as carefully as possible with a red Sharpie. In retrospect, she should've picked a different color marker. The numbers blend with the vital maroon of the bag's contents, making them almost illegible.

If Beth gets close enough, she can hear it beating. She wonders if it belongs to a woman or a man, an adult or child. She once read somewhere that a heart usually corresponds with the size of a person's fist, and holds her own against it. It's probably an adult heart—a man's—judging by the size of it. Her hand brushes against the bag and the heart begins to beat faster, pulsing so frantically, it tips toward the shelf's edge. Beth cups it in both hands and holds it against her chest. She can't leave the thing on the shelf if it's going to work itself into a frenzy and wind up rolling onto the floor.

At one point, Beth begins rocking back and forth, humming *Silent Night, Holy Night* (it's the only song that pops in her head despite it being July and she feels stupid for it, wondering if the heart thinks she's dim also), in an attempt to lull it back to a normal pace. After a few minutes, the heart's pounding finally slows, its electric pulse coursing through her fingertips.

This time, she places the heart inside a bin before putting it back on the shelf. The bin will keep it from rolling if the thing gets jumpy again for whatever reason. She watches it for a minute or two then walks away. She'll never get much work done carting around a heart all day. She needs to get started on the heart's paperwork. Can't waste another second worrying about someone else's forgotten organ if she wants to leave at a decent time. Although, ever since Gabe's accident, she can't say she minds working longer hours so much.

Beth presses a pen into her palm, but can still feel a phantom beating along her fingertips. It's hard to think about timestamps and carbon copies when a human heart is throbbing in the same room, out in the open, like having a body to supply oxygen to isn't its sole purpose.

It seems unnatural for a heart to be squeezed into a plastic bag, she thinks, as she holds it against her chest for the second time in as many hours. The heart is beating in time with her own, radiating warmth from inside the plastic.

Can a heart suffocate and die sealed away?

She knows it supplies oxygen, but doesn't it need some too?

Beth fumbles it out of the bag and sets in on her lap. Her slacks are black, so if she gets some heart on her, no worries. Up close, she can see how dirty it is. There are balls of lint,

a strand of hair—short, black, suspiciously curly—crumbs from some kind of baked good (a muffin? a scone? a dog biscuit?). She's curious as how to dust off a heart. Spraying it down with Windex just doesn't seem like a good idea. Running it under the tap: another impossibility.
Who could be so careless?
It is the end of her shift. Beth can't see putting the heart back in the baggie and leaving it overnight. Besides, who will ever claim it? A person can't just ditch their heart behind a nightstand and go on like everything is hunky-dory. Hearts don't slip out of bodies unnoticed, without detrimental effects, right? The heart is obviously left behind by someone long dead. No one will miss it.

Beth considers putting the heart inside her lunch bag, but can't see zipping it into the nylon, which still smells of chicken salad. Instead, she slips the heart inside her sweater. The heart's paperwork, which she barely began, lies at the bottom of her purse, torn and crumpled, inside the smeared and dated Ziploc. If anyone asks about the heart, it'll be her word against the maid's. Maybe it's not that simple, after all, there are surveillance cameras along the corridors of the hotel. But none in the lost and found room, that's for sure. The heart beats against her own, almost synchronized. A Phil Collins song pops into her head, but Beth is decidedly against Phil Collins, so she pushes the song away and replaces it with *Silent Night, Holy Night* once again. As she nears the lobby, Beth prays no one will stop her with a question or for some random conversation. She's praying after all, so maybe it is appropriate that she's humming a song about Baby Jesus.

The lobby is nearly empty as she walks out, her arms

crossed in an attempt to conceal the bulge of the extra heart in her sweater. At the reception desk, a balding man is slumped against the counter, his skin pale and gray. He's trying to ask the receptionist a question, his right hand clawing at his chest, his lips working soundlessly. The girl—she couldn't be any older than sixteen—frowns and asks if he needs a manager or a doctor in a tone both sarcastic and incredulous. Beth can't help smiling a little as she observes their exchange. As the girl reaches for the telephone, the man closes his eyes and slides to the ground, now both hands gripping and tearing at his chest. The receptionist cranes over the counter, the telephone pressed between her shoulder and her ear, and yells for help.

Beth hurries on. She can't stop and help. She doesn't even own a cell phone or know CPR, nor is she capable in any other way to help a random man who is obviously beyond help. The man is probably having a stroke or something. She tells herself these things as she pushes through the revolving doors of the hotel. She tells herself the man is probably better off as she prays silently that the roar of two hearts is only audible to her, a Christmas song in rotation somewhere in the recesses of her mind.

Loose Ends

BY
CRAIG WESSEL

The meeting started off a bit shaky, but it looked like it was going to end well. Cain nodded as his counterpart across the table, Landon Hopkins, suggested they meet again in two weeks to finalize the details. After exchanging a few more pleasantries, Cain stood, shook Hopkins' hand and was shown out of the conference room by an assistant. As he was led down the hall, Cain smiled, convinced that the upcoming deal was going to cement his company's position in the industry. It had been a very important meeting, and from his perspective, it could not have turned out any better.

The assistant led him around a corner, opened another door and gestured for him to enter. He walked into a featureless, windowless waiting room, and before he could question the assistant, she smiled and closed the door, asking him to wait one moment, babbling something about security. Cain was confused, but shrugged and paced around the room. He waited awhile, and then decided to take a look into the hall to see what was holding things up. He was shocked when the door to the room would not open. He tried the knob several times, but was unsuccessful.

He was a man who was used to getting what he wanted, and right now, he wanted out of this room. He pounded on the door, and began to yell for the assistant. He looked around the room but there was no other exit. He opened his briefcase and took out his phone, but there was no signal in this room. He took out his laptop, but could not find a local connection to the net. Frustrated, he slammed his laptop back in his briefcase and sat at the featureless table, brooding.

The door opened, and Cain stood at once. Before he could protest, the man who entered walked over and shook his hand.

"I'm terribly sorry Mr. Cain—I was tied up in another meeting and it took me much longer to get here than I intended. I'm Carl Jenkins," he said, and offered his hand.

Cain, being a pro at this sort of thing, smiled and said that he understood, shaking Jenkins hand. Cain asked why he was being detained, and Jenkins smiled, gesturing for him to sit again. Cain sat, and Jenkins joined him at the table.

Jenkins steepled his fingers, and Cain noticed that he seemed a bit uncomfortable. Jenkins looked at Cain over his fingers.

"Mr. Cain, there's really no easy way to tell you this but, we have a problem."

Cain raised his eyebrows, flashing his most charming smile, and asked what the problem was.

"Mr. Cain, the problem is that you aren't supposed to be here." Jenkins looked embarrassed.

Cain stared, and began to become upset. He sat up in his chair and fixed Jenkins with a disapproving look. He began to tell Jenkins that the only reason he was still here was because he had been detained, but Jenkins raised a hand and interrupted.

"Yes, Mr. Cain, I'm aware and I assure you that it is our fault. However," he said, clearing his throat, "we have a problem. Let me explain."

Jenkins stood and began walking back and forth, his arms crossed.

"You *were* supposed to be here—you were sent from New York for the meeting that just took place. That much was fine—we have received word that New York was very pleased with the outcome of the meeting."

Cain wrinkled his forehead, confused.

"Yes, I can see you're confused," said Jenkins, " and I assure you, I don't blame you one bit." He stopped pacing and placed both hands on the table, looking at Cain. "You see Mr. Cain, you are not supposed to be here anymore. You're a fax."

Cain stared at Jenkins and repeated the word.

"Yes, Mr. Cain, a fax." Jenkins started pacing again.

"You are a facsimile, a copy of the real Mr. Cain, who is sitting in his office in New York. You were ported over for this meeting, and of course you did an admirable job, as Mr. Cain himself would have done." He gave Cain a patronizing smile. "Most of the time we don't have this problem—faxes come and go, they do their job and then we bring them here to the sh—to this room, and they just disappear." He looked at Mr. Cain, and it was obvious he was even less comfortable than before. "But sometimes—and I can assure you it's rare—faxes don't um . . . well they don't go away."

Cain stared. It was obvious to him that this man was insane. Faxes? Cain was beginning to get upset. He told Jenkins that he was Malcolm Cain, President of Cain Holdings, and he demanded that Jenkins stop spouting this nonsense and show him the exit.

Jenkins looked even more uncomfortable. "I'm sorry Mr. Cain, but I can't do that. You see, I told you we have a problem, and it's this: can't let you leave."

Cain begged his pardon.

"Yes well, you see, there's only one Mr. Cain in the world—the one that sent you. You, well, you shouldn't be here, and I cannot let you leave the building. I'm sure you understand the havoc it could cause to have two Mr. Cain's wandering around."

Jenkins gave Cain another patronizing smile, but Cain was having none of it. He stood and leaned over Jenkins, demanding that he put an end to this foolishness. He threatened, he glowered, he shook his fists, he threw his briefcase. Jenkins frowned and asked him to take a seat again. Grudgingly, Cain did so and Jenkins continued.

"I understand, Mr. Cain—to you this is all surreal. After all you, you think you are the real Mr. Cain, not a copy, not some fax sent across the world."

Cain nodded, glad to see where this was going.

"Can you answer a question for me, Mr. Cain?"

Cain assured him that he could, indeed, answer his question.

"Good. Tell me Mr. Cain, what did you have for breakfast this morning?"

Cain stared, thinking this was the most ridiculous question he could have been asked. He started to tell Jenkins what he had eaten this morning, because he could remember . . . he could remember . . . the thing was he couldn't remember. Cain struggled to recall coming to the office earlier this morning, and as hard as he tried, he found that he could not remember a single thing. Not waking up in his hotel (as he must have surely done), not having a nice continental breakfast in his room (as he always did when he traveled), and certainly not the car ride over. He stared at Jenkins, who was looking at him sympathetically.

"You don't remember do you, Mr. Cain?"

Cain shook his head, claiming fatigue.

Jenkins nodded and stood.

"Mr. Cain, in these situations, we have found it best to let you sort things out on your own. Obviously you'll need to wait here, but I'll be back in a bit and we can chat some more."

Before Cain could object, Jenkins quickly opened the door and darted out into the hallway, shutting the door behind him. Cain sat at the table, thinking, or trying to think about his breakfast. The more he thought, the harder it became to remember it, and then he realized that it was harder to remember other things. He thought about the meeting, and found that even that was beginning to become fuzzy to him. Who had he met with? Hopkins? Hopewell? He couldn't quite remember. He rubbed his forehead and found he was suddenly very tired.

Twenty minutes later, Jenkins entered the now empty room. He gestured to a technician who entered and scurried over to open an access panel on the wall, checking to make sure things were back to normal.

"This is the fourth time this month we've had this problem, Perkins!" Jenkins was not pleased. "I suggest you figure out what is wrong, and take care of it. I hate having to talk to faxes!"

He stormed out of the room, followed closely by Perkins, who closed the door to the room, but not before putting a SHREDDER UNDER REPAIR tag on the doorframe.

To Read or Not to Read

BY
VINCENT HOBBES

"Welcome. Welcome. Please *do* come in," said a friendly voice.

A chime chingled, and Shelby hesitated at the door. She wasn't sure why she had entered, and nearly turned away. But something was enticing about the place, she had time to kill, and was curious.

The store was small, quaint. The room was dimly lit, and smelled of leather and pine wood polish. It had a soothing feel to it, and Shelby took another step inside.

"Welcome to my humble store," said the voice. It was a heavy dialect. A familiar accent. The words were guttural, and deep.

"Hello," she said.

"Strauss Books. I know the name is plain, but how could I possibly explain *this* place?" he asked with a laugh. It was high pitched, cackling.

"W . . . where are you?" she asked, still paused in the doorway.

Poof!—like a magician, he appeared from behind the shadows of piles of books.

"Allow me to introduce myself—" the man said boldly. He moved like a flash of light. One moment he was rounding the counter, the next he was directly in front of her. With a flick of his wrist, he eccentrically extended out his hand.

She took it by habit.

The man shook Shelby's hand vigorously, a wide, curved smile on his face.

"My name is Günter von Strauss," he said. "And it is a pleasure to make your acquaintance."

"*Uh*, nice to meet you too, Günter."

"Herr Strauss," he corrected.

"*Oh*, my name's Shelby—Shelby McClain."

"A beautiful name for a beautiful woman," he complimented, winking.

She smiled at this, and relaxed. His hand was soft in hers. Frail. Cold. Now that Shelby could fully see him, her apprehension drifted away.

The man was elderly. Perhaps in his seventies, maybe older. He wore a black suit, tailor-made. His shirt was maroon, flashy at the collar, but still proper.

Strauss' hair was full, and swiped back with a dime-size bit of grease. It was gray, and he had a distinct widow's peak. A few wrinkles covered his hollow face. He was clean-shaven, and wore thin glasses that drooped down on his nose.

For some reason, the man reminded Shelby of a circus ringleader.

Strauss' body might have been old, but his eyes flurried with life. Shelby could see it—a passion that still burned inside him. Youthfulness—mixed with a friendly smile. Shelby could not help but feel welcomed.

"Your accent—" Shelby began. "German?"

"Indeed," he responded. "Now that we are introduced,

might I ask a question?" Again, another smile formed across his face. Sincere. Grandfatherly.

This brightened her, and she responded, "Of course."

"What brings you into my humble store?"

She blushed, lowering her head shyly. "I'm just passing some time."

"I see. Let me guess—your kids are at the roller rink across the street."

"How did you know?" she asked, looking up.

Strauss leaned in close. "I'll admit, most of my business is women waiting on their children." He leaned his head back, chuckling softly.

She joined, easing the tension of talking to a stranger even more. "My oldest is at a birthday party. I couldn't stand the music," she said with a laugh.

Shelby looked around. The bookstore was small—paling in comparison to the mega-chain retailers she normally shopped. Yet, something about the place made her feel comfortable.

Strauss stepped back a few paces and wildly extended both his arms. He gestured grandly, saying proudly, "Strauss Books. I stock only the finest collection."

He bowed extravagantly.

Shelby giggled at this. "You have a nice place," she complimented, taking a slower look at the vast selection.

"Thank you," he replied. Although his accent was heavy, Shelby understood.

"*Do* look around," he offered.

"*Oh*, I . . ." she began. ". . . I'm afraid I don't have much time." She looked down to her watch, knowing that was un-

Vincent Hobbes Presents

true. She had forty minutes to spare—plenty of time.

"Nonsense," Strauss responded. "There are only two options on this block. My place, and McGraw's Lumber. Now, I don't think *that* sounds very fun."

"No, it doesn't," she chuckled.

"Stay for a moment. It is chilly outside. I just finished brewing some tea. I'll make you a cup."

"You don't have to."

"It's my pleasure. Take your time and look around. I'll be back in a flash," he insisted, passing behind the counter and into a room behind it.

"Is this a rare book store?" she asked loudly, hoping he could hear.

"*Oh*, no," he replied from the other room.

Shelby could hear the clank of mugs.

"I carry something for everyone's taste," Strauss added.

"I don't have much time to read," said Shelby. Her fingers traced the outline of a shelf of hardback spines.

"Do tell—why not?" he said from the kitchen.

"Well, my husband travels a lot. With three boys, I hardly have the time. Soccer practice. Music lessons. School. *Ugh.* It's hard enough to find time to watch a television show, let alone read a book."

"I would suppose so," he chimed, his voice friendly. "You look much too young to have three little-uns."

She laughed at this. "Thirty-two, and I'll take that as a compliment." Her fingertips drifted to another row.

Strauss appeared around the corner, carrying a mug of warm tea.

"Thank you," she said, gripping the mug.

"Please, take your time and peruse my selection. I think you'll find it very diverse. I have Mark Twain and Sherlock Holmes. I have Socrates and Plato if ancient philosophy is your thing."

"*Ugh*. No thanks," she said, sipping her tea.

"Greek mythology?"

"Nope," she said with a smile.

"*Ha*. Very well, perhaps you prefer something more modern. I keep up with all the bestsellers. Although I prefer the classics myself, I don't expect my patrons to. New titles are on the far shelf. Paperbacks are to the left."

Shelby turned and walked to the shelf. She was merely being polite, having no intention of buying anything. There was a pile of unread books on her nightstand, and the last thing she needed was to add to her collection.

"Horror on the left. Science Fiction below—I'm afraid I don't carry much of that. But I do have action and adventure. Mystery. Perhaps you're looking for romance. *Hmm*," he said, with a quick lick of the lip.

"No thanks," she said bashfully. "I usually stick to crime novels, stuff like that. I like James Patterson. Michael Connelly. A few others. But I'm not into romance novels. Not at all. I've never understood how women get into such things."

"I see," he said, looking almost suspiciously at her. "Most of my regular clients like romance. Married woman, especially. I suppose their husbands don't give them much attention. Although, I do not judge on what book a patron chooses. I merely sell a service. Your privacy is safe with me."

Had he said he sold a service?

Didn't he mean a product?

Vincent Hobbes Presents

Perhaps she heard him wrong. He had simply misspoken, she convinced herself.

Shelby took her time at the shelf, recognizing many of the names. They were new bestsellers as promised, although she had no real interest. Shelby was merely being polite, and sipped her tea while browsing. She even set her mug down a few times, flipping through the pages of a few books, acting as if she was interested.

Again, Shelby looked at her watch. Thirty-five more minutes.

"Do you see anything you like?" Strauss asked. He was close behind, peering over her shoulder. For an instant, it appeared as if his neck was extra long. It stretched like a snake, moving his small head past her shoulder so he could see better.

She snapped her head, but Strauss was a few feet away, and not invading her personal space.

She thought it strange, but dismissed it, shaking her head at the notion.

"*Oh*, a few authors I enjoy. I didn't know Dan Brown has a new book out."

"As I said, I carry the most up-to-date titles. My patrons insist upon it."

"I see."

Shelby heard a chime.

"*Oh*, pardon me," said Strauss with another bow. "I must tend to a customer. Her time is up." He turned to walk away, but she interrupted his step.

"What do you mean?"

Strauss looked oddly at her, as if she should know. "Her

time is up. *Frau* Tinkleton is a trooper—over twenty minutes inside." He smiled and turned again, walking down a short hallway.

Shelby was curious now. She set down her tea and grabbed another book. It was a Stephen King novel, and it was heavy. She held it up, flipping to the middle, pretending to read a page. Her eyes watched as Günter von Strauss stood at the end of a hallway on the other side of the store. Three doors lined the wall, and he stood in front of the farthest. He knocked softly, and then jiggled the handle. Another few seconds and he gently opened the door to a room.

At this angle, Shelby could not see what was inside. Strauss entered the room for a moment, and she could hear soft words, although not what was said. Eventually, Strauss came back down the hallway, and Shelby's eyes flashed back to the book in her hand.

"I'm terribly sorry about the interruption," he commented as he approached.

"It's okay," she responded, setting down the book. She followed the row with her eyes, spotting the paperbacks at the far end of the shelf. She neared, reaching down, grabbing another familiar author. She then took a final sip of her tea, and began walking toward Strauss. They met at the counter.

She handed him the glass, saying, "Thank you. That was wonderful tea."

"Would you care for another cup?"

"*Oh*, no thank you. I must be going soon."

He nodded, but said nothing.

She didn't want to hurt his feelings. Strauss was a nice enough man, and most likely his store saw little business.

Vincent Hobbes Presents

Shelby felt sorry for the old man, and knew a few bucks spent on a book would make her feel good about herself.

She twisted her wrist, looking down at it.

"How much for this one?" she asked, flashing it his way.

But Strauss did not look at her selection. Instead, he stared straight into her eyes, saying, "*Oh*, these books are not for sale."

"They aren't?"

He chuckled. "*Oh*, heavens no!"

Shelby looked at him oddly. She figured this must be a joke. Any moment he would laugh at her. Any moment, they would have one last chuckle, she would spend eight dollars, and be on her way.

Any time now.

But it was no joke. It was not of Herr Strauss' nature to tease anyone, especially a customer. He was a gentleman, and would never do such a thing.

Tilting her head, a humorous look on her face, Shelby asked, "Then what is this place? A library of some sort?"

"You're allowed to take the books home at a library, but not here. I rent time for people to read, *Frau* McClain. Time for people who have no time to spare." Strauss' eyes twinkled.

"I don't follow. People . . . read here?"

"Yes, ma'am. It's a wondrous concept."

The door chingled, and Herr Strauss excused himself once more, this time to greet a customer entering his store.

It was good timing, because Shelby could not help herself, and giggled uncontrollably. She covered her mouth quickly; the thought of renting time was as odd as anything she had ever heard.

A large woman came through the door. She was in her fifties, and walked in from the cold, stomping her feet at the doorway.

"Hello, *Frau* Huddleston," Strauss bowed flamboyantly.

"Herr Strauss," she said loudly. There was no bashfulness to this woman, Shelby could tell.

"Would you care for some tea? I just made some," he asked.

"I would, thank you."

As he scurried back to the kitchen, the woman asked, "Do you have any new ones in yet?"

"Far shelf. Top right," he responded from the kitchen.

Shelby had already decided to make her exit. She looked at the book in her hand, and thought of leaving it on the counter and making a quick getaway. But Mister Strauss—or Herr Strauss, as he had introduced himself—was much too nice for such an act of cowardice. He might have been slightly odd, but that did not warrant such an insult.

She turned back to the shelf, meaning to return the book in her hand to its rightful place. She would thank him again for the tea and go back to the skating rink.

Shelby looked at her watch. Twenty-nine minutes.

The thought of the newest breed of pop music blaring on loudspeakers, and fifty kids skating in circles under annoying lights, did not sound at all appealing. Still, she felt awkward in this store, and was ready to leave.

The woman, Marge Huddleston, neared a moment later,

looking at the same shelf of new releases. Shelby gave her a brief nod, and then continued searching for the place she had gotten the book.

"Watcha reading?" Mrs. Huddleston asked.

"*Huh? Oh*, nothing really."

"Let me see," said the woman. She was much larger than Shelby, who had worked hard at maintaining her figure. The woman didn't allow her much choice, extending her hand out and turning the book in Shelby's hand.

"Michael Crichton?" asked the woman curiously.

"Yeah," said Shelby.

"Never heard of him."

"*Oh*, well he's quite good. This is one of his best. It's about cloning technology and . . ." Shelby trailed off. She could tell by the look on the woman's face that she was uninterested, perhaps even confused. Shelby quickly said, "It's just something I've read before. What are you buying?"

"I ain't buying nothing," the woman said with a short grunt. "You don't buy books here. You rent time to read them."

"*Oh*, yes. Mister Strauss—"

"Herr Strauss," Mrs. Huddleston corrected.

Shelby rolled her eyes. "I mean, Herr Strauss. He said you don't buy books here, but I don't know what that means. What's the point of a bookstore, if you can't buy any books?"

"*Ah*, I see. You've never been here," said the woman, finally turning her attention fully to Shelby. "Okay, let me explain. First, very few people know of this place. Those who do know, either come back often, or never come back at all. Either way, we don't talk about it."

"Why not?" Shelby asked.

"Because if we did, all the rooms would be taken. I hardly have any time to spare as it is, and I appreciate not having to wait in line."

Shelby was beyond confused. "What do you mean, wait in line?"

"You see those rooms?" Mrs. Huddleston said, pointing. "There are only three reading rooms. This place won't hold more."

"I see. How much do you pay to . . . read?"

"Ten bucks. I usually stay for ten minutes. A bargain if you ask me."

"What?" Shelby said. "Are you serious?"

"I am."

"So, you pay a dollar a minute—"

"Yup. That's exactly right."

"But I can buy this book at the store for seven," said Shelby, perplexed. She laughed at the absurd nature of renting books—especially at such prices.

"You won't need more than five minutes your first time," assured Mrs. Huddleston. "Five bucks should be enough. It took me months to get up to ten minutes. It's a good thing, though. My old man hardly misses ten bucks from time to time. He's at the lumber store right this moment. God knows what he's building. I promised I'd drive him to town if he'd let me stop by here for twenty minutes. Ten to sip tea and talk with Herr Strauss. Ten to read."

Shelby shook her head. "You'd be lucky to read a chapter or two in ten minutes."

"Pardon me, am I interrupting?" questioned the accented voice from behind them. Both women turned, and Strauss was standing in the middle of the room.

"Herr Strauss, you have confused this young lady," said Mrs. Huddleston with a grin. "She doesn't understand your store policy."

He turned to Shelby, an apologetic look on his face. "I am truly sorry, *Frau* McClain. At my age, I tend to forget things. It's happening more often lately, I'm afraid. I thought I explained."

"It doesn't matter, though. I really must get going," Shelby insisted.

"Give Herr Strauss a moment to explain. Trust me, this is the greatest bookstore ever! The books here are magical!" Mrs. Huddleston exclaimed.

Shelby smiled, but it was weak. She was feeling pressured. But, she remained polite, as was her nature, and listened as Strauss spoke.

"I stock only the best novels. I hand select them myself. I personally read each and every one to make sure they are safe for my patrons."

"Safe?" asked Shelby.

"Of course. I wouldn't want any mishaps. I stock only books that are appropriate—ones that will not endanger those who read them. Some books have limited dangers, so I usually rip out the pages. I'd hate to take away from the beauty of a story because of one scene."

"You rip out the pages?" Shelby asked.

"Let me give you an example," replied Herr Strauss. He walked to a nearby shelf, took a moment, and then made a selection. He flipped the book open, showing it to her. "See.

Moby Dick. A wonderful novel if you haven't read it."

"Perhaps in high school. I don't remember."

"Well, no matter. It's an elegant story. One that will capture your imagination. There are only a few parts that are dangerous. I'd hate for one of my patrons to be eaten by a whale, or God forbid, fall overboard in a storm. So, I took the liberty of tearing out those sections. See?" he asked, showing her the missing pages.

"I see," she muttered. Shelby was most definitely uncomfortable, and she had no clue what Herr Strauss was talking about. The fact that he took the liberty to censor books did not sit well with her. But, before she could respond, the door to the room down the hallway opened. Herr Strauss turned as an elderly woman exited.

"Ah, *Frau* Tinkleton. I presume your reading went well?" asked Strauss, approaching the woman.

She was elderly, probably in her seventies, as well. She had silver hair and used too much hair spray. She was one of Strauss' regulars, visiting three days a week. Her selection was usually poetry, or one of the classics.

"It did," she replied, her voice cracked as she spoke. The two met at the counter, and began chatting.

"Shit," exclaimed Mrs. Huddleston.

"What's the matter?" asked Shelby, turning.

"Mrs. Tinkleton goes to my church."

"So?"

"She surely won't approve of this," said Mrs. Huddleston, holding a book out in her hand. It was one of those sappy romance novels Shelby so desperately hated. It had a cheesy

Vincent Hobbes Presents

title with a picture of a man and a woman on the front cover. The man was well built, and had long, flowing blond hair. Of course he was not wearing a shirt. He held an attractive woman in his arms.

"It's the third in the series," commented Mrs. Huddleston. "Lots of juicy scenes," she added with a grin and a wink. She quickly cast the book aside, searching frantically for another. Finally, she chose one just as the elderly woman strode near.

"Mrs. Huddleston," the old woman said, nodding her head.

"Mrs. Tinkleton," she replied.

The old lady had a scoff on her face. Shelby guessed she was the judgmental type by the way she looked Mrs. Huddleston up and down.

"Hi, I'm Shelby McClain," she said with a smile.

"Edna Tinkleton. I've never seen you here before," the old woman stated, looking sourly at Shelby.

"First time," replied Shelby.

The woman nodded her head, taking a few moments to stare down Shelby.

Again, she felt uncomfortable. Shelby looked at her watch. Twenty-six minutes.

The elderly woman looked back to Mrs. Huddleston, staring at the book in her hand. "*Pride and Prejudice, eh*?"

"It's a classic," replied Mrs. Huddleston.

"I would have guessed something different," replied the elderly woman with a sneer.

"Such as?"

"Something filthy," the old woman snorted.

The Endlands

Before Mrs. Huddleston could retort, Herr Strauss reappeared from the kitchen, carrying yet another mug of hot tea. He offered it to the old woman, who took it from his hands, exchanging it for the novel in her own.

He looked down at it, stating, "*Gone with the Wind*. A beautiful story."

Mrs. Tinkleton smiled at Strauss, and then turned her head, glaring at Mrs. Huddleston with a sneer. "At least it's not smut!" she scolded.

"*Pride and Prejudice* is hardly smut," replied Mrs. Huddleston.

"I know what you come here for. Filth. Trash. Smut!"

Strauss cleared his throat. He realized the tension between the two women, and offered a bit of conversation to ease everyone. He took Mrs. Tinkleton by the arm, escorting her away politely.

Shelby remained still, holding her novel in her hand. She was dumbfounded. She felt like she was in a movie. Everything around her was surreal.

Mrs. Huddleston was insightful, though, and realized Shelby's angst.

"She's an old hag," the woman whispered. "The type of woman who judges everyone she meets. Do not worry about her."

"I'm not," said Shelby. She was defensive. Ready to leave. "I don't understand this place, and I really must get going." She reached out to lay the book down, but Mrs. Huddleston stopped her.

"You really must give it a try. Just five minutes. Trust me, you'll enjoy every moment."

Vincent Hobbes Presents

"You want me to pay to sit in a room for five minutes?"

"Yes. Please, pick a selection you'll like." Mrs. Huddleston winked at her again. She leaned in close, saying, "I suggest something a bit more . . . intense. A woman can't have too much romance, now, can she?"

"I . . . I suppose not."

"This is how it works. You pay for your time. Go into the room and relax. Flip open your book to a hot scene, and presto!—you're *in* the story. You'll experience everything firsthand."

"*In* the story?"

"Yes. Herr Strauss' books are magical. Open up to an interesting part and start reading. The next thing you know, you'll be inside the story. You can watch the sacking of Troy if you wish. Sail the Mississippi with Tom Sawyer. Anything is possible!"

"I . . . I don't understand. How can that be possible?"

"I don't know, but it's true. You can meet your favorite characters. Travel through time. See other parts of the world and have great adventures. Trust me, buy some time and you'll see."

"I'm sorry, but I don't believe you," said Shelby bluntly. She couldn't help herself. This was too bizarre to believe.

"*Oh*, I didn't believe it, either," returned Mrs. Huddleston. "But Herr Strauss has a money back guarantee. I'm sure you have five minutes to spare."

Shelby looked at her watch. Eighteen minutes.

"I suppose," she answered.

"Great. Now, choose a book you like, although I still recommend something erotic. Perhaps at your age, you still have romance at home. My husband could care less about romance, which is why I come here."

"So . . . you go *into* the story?" Shelby stammered, still in disbelief.

"Yes," responded Mrs. Huddleston eagerly. "You go *into* the story! Just last week I walked the beach with an Italian prince. We did other things, too." She grinned wide. "I've traveled the oceans with Captain Ahab, and met Dracula—in the daylight, of course. I know it sounds strange, but you *must* trust me. Once you find a book you like, just give it a try."

Shelby nodded, but wasn't convinced. She hesitated, and Mrs. Huddleston had to pat her on the shoulder for encouragement.

"Go on," she urged.

Shelby had no interest in a romance novel. She decided what the hell, and approached the counter with the Crichton novel in hand. Herr Strauss and Mrs. Tinkleton were chatting eagerly.

"Did you decide on anything?" he asked.

"I . . . I suppose."

"What did you pick?" asked Mrs. Tinkleton. She was nosey, and stared at the book in Shelby's hand. "I've never heard of that. Is it more filth?"

"No. It's not filth. It's an adventure story, written by a bestselling author," Shelby answered defensively. She was annoyed at the woman.

"No matter what you choose . . . it is none of my business," said Herr Strauss, realizing the tension, and giving Mrs. Tinkleton a look. "How long do you wish to read?" he asked Shelby.

"*Um*, I don't really know."

"Let's start you with five minutes. That should be more than enough for your first experience."

"Okay." Shelby dug in her purse, looking for cash. She pulled out a five, handing it over reluctantly.

Herr Strauss took the money in his hand. Shelby realized his nails were painted black. They were long and pointy.

"Room three," he motioned to the hallway.

"Alright," she said. Slowly, Shelby walked to the room.

At the same time, Mrs. Huddleston placed *Pride and Prejudice* back on the shelf, snagging the romance novel, keeping it hidden from Mrs. Tinkleton's prying eyes. She handed Herr Strauss a ten dollar bill, and walked away from the counter.

"Enjoy your read," he responded with a grin.

Mrs. Huddleston waddled down the hall. She smiled at Shelby before entering room two. "Trust me, you'll enjoy it." Then, she disappeared.

Shelby sighed before opening the door, unsure of what to expect. The room was small, housing only a recliner and two pictures on the wall. It was dimly lit, and Shelby questioned why a reading room would be so dark. It didn't matter, though. She wasn't interested in reading.

She closed the door behind her, looking around once more. The recliner seemed comfortable. Sitting down, she pulled the handle, easing back the chair. She lay there a minute, unsure of what to do. The dark room made her sleepy.

Finally, Shelby held up the book.

The Endlands

She had read it before. It was a wonderful novel and a popular movie.

She flipped through the pages, skimming them. Shelby read a few words here, and a few words there, and noticed no pages were ripped out. She thought it odd, after what Strauss had said about censoring them.

Herr Strauss had found nothing to 'protect his patrons' from, she thought, shrugging her shoulders with a smile.

And she began reading. As she did, Shelby began falling—deeper and deeper into a world far different from her own.

The chime sounded.

Herr Strauss looked up from his book.

"*Frau* Huddleston," he remembered. Strauss gently made his way to the hallway, and rapped at the door, jiggling the handle before opening it.

"It's time," he said in a soft voice.

With that done, he went back to the counter. A minute passed and Mrs. Huddleston returned from her reading time. A blissful look was upon her face. She was relaxed—this series was indeed a good one.

"I hope you enjoyed your time," Strauss said pleasantly.

"I did, Herr Strauss. Amazing book!"

"I have a new shipment of titles coming in next week."

"Great. I'll stop by, same as always."

"Wonderful," he said, taking the book from her hands and placing it on a cart. He took special care to not invade her privacy, and did not look at the title. Whatever his patrons wanted to read was fine by him. He did not judge. He turned to say goodbye, accidently brushing against a pile of books. A few fell as he reached out to catch them.

"Here, let me help," said Mrs. Huddleston, stepping close and securing the pile. "New shipment?"

"Thank you. Yes, I just got this in. I haven't had time to go through them yet. It takes awhile, you know—going through all these books. Making them safe to read."

"I'm sure it does."

"Every once in awhile, I forget if I've checked a book or not. My memory is failing me, I admit. I'll sometimes read one three or four times before placing them on the shelf. Can't be too careful."

"Ever forget to check one?"

"*Oh*, heavens no," Strauss replied. "At least, I don't think so." He took a moment, staring absentmindedly into the distance, as if trying to remember something.

Mrs. Huddleston helped him stack the books. After doing so, she turned to leave, then she remembered. "Herr Strauss?"

"Yes, *Frau* Huddleston?"

"That young woman—Shelby."

"*Eh?*" he replied.

"She went into reading room three," reminded the woman. "I was just curious if she enjoyed her experience."

It took a few more moments for the man to remember. "*Oh*, my!" he exclaimed. "I forgot." He dropped the remaining books on the counter and scurried down the hallway. "My mind tends to forget things," he mumbled.

"How long has she been in there?" Mrs. Huddleston asked, rushing after him.

Strauss looked at his watch. "Eleven minutes. Much too long for a new patron," he said glumly.

"I'm sure she's quite alright," said Mrs. Huddleston, following Strauss to the door.

A light tap.

A jiggle of the door handle.

He cracked the door, saying, "*Frau* McClain, your time is up . . ."

He looked inside.

The scene was horrific.

Shelby McClain had been ripped apart. Appendages were flung haphazardly around the room. Blood soiled the recliner. It was smeared on the walls, and pooled on the floor. Hardly anything was left of the poor woman.

Mrs. Huddleston peered past Strauss, and gasped.

Her screams filled the store.

Strauss took a step in, leaned down, and picked up the tattered book Shelby had been reading.

"*Jurassic Park*?" he asked, flipping through the pages.

"I do not remember checking it," he added, still flipping.

"I like the classics, you know," he muttered.

"I only buy the modern stories for my patrons. I must have forgotten this one," said Herr Günter von Strauss, muttering like a confused old man, scratching his head.

"I must have forgotten."

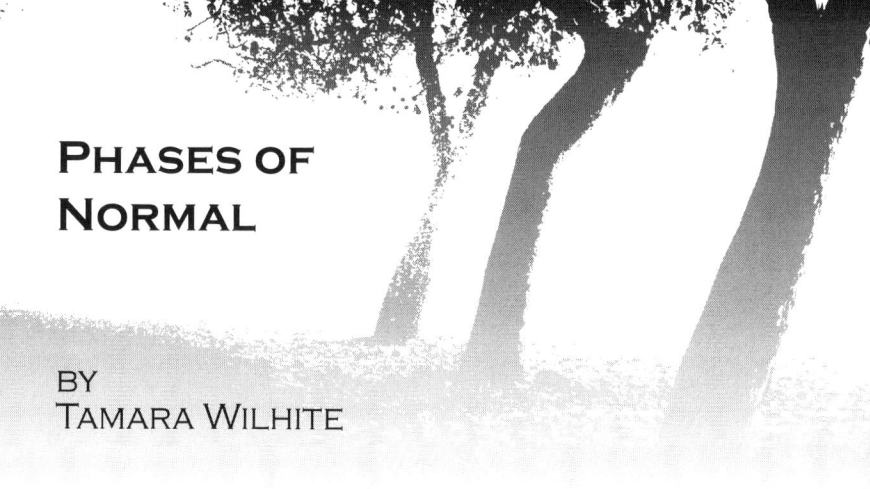

Phases of Normal

by
Tamara Wilhite

"Why do they always do the experiments on slow ones?" Marissa got the nerve to ask.

"Would people accept experiments on normal ones?" Doctor Ramirez asked, his hand never ceased typing notes on the digital pad as he spoke. He kept his eyes on the boy behind the one-way mirror. The child continued to draw his repetitive, yet ever so straight lines.

"How does this happen? With all the testing, I mean."

"Some people refuse testing for religious reasons," Doctor Ramirez remarked, surprisingly no disdain in his voice. "Then, there are the false negatives, those the tests don't catch or with low quality control."

"I thought quality was going up," Marissa remarked.

"Quality goes up, so standards tighten. Thirty years ago, this subject would have been placed in a special education environment, carefully trained for a remedial job."

"Those jobs still exist," Marissa said, keeping her voice cool and calm. She needed this job, having been rescued by Dr. Ramirez himself from a menial genetics lab job. Work humans or robots could do, but delegated to humans to keep employment up. And save electricity.

"And with increasing mechanization, those jobs tend

to go to the underemployed who need physical labor to feel useful. Those who can contribute in such a way, saving power and robotic wear, are better utilized as such. The non-useful, those who require more resources and require much more supervision, are not worth it."

"What happens next?"

"He will acclimate to the environment."

"His behavior hasn't changed."

"The stress indicators from his biosensors indicate that it has happened."

He. It. Never a name used, Marissa noticed. "What's his name or designation?" Marissa asked.

"Can't you read the ID bar code?" Dr. Ramirez snapped.

She could. She did. Long, but she had a good memory. That's one reason Dr. Ramirez picked her. She could put less data in computers in order to keep track of things, which was less data that could be analyzed and picked apart by others.

There were people who would disagree with what Dr. Ramirez did, preferring that these unacceptable children just be put down. In fact, some of them might have been listed as such in the database when Dr. Ramirez had them delivered here. Others would see his work as immoral. As if giving them a chance at a better life—any life—was immoral.

"How long?"

"However long it takes for him to acclimate." Dr. Ramirez took his eyes off the child briefly, a sharp flicker to her, a visual cold stab. "Take a break if you need it." His attention went straight back to the child.

Marissa kept herself from rushing to the bathroom. Racing away would look bad, overly emotional; unprofessional. She didn't want to be medicated as an adult, as she'd been as a child. She knew the violent and unfocused were drugged into peaceful stability. When emotional extremism was recognized as the source of violence, suicide, even unsocial acts like social harm and gossip and stress, even the naturally exuberant like her were brought under control. The too low extreme simply flowed down the drain by suicide. Those like Dr. Ramirez, controlled and naturally calm, flourished. The new ideal. The Middle Way, beyond rage and hate, joy and pain, was the new normal. Her way, now, though by effort.

    Marissa used the bathroom, only to justify being there. She washed her hands overly thoroughly, letting the sensation of getting clean restore her. She mentally chanted Middle Way mantras, to restore calm and certainty and peace. Restored to herself, she stared at the couch in the bathroom. Did she want sleep? Yes. The day was already emotionally draining and she felt tired. Did she need sleep? Not for another couple of hours. She did a delta wave buzz with her neural implant to drive away the muzzy thinking of exhaustion and headed back to the lab.

    Dr. Ramirez did not acknowledge her return. "What condition is this case?" she finally found the nerve to ask.

    "Borderline autism."

    "What causes it?"

    "Chemical exposure causing decreased mental capacity is the leading cause."

    Marissa remembered some details of autism. Couldn't understand the emotions of others. Emotions were bad, she had learned in her training. However, the ability to understand others sprung from that ability to understand the emotions of others—a step on the road to sentience.

"Autism is typically diagnosed by one year of age. He's older."

"Other circumstances delayed symptoms until this age."

Was the boy ripped from a family that refused to hand him over for treatment, afraid he might be killed? Or gotten rid of by a family that had been hiding him to hide the shame?

The child had started on the last clean paper. Marissa wondered what he'd do when the paper ran out. "Why did you give him paper instead of a digital pad?"

"Less digital data."

Marissa wondered how Dr. Ramirez wasn't tired yet. Maybe he was enhanced to need less sleep. Her need for sleep caught up and she sat down Lotus-style to rest.

She woke to find the answer to her prior musings.

The child was rocking back and forth. Normal, for a child. Dr. Ramirez had entered the observation room, typing even as he kneeled down by the boy. The child's keening, repetitive cries had woken her, carried in by sound systems she hadn't known were there.

Dr. Ramirez did not touch the child. He took the paper sheets, turning each one over in turn. The child's keening shifted to moaning. Dr. Ramirez disturbed the child, but paid attention to the revealed solution. When Dr. Ramirez had turned each, he took the pencil from the child's hand and put it as it had been previously. He then left the room and returned to the observation room. The child's cries stopped. After a brief puzzled interval, it began drawing again.

"Trust building?" Marissa asked.

"They don't trust. This was a demonstration that I can resolve the problems."

"Will he see you as a caregiver?"

"Autism case," Dr. Ramirez reminded her.

"Now what?" she asked.

"It will keep going until asleep."

Marissa took note of the child's behavior, and that Dr. Ramirez seemed practiced at this routine, and returned to sleep herself. She'd need to be refreshed to help at the next phase.

Dr. Ramirez woke Marissa with a tap of his foot on her leg. He had a gurney in the hallway between the observation room door and waiting room.

The child was curled around the hand with the pencil, sleeping on the paper as if a bed. "I'm surprised he's not hungry," Marissa remarked.

"I did not introduce food because an empty stomach is required before surgery. This is less invasive than a stomach pump."

He motioned Marissa to hold the gurney. He walked in and picked up the child. The sleeping child reacted instinctively to being picked up. To Marissa's surprise, Dr. Ramirez did not sedate it. He put it on the gurney, untied. The child curled up in a tight ball, sleepy but unable to sleep. Marissa then followed Dr. Ramirez, pushing the small burden.

Now it was phase two.

The surgical suite was two security doors down the same hallway. A short physical distance, except for all the security procedures. It took nearly twenty minutes to get through.

Vincent Hobbes Presents

Decontamination and security were layered into one sequence, twice. Authorized visitors saw the decontamination. Unauthorized visitors saw the security. As a new arrival, both fascinated Marissa. Did unauthorized users get hit with an extra high "sterilize" cycle of radiation, thus preventing them from causing damage to the facility? And could they be disposed of as the infected would be, reducing the need for a security clean-up detail?

The surgical suite was sparser than Marissa expected. It was almost disappointing. Dr. Ramirez pushed the gurney to a standard operating table array. He finally sedated the child, who had begun keening again. He used the mechanisms to uncoil the child and strap him down. This part was familiar to Marissa. The sick, the insane, the unstable all sometimes had to be forced into position for the machines. She'd faced it once, as a child, curled up with a case of appendicitis and pried to proper position by the surgical unit. It saved the nurses and surgeon the need to physically handle her. Less disease risk, as well.

The child's eyes darted about, staring in terror at the machine and at the doctor. "Do I need to administer sedative?" Marissa asked.

Dr. Ramirez did not pull his attention from the control panel he'd taken position beside. One hand flowed over the control panel in a flurry of motion. The other hand continued adding notes to the note pad. The ambidextrous nature was a wonder if Marissa was willing to allow it. But awe could be as destructive as anger, and more demeaning. She took the position of observer.

The neurosurgical unit descended from a cache in the

ceiling. *That* unit was the high-tech she'd expected. Hidden? Or simply better stored there?

When it was just above the child's head, Dr. Ramirez began doing all the manipulation in person, by hand. Mouth insert to protect the tongue. Forehead protection. Restraint checks. As if this mattered to him so much he would not let the machine do it. As if it was a patient, not an experiment. Marissa felt a little relief. Maybe this child was receiving an experimental treatment and wasn't just the experiment?

The child was given another set of injections. Not quite asleep, but quiescent.

"Why not unconscious?"

"There is a need for neural feedback during the process."

The child strained briefly at the contact before going limp. The eyes were wide, not quite awake, definitely in shock. IVs snaked down from the surgical unit and joined the child, sliding in and around its clothing. A catheter snuck into place just as the child relieved itself.

Dr. Ramirez returned to the console. When the probes and implantation device activated, Marissa jumped back involuntarily. The devices were small, but the sounds of metal drills on bone were unmistakable. Marissa controlled the violent regurgitation in her stomach. Getting physically ill here would be the end of her life, not just her career.

A three dimensional display of the brain appeared. A biochemical map of the same brain appeared nearby. Many more IVs and sensors descended, covering the child like a nest of snakes. Chemicals in, biochemical wastes out, a few more probes inserted. The biochemical map of the child's brain began the change, colors slowly shifting. It would have made for an interesting case study if she hadn't seen the intrusive means by which it was accomplished. Over the course of several hours, the physical structure of the brain, too, shifted. Closer to normal, Marissa knew. The new and improved normal.

The flow of chemicals and fluids stopped. Marissa started forward to be of assistance when Dr. Ramirez commanded, "Stop." She froze in place. "Come here," he demanded.

A map of the new brain structure and biochemistry was compared to a structured map. "Do you understand these visuals?"

"One is how the child was; the other is how the child is."

"No. One is how the child is now. The other is how the child should be. The structure map shows the acceptable ranges of biochemistry and biological structure."

"Is the child where it needs to be?"

"There is no perfect, only acceptable ranges. The question is if the current state is within acceptable ranges. Review and comment."

"I'm glad there's not one perfect—"

"No!" Dr. Ramirez snapped, very annoyed with her. "Review the current state to the structure map of what is acceptable, and comment on what else needs to change."

Marissa felt a sharp wave of anxiety. Visual review of brain structures, looking at is and what should be, that was an analyst's job. Saying what should be done to make what is to what should be . . . that was responsibility.

Responsibility. A strange thought, something that had only before come into her vocabulary when she'd broken rules and should have known not to.

That he'd ask her to do that . . . this was a job computers couldn't do. A big responsibility. Had she blown it?

"Uh, here?" Marissa jabbed a finger into the display. "Needs more red," she offered.

"Your resume indicates you should know the biochemical indicators involved," he accused her. Was he intending her to be his equal and partner or a subordinate? She knew, vaguely, but wasn't certain.

"Serotonin," Marissa said. "Those levels need to be higher."

"Does that necessitate adding more biochemical now or increasing the body's ability to produce it?" he asked her, no longer angry. Back to calm.

"Increased ability to create," she said with more certainty than she felt. She held a hand over the frontal lobes. "And the electrical activity here needs to be lessened. The sensory integration protocol should be used." This demonstration had to be the next phase of the job interview, she decided. She had to prove she knew what they were doing before they'd let her contribute.

"Noted," Dr. Ramirez said, literally noting it in his pad before proceeding. He then took the controls once more and made a few changes. Then the machines worked and the brain maps changed. Marissa felt a rush of pride. Her suggestions made reality. In a child's mind, she remembered, and then felt less pride and confusion as to why.

The flow of fluids and tubes stopped again. The new map was generated and compared. "Review and comment."

It looked all right. All the colors were within the lines, Marissa thought. "The ranges of acceptable parameters are within the scope of the new current state," she said.

The equipment unplugged from the child and retreated to a sterilization unit. The child lay staring at the ceiling, unresponsive. Shock? Dr. Ramirez was back to taking notes.

"Go to him," Dr. Ramirez commanded. Marissa blinked at the command. She walked to the child's side and stopped. "Be emotionally interactive," he demanded. She then took the child's hand. "I will not say maternal. You are not the maternal unit. However, his brain is processing input on an emotional level now. Act . . . concerned. Act caring. Consolation. Reassurance." Dr. Ramirez stated the emotions as emotionlessly as a Middle Way member.

This *is* a child, Marissa reminded herself. A solid, stable, certain emotional environment was necessary for a stable mental foundation, she told herself. The exuding of gentler emotions would calm the child's incipient emotional storm. Middle Way wasn't cruel, but candor. It wasn't cold, it was cool. And some warmth was needed with the young so they didn't die inside and become violently insane. Candor and loyalty, she'd been taught. That brought out the best of human nature. Be natural, within those constraints. Neither wild nor without emotion.

The Middle Way.

The ID flashed through her mind, but meant little. He was little. She saw the terrified child as he was. "We're done now. The pain is over," she said, her eyes flicking to Dr. Ramirez for confirmation, which he gave. "No more to worry over. The fear can be over." She stated the platitudes that were truth to the child until he began to respond. He'd been in shock and slowly began to come out of it. Toward life. Toward a normal life.

The child's hand clenched tightly around hers. Physical reassurance, the most basic kind. She wanted to let go, but reminded herself to have compassion for his intense experience. She kept talking. The child's eyes focused on hers for the first time, as if he'd never truly seen her before. Life-like. Alive. Would he now be allowed to live?

Dr. Ramirez waited. Marissa wondered when they'd be done. This, too, might be part of her future job. She was growing bored of the role. She turned to him. His eyes were on a new 3D display. She saw a biochemical and electrical map of the child's brain, current state. "You're not done yet," he said.

She sighed and obeyed. This was, indeed, part of the job description. The child took her every motion and emotion in. It was old enough that it might even remember this. Its fascination would have been fascinating if the child had been cuter. "That is sufficient," Dr. Ramirez stated.

Marissa stood up and tried to take her hand from the child's. It wouldn't let go. She saw the biochemical and electrical activity map. She understood only a little of the brain structures, but she saw that the colors were all within the acceptable lines. How long before they were done and she could leave?

Marissa tried to remove the child's hand, but Dr. Ramirez stopped her. "Not yet," he scolded her. Dr. Ramirez pushed the gurney away from the operating table. The child's eyes never left her face, despite the new set of doors they went out.

Marissa was fascinated by the new place they were in.

Vincent Hobbes Presents

Geometric designs on the walls with contrasting colors on the floor tiles. Suitable for young children, she knew, vaguely remembering her own days in the crèche.

"Is this his new home?"

"Next transition phase."

"Where are the caregivers?" Marissa asked.

"You will stay here and help him explore and acclimate," Dr. Ramirez stated calmly.

"How long?"

"Until his bio-signs return to a calm state."

"Where will you be?"

"You should know that by now."

"Observation room," she replied. He didn't confirm or deny, but instead retreated to a door that would be hard to otherwise notice among all the exploratory toys. Marissa then dedicated herself to acclimating the child to the toys and environment. To take his attention from her to toys, so that he could then transition to a full time caregiver with those toys in tow.

They slept that night in the playroom, the child curled up against her, as she was flat upon a stack of beanbags. She woke to the strange sensations before reorienting herself. Why wasn't Dr. Ramirez doing this? Did young children prefer females at this phase, or did Dr. Ramirez have other work that was more important than this? Or was he observing the whole time, taking more notes?

Finally, a new door opened. A woman not unlike Dr. Ramirez entered. Marissa didn't want to assume they were related, given how unlikely that was. She'd seen so few people here; someone of an opposite race might have even looked a little like him.

The new woman knelt down beside the child and stayed with them a while. Marissa tried not to look relieved. This was the caregiver. This was whom she'd transition the child to. Then, she'd be done. The new woman let the child interact with Marissa. Then she left again. Marissa was annoyed until she returned with food and offered it to the boy.

The child devoured it. No food for two days, though plenty of IV fluids had been given. The woman ate the food with mild boredom, freely offering the child his next serving, getting his unconditional gratitude in return. Marissa tried to reach out for a food cube when the woman slapped her hand. Marissa pulled her hand back and yelped. The child jumped, terrified. The woman took the food Marissa had reached for and gave it to the child instead. The child beamed, happy, and began devouring it.

Dr. Ramirez flashed the observation room lights. Marissa saw it, and realized her cue to retreat. The child was bonding more strongly to the person who fed it. Pure mammalian behavior. This was the transition to a caregiver she'd wanted, and Marissa had almost blown it.

When the observation room closed, Marissa saw meal bars waiting. "Are those for me?"

"You need to eat, too," he answered.

Marissa wolfed down the bars. "It's hard to not eat when they are," Marissa stated.

"You have Middle Way training. Use that to control the hunger impulse."

By the time she was done, the caregiver and child were gone. "Where are they?"

"Next phase," was all Dr. Ramirez said.

"What now?"

"We go to our quarters and sleep and eat. Then, we do it again."

"Again?" Marissa said, not quite believing. "Again?"

"That is the job assignment," Dr. Ramirez said.

"You do what we just did as a job? Full time? There are enough patients to make this a full time job? How can you do that, stand to do it—"

"If you cannot perform this job, you will be put in a different capacity."

"That's not what I meant."

"If you cannot act in this capacity with me, you can fulfill the same capacity elsewhere."

"There are other places like this? Other people who need this . . . this procedure done?"

"Every case is unique, though the outcome must always be within parameters."

The way Dr. Ramirez said it rankled at her. "How can there be so many cases, when we're trying to perfect humanity?" Marissa demanded.

"Children such as this are born, and then brought within parameters."

"They shouldn't be born at all."

"They are more likely to fulfill parameters and later job assignments than natural-born," Dr. Ramirez said.

"He's a genetic mistake? The lab didn't miss him, it made him—"

"That is correct," Dr. Ramirez confirmed. The same cool tone was beginning to bother her more. It wasn't Middle

Way, it was a different way.

"Was he engineered like that?"

"Yes," Dr. Ramirez said. "As is the next case we will be processing soon."

Next case processing. Assembly line style? That implied a mass production operation. Marissa tried not to stare at the doctor in horror. She could see a likeness in him that she'd seen in the woman. In the child that looked like the woman. He was like them. He was different, like the child. The dawning horror of realization grew through her, giving birth to an outburst she couldn't control. "You're engineered, too, like that child!"

"His generation's upbringing and regimen are improved over my generation."

Not "his own upbringing" but "his generation".

"How can this be? A generation? A whole group? But the imperfections should be weeded out, not bred!"

"Natural breeding has a high risk of imperfection, as your own behavior demonstrates. Genotypes easily managed and easily brought into required standards are of greater benefit than those that must be managed to stay within standards all of their lives."

He didn't say "like you", but he might as well have. "You can't do this!"

"This is my job function."

"But how can the normal—"

"The child is now within normal parameters."

"How can everyone allow this? Making kids, making them fit standards, making—"

"That is why there is such high security at these facilities."

"There are others?"

"There is the option to transfer, if you require it to function. The emotional imprint of stress of the observations sometimes negatively impacts the work relationship."

"You need me to be the emotional anchor because you can't be," Marissa accused.

"Correct," he stated mechanically.

"I can't do this," Marissa said. "I can't help you make these kids, do this, make these . . . these . . ."

Forget the Middle Way, she thought, this was a new way, a new and improved form of human. People not capable of wild emotional swings, bad thoughts, programmed to the ideal emotional state parameters before they could even ponder the imponderable. The defective made normal, the new normal, which normal people struggled to attain. Making her, all natural born people, obsolete in the process. Processes. Processed. He said other facilities. How many were like this? Dr. Ramirez was an adult, as was the woman. The child was another generation. How long until there were many like them? How many more were there like them? "I can't do this," Marissa repeated.

"You are overly emotional, thus cannot serve as a comforting caregiver during the reprogramming process," Dr. Ramirez stated matter-of-factly. "You cannot act in the capacity you were trained for."

He swiftly pushed a hidden button, gassing the room. With no concern for him falling down, she saw, even as she fell. His only thought was to ensure she could do nothing that could harm the equipment or the project. No hope of escape, she thought, before blacking out. She wondered if she'd ever wake up after failing such a test.

Marissa did wake up, in another surgical unit, though not the one she'd been in with Dr. Ramirez. She felt the surgical hoses and tubes inside her. Were they going to make her into the kind of person they wanted her to be, closer to the new and improved normal?

"Where is Dr. Ramirez?" she demanded of the new doctor's shadow.

He turned to face her. The face was almost, but not quite Dr. Ramirez. Same model, though, and probably same edition, too. Marissa tried to get up instinctively and found herself strapped down, and without clothes. Even the child had been allowed clothes.

"He works with subjects phasing to more normal brain function."

"And who do you work with?" she asked.

"I create breeding units," the new doctor stated.

Marissa tried to scream in protest but was promptly covered as a biochemical manipulator dropped from the ceiling. It drowned out her cries even from her own ears before it began changing her.

Breeding units.

She wished she'd remembered the Middle Way, and not reacted so badly. She'd been working there to make children a few steps closer to normal. This room, perhaps just down the hall, moved her a few phases away from normal. All for the same grand purpose. Making more people; better people.

The chemicals were flowing through her, calming her

stress response before a probe snaked inside her. Worse than the men she'd known, far worse knowing what it was going to do. The next drugs, though, took her from her thoughts altogether. She felt her body relax even as the thing inside her made her ready to receive their engineered embryos.

At first, she felt the electrodes and chemicals rushing in. She knew her own mental map, from her Middle Way training. As the chemicals flowed and ebbed, she lost the map in a tide, all flowing into a warm, blood-red sea of her own eyelids. For a moment, there was peace, no anger or anxiety, as she'd felt when consigned to this fate for not being enough of a cog in the greater machine that sought to create correctly made workers for society. For a moment, the detached acceptance was what she'd been trained to seek to attain for her life—the ideal. That it was imposed by a machine didn't matter then.

Then it did matter, as she struggled for full consciousness. She felt changes, and tried to imagine what the mental map of her own brain would look like. She saw the child's scan, a strong recent image, and then the child's face, and then the doctor's face and his harsh rejection—his sentence, her punishment. Her harsh emotional recoil was more than she could contain under the drugs, and the machines promptly corrected it.

As a deeper blackness threatened, she felt no fear. That wasn't allowed. Not out of compassion for the patient, but because a calm patient was easier to work with, thus more efficient for the operation. Then the coherence, a bubble of higher thinking, seemed to pop. No more thoughts or memories, and with it, no more wonderings or worries. It would have been a perfect Middle Way sensation if she were capable of appreciating it.

She could barely feel the start of the new life even as the machines gradually took away her ability to control her own. Then, she was unable to feel or care if she felt anything at all. As the life grew, the hoses and covers were removed. Yet she couldn't see more than a blur or hear much farther than the equipment. Even her body felt distant. There were only the sensations of the growth of the new life, the warm glow of it, and wonder as they grew.

When the pain came, she knew that the lives would be leaving her. Then, the medics swarmed and took the babies away. The cocoon fell from the ceiling again, taking the pain and placenta and worry away.

She felt a brief wonder of how long it would be until those children met Dr. Ramirez. They would know him more than they would know her. That emotional pain caused the computer to take the pain away in a new wash of drugs. She slept then.

She awoke, eventually. Time ceased, even as it passed. Her body was healing, but she didn't care what happened to it. She didn't care about anything anymore.

Then, she awoke one day and felt them begin the cycle again. She was briefly surprised and eager to be filled with new life again. She couldn't remember how they remade her brain, or what had been done to her body, nor could she think of much more than the sensations any more. All she could remember was that this wasn't the job she had originally wanted, but they'd made her willing to be fulfilled by it.

She recited the Middle Way credo when she could, to remind herself of being normal, though there were only phases of normal left anymore.

Propaganda

By
Nathan Palmer

The road was an endless corridor of triple-stacked houses. The dwellings appeared to cave in on him as his boots clacked loudly on the cobblestone sidewalk. His steps echoed throughout the streets. He felt nauseated from the claustrophobic feeling the buildings gave him. Crickets chirped their night song through their hiding spots in the bushes. They would not show their faces to this man, even in the damp night.

He was a man to be feared. The foggy night, the dimly lit lamps, and the staleness of the air added to his intimidation. This soldier wore a distinct uniform. The long, grey overcoat proudly displayed his patches, informing everyone he was on the right side. His neatly combed, blonde hair contrasted with the darkness of the night sky. He had his machinegun strapped across his shoulder, a pistol on one hip, and a long knife resting on the other. He was trained and ready to carry out his orders, just as he was taught.

He passed a few people along the way. They braved the dismal fog just as he had. He approached a group of children playing in the street. They stopped their innocent banter and saluted him. He returned the salute with a smile; these children were the future of his nation—the survival of his kind.

Vincent Hobbes Presents

It was them he was trying to protect.

The kids had read the posters:

'Loyalty is honor'

He passed a man watering his flowerbed. The older man stopped what he was doing and gave the same salute as the children. He halted his stride and looked at the old man. Proudly, they stared at one another. Then, he raised his hand, and returned the salute. The two held their pose for some time. It was an honor for both. The older man had done his job to secure the survival of the previous generation. Now, there was a youth in front of him doing the same thing.

'Never forget'

This is what the people's job was—morale. It was a hard fought battle, but they were there to help him succeed in his mission. Every one of them was doing his or her job. He even passed by a couple standing in front of their house, smiling at him and nodding their heads. They understood the posters:

'We will never be destroyed if we remain united and loyal'

The soldier was given a short briefing as to who his enemy was, and what *they* were. He was informed what would happen if he failed. The training films showed him the extent of their wrath. But he did not need the films. He knew what they had done to his proud people. They were creatures of the night; cannibals, vampires, werewolves—monsters. They would snatch babies from the good people of his country. They dined naked around flames of human flesh. They were hard to capture, as they blended in with society during the day—leeching all the money from his people, leaving so many unable to fend for themselves.

It took one man, his grand leader, to say it openly. He

spoke in front of the masses, telling of the atrocities these creatures were committing. He told of the plague that the others were spreading across his good country. It had been there all along, but the people were too blind to see it. His leader blamed all, even himself, for not knowing this would happen.

Now, it was time to fight back!

Now, it was time to cleanse the land!

As the soldier's boots clacked against the street, he thought of the films. They showed what *they* were capable of. He recalled horrendous sights of *them* stalking in the bushes, waiting to prey upon his people. He saw how they sacrificed their own children.

He tried to shake the scenes from the films out of his head, but they also helped. They fueled his anger. They were the sole reason he decided to enlist. He wanted to *'be part of the solution, not part of the problem'*, like all the posters said.

Most had already been rounded up, but a few loose stragglers were still out there. They were hiding, waiting for their opportunity to strike. This he knew to be true, for his leader told him so. He told him that they would kill his father, then his mother, then every last one of his people if they were not found and destroyed.

This was his mission. He was sent alone—to investigate a home where one was said to be hiding. This was his time to prove that he loved his country, and be part of the solution. He would be praised as a hero for doing his part.

He counted every number on the houses. The street seemed to last forever, but the numbers were getting closer.

Vincent Hobbes Presents

He was almost there. His hands became clammy. He knew his cause was just, but nothing could prepare him for what he was about to do, no matter the training. He was like an athlete about to play his first professional game. It was a world of which he was unfamiliar.

He found the address. The lair was concealed as just another home, but he knew something else lurked inside. He walked up the stairway and saw the lights of the living room fully lit. He looked around some, trying to figure out what he was up against. He was armed, but according to his leader, these creatures were quick and hard to kill with human weapons. He thought of this as he grasped his rifle and attached the bayonet.

Inside, shadows moved across the room. There were more than one inside the lair. They were moving rapidly; the shadows clashed and intermingled, then split again. Laughter came from the house. But he knew it was all for show. They were trying to act like one of his kind. They were up to something big inside their lair.

He should have gone back for reinforcements, but this was his mission. He wanted to prove he was capable of engaging the enemy, that he could carry out his mission at any cost. But his enemy was smart, and he would have to use his wits.

He looked inside the window. He could see them dancing in circles. Their robes twirled around in the shadows of the fire-lit room. He could hardly make out their faces through the dimness, but he could see that they were not human. Their faces looked distorted, like that of demons. Fangs hung outwardly from their mouths, like something the soldier had seen in a comic book. They hissed and shrieked, dancing around a baby in some manner of ritual.

At the sight of the infant, the soldier feared the worst. The fact that they were dancing around a youngling with fangs as large as theirs meant they were reproducing. The films were right! If they reproduced, then soon they would have an army big enough to kill all his people.

Then, the light brightened and the soldier could make out all the details in the room. They changed. They morphed into human form. In an instant, they were no longer demons. They now appeared as normal human beings. They held the baby in the air. They sang songs to it. They played with it. A mother, a father, and two older children surrounded the infant as it laughed with glee.

He panicked. They knew he was there. They had changed their form to *seem* like humans. He knew their tricks, though. If he did not move in immediately, they would come out and kill him. They would snatch his body and do unthinkable acts, just like the films said. Every part of his training was coming true. Everything he had learned about them was being shown to him—firsthand.

He looked down the road. Nobody was around. The streets were empty, and the fog sat heavier than before. He took one last look into the window and their true form showed once again. They were dancing once more, their fangs protruding as they held the baby in the air.

It was time.

They had to be stopped.

He readied himself for impact. He wiped the sweat from

Vincent Hobbes Presents

his hands and brow and put his boot against the door.

Three... Two... One!

He smashed his way in, rifle drawn—ready to kill.

The family jumped and looked to the door. As if on cue, their bodies morphed into humans, once again.

The soldier was terrified. They tried appearing as his own kind, but he could not let them succeed. He attempted to speak, but no words would surface. Pure rage burned within him as he thought of the films. He imagined the infant killing the young children he had seen only moments prior.

The look of a killer formed across his face.

They scattered like roaches. He knew he was at the right place. He was told they would attempt to flee. They moved quickly, just as his leader had said they would. Everything he had learned in training was true.

The creatures morphed again, back into the ungodly beings they were. A little one tried to approach him; she spoke a language that he did not comprehend. He screamed at her to lie on the ground, but she would not.

He feared for his life.

She approached within paces.

The father took the baby and ran upstairs.

Screams—shouts—pandemonium.

He knew his mission was quickly going sour. He had to act, as they were about to take his life—just as the films said they would. He stuck his bayonet into the girl's stomach, pushing deep. Her eyes lit with a sense of pure shock—but the soldier knew they felt no pain.

The mother screamed, rushing over to her child.

He pulled his bayonet out of the girl, and proceeded to

open fire.

The mother let out one last cry before a bullet split through her head. Her last sight was of her daughter's death. Her last thoughts were fear and panic, not peaceful as they should be before death.

The soldier put two rounds into the other child, who was waving his hands, speaking the same language, pleading for mercy. He would find none.

Then, the soldier slowly walked up the stairs. His boots clacked against the wooden floor. The boards creaked under his weight. Rifle at the ready, he opened the bedroom door and found the father holding the child. He spoke the same language, but appeared to be praying. He looked to the sky, mumbling his gibberish.

The soldier took steady aim, and then spat a bullet into the infant, splitting it from the father's grasp. Then, he pointed his rifle at the father. Tears fell from the man's eyes. He had just witnessed the demise of his family—a lifetime of work ended in an instant.

The soldier squeezed the trigger without remorse.

It all happened in a matter of seconds—they were all dead.

As they lay on the ground, they changed back to their human forms. At first, he thought they took human form in death, but quickly deduced this was not the case.

These *were* humans.

He looked around. Blood pooled on the tiled floor, contrasting against the white of the walls. It spattered everywhere, dripping down. A few squirts even found their way across his face.

Vincent Hobbes Presents

* * *

He realized in that one moment that these Jews were not his enemy.

These Jews were not the creatures he was told they were. They were just as much human as he. Everything he had been taught was a lie. This was a false war—one without an enemy—but people would praise him for killing an innocent family.

His hands shook.

The films had lied to him. His leader had lied to him.

He vomited.

His training was nothing more than a series of propagated segments. He was made to believe that the Jews were the enemy, when, in fact, *he* was the enemy. He was a soldier of the Reich, and was taught to hate these people—these Jews. He searched for some justification within himself, but fell short. He searched for a reason as to why, but there was none. He had killed an innocent family, and within that family were innocent children.

Guilt welled up inside of him as he looked at the aftermath of what he had done. He had committed an atrocity. He only hoped that God would accept his most sincere apology.

He pulled his unused pistol from his hip. Tears leaked down his face. He would give this family retribution for what he had done to them. It was the only way.

There was no excuse for the thousands that were being killed.

There was no excuse for his people.

He swallowed the barrel of the pistol and clenched the

trigger without a second thought. In the fluster of bullets that had occurred a few minutes prior, one more joined the others.

One last pop thundered in the lair to ensure a successful mission.

Success—he had killed the enemy.

'Through might, we build strength'

Propaganda—a nation united.

King of the Jungle

by Jordan Benoit

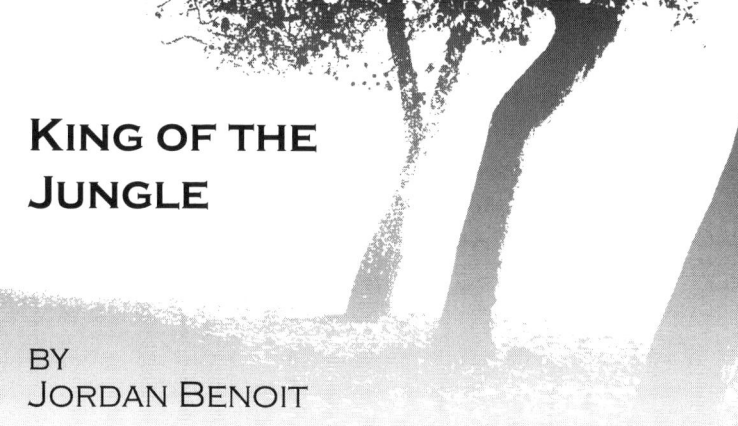

He ran as fast as his legs would carry him. Fatigued, heaving for breaths of air, Odisi lunged over the obstacles in his path. Rocks, bushes, fallen logs—his long legs propelled him forward across the great tropical landscape. The jungle expanse spread far and wide, covering much of the domain beyond his homeland. Sweat covered his body, the blue hunting paint upon him now running. Odisi's eyes intently searched ahead for danger if his nose did not first smell it.

He sustained his frantic movement, his stride increasing in length the further away he drew from the cave. What he had seen there had been a nightmare. Odisi did not wish to think about it anymore—at least not for now. He was a hunter, but he had not been prepared for this particular hunt.

Odisi wanted to get back to his camp. Famished, he needed to eat, rest, and decipher his next course of action. He ran until he felt his legs could not do so any longer, and then eventually calmed, slowing down his stride to a hurried walk. The sun slowly faded beyond the immense treetops, and darkness engulfed the lush landscape. Odisi looked around at his surroundings as he walked through the thickets of bushes and vines, all the while keeping a wary eye for other hunters of the night.

Vincent Hobbes Presents

As his heart rate returned to normal, he smelt the air around him, the jungle's moisture hurling vivid scents of vegetation and small animal life up his nostrils. Odisi grasped his musket tightly in his palms and kept walking. He had a keen sense of direction, and would encounter no setback finding his way to his camp, even in the darkness. That was not what bothered him. It was the monstrosities he had seen in the cave that gave him angst. They caused him to fear this jungle in which he had hunted game most of his young adult life.

Odisi always hunted alone, for he truly believed he was a better huntsman than his peers and, in his gut, he knew others would only slow him down, or give away his position whilst stalking prey.

Many stories of a large monster that lived in the deepest depths of the jungle passed along amongst the people of Odisi's society. It was the fascination with this monster that led him to be out here alone. The story claimed there existed a monster amidst the jungle that preyed upon Odisi's people. Yet it was not a tiger, or a lion, or even a giant python. It was something much fouler. Several men from his hunting guild had taken to the inner reaches of the jungle to track this beast with hopefulness of bringing its malice to an end; yet, the tale of this monster had struck much fear in the hearts of Odisi's brethren. All who had ventured into the jungles in search of this beast had been pronounced dead, though none of their remains had ever been found.

The monster had become a legend, and this hunter, Odisi, bravest of his village, was determined to put the legend to rest. He told almost no one of this excursion. He did not proudly announce to the people of his village that he was going to hunt the renowned man killer of the jungle. He had departed without incident, except for his friend, Killin, whom had unexpectedly surprised him before he left. Killin had always been a good friend to Odisi. He had merely been going to visit his friend when Odisi was setting out in the early morning. Killin could sense he was going hunting, but had agreed not to spread the word to anyone of *what* he was hunting.

Odisi trusted his whereabouts only to Killin, and he knew Killin would keep the secret safe, despite being completely distraught that his friend was surely going to his death. Odisi thought about his last encounter with his friend as he continued to make his way back to camp. He recalled the look on Killin's face when he told him he was going to track down the legendary monster of the jungle, the one who no one could describe, since no one had seen it and lived to recount the tale. Killin genuinely feared for his friend's life and begged him not to go but, deep down, knew there would be no convincing him otherwise.

Odisi smiled; he hoped he would return to see his friend.

He finally reached his camp, without incident. Relieved, yet still cautious of his surroundings, he set his musket on the ground next to him as he sat, igniting flames in his fire ring. It had not been easy to find fully dry wood and kindle that would take to flames but, having enough experience, he had managed to find a sufficient supply not far from where he made his camp.

Once the firelight aided his ability to see, he reached into a small satchel he had secured high in a tree—so ground-

Vincent Hobbes Presents

dwelling animals could not get to it—and pulled out some smoked deer meat. As Odisi chewed on his food in scrupulous fashion, he took the time to reflect on what he had seen in the cave.

Trophies.

There had been so many of them—skulls of creatures from all walks of jungle life, neatly arranged in precise rows, hanging along the cavern walls as though a warning to intruders to be mindful of the beast that lurked within—that is what Odisi thought, anyway. The hunter had seen much death, especially of wild game, but never put on display like this. Even as a hunter himself, he had never hung such morbid trophies of the dead in his own dwelling. Odisi's people ate the game they hunted, and used all parts of the body for several different uses, but never for vanity, and always with respect. His people would not use the bones of dead animals for their own personal gain, and they had no use for rendering them into crude weaponry, either. His people were beyond that. They had evolved and migrated from another part of the world long before Odisi's time. They had brought with them black powder and most indigenous creatures of these lush lands had bent to their every will.

Not this one.

Odisi scratched his head and took a swig from his water flask. How could such a beast lurk in this jungle? How could it act so morbidly civilized? Now, of course, Odisi did not believe the beast to be as civilized as he. That would be preposterous. However, by putting the skulls of its prey on decorative display, he believed the monster able to reason, rather than act purely on instinct. This was a sign of something oddly peculiar to Odisi. Were there other species in the world that could use reason and logic, as well? Was this monster of the jungle merely a lesser-evolved person?

No. That could not be the case. Odisi rashly shook away such thoughts from his mind. He leaned back as he put more of the dried deer meat in his mouth. It soothed his innards as it deluged into his stomach. His good friend, Killin, had prepared the jerky, smoked it, and seasoned it to perfection. Odisi thought it quite delectable, and Killin always made sure he had a fresh supply prior to embarking on a hunting excursion.

As good as it tasted, Odisi made sure he saved some for later. He did not know how long this expedition would take, and now that there were new complications, he thought he might be out here longer than he had originally planned. Odisi took one more strip of the jerky and then put away the rest in the satchel, replacing it on the tree.

He leaned back against the tree and thought about the advantage he might have if he were to go back to the cave now that it was dark outside. Perhaps he could trounce the beast as it slumbered. But, then again, perhaps the beast was nocturnal, and Odisi knew he would be put at a severe disadvantage if that were the case. After all, he could not see in the dark as well as other creatures of the night, and he had no desire to take the risk that this jungle predator might be a nighttime hunter.

The thought of such a prospect had yet to cross Odisi's mind until now, and he immediately began searching his guarded eyes around the darkness abound. He realized the campfire would be a dead give away to his whereabouts if the

Vincent Hobbes Presents

beast were currently on the prowl, so he took quick action and smoldered the blaze with dirt. The air suddenly cooled and darkness engulfed the entire campsite.

All became dreadfully quiet, but Odisi knew the life of a lone hunter all too well. The eerie silence was not what bothered him. No, it was the fear that the beast might be watching him this very moment. There was no rest for him now, not this night. He needed to remain awake and alert. And at the first sign of dawn, he would set out to the cave once again.

But, this time Odisi would be prepared.

Thin streams of light punctured their way into the jungle landscape as the sunrise of the new day took hold. Odisi rubbed his eyes, which had become dry and red over the course of the night. He had stayed awake and alert all those long hours of darkness, much too cautious to have let his guard down whilst alone, and now wished he had attained at least some shuteye; for to hunt with fatigue is one of the fundamental situations a good hunter should always avoid.

Odisi heaved himself to his feet, using his musket as a crutch to rise from the ground. The morning insects buzzed around him in soothing timbre. The thinner branches of the massive trees swayed, their leaves rustling in the quiet breeze. Odisi took in a long whiff of the fresh dawn air as he broke camp. He had spent the night gathering his wits, harnessing all the mental readiness he would need for the hunt. Now, he was ready. He had patiently waited all night, calmed his nerves, and relaxed his muscles. Odisi's composure had recoiled at first sight of the trophies in the cave, but now he was back to his confident self. After all, he was proclaimed the best hunter of his village. If others were to have smelt the fear he showed the night before, his reputation surely would dwindle amongst his guild.

 Odisi gnawed on the last bit of deer meat as he began walking away from the campsite once again. It would give him the energy he needed to complete his mission. Traveling lightly, he carried with him only the meat, his musket slung across his back, a long machete sheathed about his waist, and a small dagger laced around his right thigh. His steps were graceful and quiet as he made his way back towards the beast's dwelling.

Odisi stopped just paces from the entrance. Still early in the morning, a thick mist covered the ground, rising to his knees. The dew had softened his stride along the way, and now he stood behind the cover of a large bramble bush, as inanimate as a statue. The savory scent of red berries from the bush helped ease the tension he felt. He thought to try one of them, enticed by their colorful richness, but then decided it would be best to leave them alone. Odisi was a hunter, not an alchemist. He knew not all the signs of what made certain fruits forbidden, and this berry was something he had never seen before. Besides, he needed to focus on the task at hand.

 This man killer must be stopped, and it was he, Odisi of the Juktel'eri Tribe, who would lay it to eternal rest.

 After taking a deep breath, he brought his musket around to his front and reached into a pouch hitched to his belt. He pulled out a charge and tore off the lid with his teeth, allowing the ball on top to rest in his mouth for the moment. Moving fast, Odisi poured the powder down the barrel of his musket, and then put in the ball afterwards, topping it off with the wadding from the charge package, which he then packed with his ramrod. The remaining powder he put in the flash pan, and Odisi was locked and loaded.

He lowered the musket between a sturdy **V** shape in the bramble's branches and looked down the barrel, taking a survey of his firing radius. The mist along the jungle floor made viewing somewhat difficult, but Odisi was used to this. His intent and poise remained undeterred.

He stayed still and quiet for a long while—searching . . . listening.

Odisi ran his fingers across his bald head, feeling the morning dew upon his scalp. He would lure this fiend out of its cave now. It was time. He had the perfect position. The beast would not see him, nor would it have time to react. Odisi would lay it down flat with a gunshot right between the eyes. Despite the inaccuracy of his weapon, he was still a master marksman. The beast, the man killer, would never know the face of its predator. Odisi was an expert, and had much faith that his plan would work. He took great care in locating the best position from which to view the monster as it exited its dwelling.

He was ready.

Odisi gave a slight whistle and waited.

Nothing.

Perhaps the monster was still in slumber. Odisi was patient, though. He would try again.

Another whistle, this time a little louder.

More silence.

Eventually, he heard something.

A rustling came about from within the cave, and Odisi readied himself. The excitement, the thrill of the hunt, was almost too much. Never before had he tracked down a beast of which he had not the slightest perception of its physical manifestation. It could be anything, large or small. It could have six legs for all Odisi knew. As his anticipation heightened in brief flashes, he let his imagination wander.

The footsteps came. They were heavy, their stride a slow, sluggish pace. From the darkness of the cave came the beast. Its head was massive, and coated with mangy chestnut fur like a lion's mane; its snout jutted more like that of a wolf, though. Odisi thought it to be a peculiar creature. Its long, muscular legs were all but depleted of fur, giving way to its rich, black flesh. It walked on four legs, as most had suspected of the beast. The monster easily stood over half the height of Odisi himself, and he estimated it must weigh at least four times his own weight.

He kept his aim steady on the beast as it lethargically wandered out into the open, appearing to be curious as to the whistle that had stirred it. Odisi managed to keep from giving away any signs of his presence, but he still did not have a clear shot. The monster grunted and frothed, sniffing the misty ground, attempting to pick up a scent through its large nostrils. Odisi stayed calm. He would wait. As soon as the beast brought up its head, facing his direction, he would have his mark, and he would take the shot.

Seeing how big this beast was, Odisi knew he better make the shot count. He figured he would not have time to reload after firing his first shot before the jungle monster was upon him, and he had no desire to come into melee combat with it. It was too big. Surely it could crush him with ease, which must have been the fate of many of his brethren before him.

He held himself steady, not a shake of his nerves to hinder his chance.

Then, the monster made its mistake. Confused as to the sound it had heard, it lifted its head, looking straight in the direction of Odisi's musket, though it could see nothing through the thick brambles.

The hunter took his shot.

POW!

The ball plunged right between the eyes, and through the beast's skull. In one second, it fell to the ground, dead.

Odisi could not believe it. How could so many others have failed when it had been so easy for him? Was he truly the best hunter from his village? His quick smile of excitement soon faded back to his usual stoic expression. He realized there must be a problem. He looked at the dead beast before him, its immense body fully collapsed on the mist-covered terrain. Odisi had studied the beast before he took the shot, but why had it not hit him before?

The hunter's mind raced as to the trophy collection he had seen in the cave the evening prior. He thought of the beast's paws. *Paws!* How could such a creature organize that kind of display? It could not! That was the cold-hard fact that now raced into Odisi's mind. This was not the right monster. No way. There had to be something else. Perhaps this was just a lost beast that got in the way. Odisi started to feel remorse for ending the poor creature's life so suddenly. It was not the man killer. He had acted too quickly, without thinking.

His thoughts were soon interrupted by another growl from the cave. Odisi reached for a second charge in his pouch and immediately began reloading his musket. As he did so, another beast came into view. This one, seemingly more alert, and possibly more aggressive, took a short moment to look upon its fallen kin. A high-pitch weep reverberated from it, but the saddening pout abruptly turned into a menacing snarl, as the beast recognized the danger in which it had found itself. Frantic now, Odisi shoved the ramrod down the barrel.

Almost ready again.

This beast looked just like the former, yet much larger in size.

Odisi gulped, knowing he was doomed if he messed up his next shot. Fortunately for him, the creature had not discovered his position, but Odisi feared it would not be long before the monster sniffed out the black powder from his previous shot.

He finished readying his musket and positioned the barrel back on the branches to help keep it steady. Odisi's nerves were now getting the best of him, though. Never before had he seen a creature this large. Its jaw looked like it could swallow his head whole if it got close enough.

Odisi aimed promptly. He squinted one eye and found his mark. The beast was sniffing the air. It knew where to go now, and growled towards Odisi's general direction. The hunter closed both eyes for a moment, trying to ease the tension some. He must let go of his fear.

The monster proceeded to walk closer, taking careful steps along the jungle earth.

Vincent Hobbes Presents

Odisi reopened his eyes, and saw the beast heading his way. It was now or never.

He took the shot.

POW!

He had done it again. The beast fell flat to the ground, but he missed the direct shot. It fell hard, but it was not dead.

Odisi needed to think fast. He had to finish the job, but he also risked making himself known out in the open should there be another one. What was he to do? He hesitated, waiting to see if anything else would come out from the cave. There was nothing, though. Just deafening silence. Odisi's ears rang from the two shots he had fired; he could hear nothing else.

After another moment's wait, he decided to move in for the kill. If there was another beast in there, it surely would have come out by now. Odisi moved in, traversing around the large bramble bush and into the clearing in front of the cave entrance. He stealthily walked over to the fallen beast, its size appearing to escalate as he drew nearer. The monster huffed huge breaths of air, its long tongue hanging out as it panted. Odisi carefully set his musket on the ground as he kept walking over to it, slowly unsheathing his machete.

Now, right upon the beast, he held his blade firmly in his right palm. Odisi took a moment to gaze upon the monstrosity. Truly, he had never seen anything like it. He felt awful for having to take its life, but he did so only in self-defense. At least, he thought, he would not be leaving it to suffer. Instead, he would ease its passage into the next life. It was the least he could do.

Odisi said a silent prayer to Ghet, the god of the underworld, and raised his machete, ready to strike.

Conversely, his plan was cut short. The beast suddenly reared up, knocking Odisi off balance. It shook its head with fervor. It snapped its jaws, ready to make this hunter the hunted.

Odisi regrouped himself, taking a few steps backwards. He tossed the machete back and forth between his clawed hands a couple times, trying to taunt the massive beast. Sweat seeped out from the pores of his moist, blue-green skin. Fear settled in. The monster got back to its feet, dwarfing him in size. Odisi would show no fear. After all, he was a professional.

The monster let out a raucous howl, causing the hunter's long ears to perk in angst. Odisi grated his teeth and began circling the clearing, never removing his eyes from the creature before him. The beast then mimicked his movements. It, too, started circling.

After some time, Odisi gathered enough nerve to attack. He lunged forward, yelling as loud as he could. The beast did the same and they met with a collision that sent the hunter flying backwards, the beast landing on top of him with unmatched might. Odisi lost hold of his machete in the process and immediately reached for the dagger strapped around his thigh. The beast was taking its time. It was playing with Odisi, which gave the hunter the time he needed to retaliate.

He grabbed the dagger and shoved it hard into the monster's belly. The beast howled in vibrant agony, but did not remove its hold on Odisi. It swiped one of its sizeable front paws across his face, digging into his flesh with its claws. Crimson now covered Odisi's face, but he was not defeated. He spat blood out of his mouth and remained focused. Harder this time, he jabbed his dagger into the belly of the beast. Twice. Three times. All the while, Odisi cried with maddening aggression.

The monster finally backed off of the hunter, consequently allowing him to get to his feet. As the beast attempted to regain its composure, Odisi, with haste, located his machete through a patch of mist and leapt for it. He picked it up, the dagger now in his left hand, the machete in his right. Odisi turned around just as the beast charged towards him again. The hunter loosened his stance, attempting to create a better center of balance.

The beast stood tall on two legs as it neared, flaying its claws in the air, taunting Odisi. It let out an insane shriek of might.

The hunter was frightened by this powerful display of physical prowess, but this was a matter of life and death. Odisi was not going to lose. He was going to defeat this monster and then figure out what the real man killer was. He still was not convinced that these creatures he faced were capable of turning bones into trophies. These were simply monsters. They could not reason. They were pure animal. There had to be something more, and he must live to learn the truth.

Odisi took initiative and charged the beast as it stood on its hind legs. He was fast, his long athletic legs boosting him with such swiftness. The beast had no time to react. The machete sunk hard into the monster's chest. The beast screamed as it swiped at Odisi, causing him to be knocked down again. But, the blade remained lodged deep in the beast's heart. It dropped back down to all fours, about to approach the fallen

The Endlands

hunter, but soon collapsed to the ground, breathing its last bit of air.

Odisi had done it. He had slain the second beast.

He stood up again, wiping more blood off his face with his forearm. Odisi took in deep breaths, regaining his center.

All was quiet now. He looked at the two dead beasts on the ground. What gigantic creatures they were. Odisi was proud, but still felt sorry for them. Again, he spoke silently to Ghet, asking him to take these jungle creatures as an offering so that he might be protected whilst finishing his hunt.

It was not over yet.

Soon, Odisi sheathed his blades and found his musket. He loaded it a third time.

After a few more moments, and still no sign of any other beast, Odisi entered the cave.

Inside, darkness covered most of the expanse; however, small beams of light shone through tiny holes in the surrounding rocks, enough light to see. Just like the evening before, Odisi took notice of how carefully placed were all the trophies of bleached bone. He was disgusted by the atrocities. Animal skulls, still attached to their spines. But it got worse. As Odisi furthered himself into the depths of the cave, he found more of these bones hanging about the walls—many of them from larger animals. Impressed, but still dismayed, he attained a tighter grip on his musket and kept walking.

Before long, Odisi stopped dead in his tracks. He saw them again, the horrors that had forced him to retreat back to his camp the prior evening. In a neat row hung the slowly decaying heads of all the hunters of his village who had entered the jungle in search for the man killer recently. These had not been stripped down to bare bone but, instead, these severed heads sat impaled on spikes, which jutted out from the cavern wall, some more decomposed than others. Odisi had known each man to whom these heads once belonged. They had been good men, perhaps not as skilled at hunting as he, but good men, nevertheless.

Odisi took in a deep breath. He was not going to run this time. He had all the previous night in which to let the horrifying picture sink. Now, he did not care about the thrill of the hunt. He wanted retribution for his fallen brethren. Odisi stepped farther into the cave, the darkness gradually taking over as he drew ever away from the entrance.

His nose caught so many scents, it was difficult to know exactly what he was inhaling. It could have been a combination of the decaying heads, the dead animals outside, or anything else. Whatever it was, it was foul.

Odisi looked around, but could see nothing. He decided it would be best not to venture too far into the cave where he could not see, so he started making his way back towards the entryway. There he would attempt to lure out the man killer.

But just as he turned around, Odisi heard a sound come from the darkness, startling him.

"*Chu lact*," the voice said.

A voice? Odisi thought.

"Who goes there?" he asked, turning back around to face it at once.

Is this the man killer?

"*Chu lact*," the voice said again.

Odisi pulled up his musket's stock to his shoulder, ready

to fire.

He asked again, "I said, who goes there?"

But, as the voice came again, so did something else. "*Chu lact!*" With it hurled an object through the air. It stuck straight in Odisi's gut.

The hunter yelped in pain as he looked down to see the bone-blade of a crude hatchet lodged in his stomach.

What beast could make such a tool?

He took it out, the squishing of flesh and blood oozing as he did so. In a dire attempt, Odisi pointed his musket into the darkness from where the hatchet had come. A sudden spark of light came and went as the flint ignited the gunpowder and the shot was fired. In the brief instant of light, he thought he saw a figure. He heard the ricochet of the ball bouncing off the cavern wall, a loud frequency of sound echoing throughout the breadth of the area.

He missed.

Odisi dropped the musket and started to reach for his machete when it jumped towards him. Out from the darkness the man killer leapt, coming down hard on the hunter. Odisi hit his head on the rocky floor as he was brought down. Blood began spilling from his scalp, but he could still make it . . . maybe.

Odisi gripped his foe's arm amidst his serrated teeth and bit a chunk of its flesh. The monster yelled in agony, but kept fighting. Before Odisi could do anything else, his face met with this creature's fist.

A fist? Odisi could not help but think as the strong, closed hand collided hard with his nose, breaking it.

"*Chu lact,*" it said a fourth time, then spat on his face.

Vincent Hobbes Presents

Using what strength he had, Odisi pushed the beast off of him and, tightly gripping his machete, he thrust it forward, but missed. Subsequently, the beast's strong hands latched his wrist and twisted until it snapped. Writhing, Odisi dropped his blade. He tried hitting the beast with his left hand, but to no avail. He was undergoing too much pain at this point to do any damage of consequence.

The man killer had prevailed. It had lured Odisi into its lair, just as it had done with all the other hunters in the past. The thought of his own head joining this monster's morbid collection sent a final chill down his spine as the man killer punched him in the face once more.

Odisi was delirious. He could not move. He could not control his muscles, but he could feel his body being dragged across the ground. Dried blood caked his face, covering much of his ability to see the goings on, but he could tell he was outside the cave once again. The light touched down on the jungle floor, and Odisi tried to smile. He thought that if this were the end for him, at least he would get to die under the sun, and not in some rotten smelling cavern.

Abruptly, Odisi's movement ceased. He could tell his arms dropped to the ground now, though he still could not feel them. Surely, it had been the beast that dragged him outside by his arms. He tilted his head to the side, coughing up some excess blood that had gathered in his mouth. He lay next to the dead beasts he had slain earlier. Somehow, it seemed fitting to him.

Then, a pair of feet stepped in his line of sight. They were a dark olive tone, dressed in animal skin sandals.

Sandals? Odisi was outright perplexed. *What is this man killer?*

He moved his eyes upward, struggling in the process, coughing up more blood. What Odisi saw, he could not believe. "No...." he said, exasperating. "It ... cannot ... be...."

The man killer stared blankly back at him.

With still much exertion in his voice, Odisi affirmed, "We ... did away with ... your resistance ... long ... ago...."

For Odisi now lay helplessly looking upon his kind's old foe ...

... a human.

The Hour of the Time

By
Vincent Hobbes

The future is as harsh as nature.
　Harsher even.
　Cruel and emotionless.
　The future is a cryptic place, where a synthetic voice is on the other end when you dial customer service, and it never understands your words.
　DOES NOT COMPUTE and PLEASE REPEAT YOUR REQUEST are common words in the future.
　The future is filled with blinking lights and chirping beeps.
　Complex highways and colossal buildings.
　One hundred foot billboards line the roads, and everything around you is a commercial for a product you do not need.
　And somewhere along the line, we lost the human spirit; self-reliance and self-worth disappeared.
　Because the future is a place where government dictates happiness, and society mandates perception.
　Welcome. I hope you enjoy yourself.

Charlie was running late. He hated being late. It was one of his biggest quirks. It was the highway again—the High 12. It was jammed tight like sheep, and his drive took longer than expected.

Vincent Hobbes Presents

"Shit," he mumbled. Charlie hated the city.

He beeped his horn and cursed his way through morning traffic, arriving at 8:47 am.

Thirteen minutes early.

Charlie peered at his summons again.

9:00 am, it read.

He did not want to be late.

As the rabbit would say, I'm late, I'm late—for a very important date!

Charlie hated being late, and right now, he was behind schedule. He was always early. It was a trait of his. Always first at the office, always first at parties—when he was invited, of course. Charlie always arrived thirty minutes early to the movies, and two hours at the airport.

This day was no different.

More important, actually.

The most important day of Charlie's life.

The parking lot was full. Charlie spat more obscenities under his breath.

"It's because they're all on time. Everybody but me!" he muttered.

He cursed again, pounding the steering wheel in frustration.

It would've been comical had someone seen his outburst, but as luck would have it, nobody did.

Why?

Charlie was a frail guy—an unintimidating character. He was thirty, yet still got carded for cigarettes. His boyish features might have been bad enough, but his 5'1" frame made it even worse for him. To add insult to injury, his hair was thinning, and the way he kept it brushed back, his pimply forehead awkwardly stood out. Charlie was a mess. He'd never been inside a woman, never ridden a motorcycle. Never shot a gun. His life was six days a week to the office, one day off. Charlie didn't mind if his boss gave him work to do. He wanted to do his part. Everyone should do his or her part. But what Charlie never understood was that his small features, his nasally voice, his obsessive ways—these things usually made for a good laugh at his expense, and this moment was no different.

"Shit shit shit!" he exclaimed.

"It's fine. It's fine," he muttered to himself.

"I don't have to impress anyone," he grumbled. "I'm here, and I'm on time."

He pounded the steering wheel one last time.

"There has to be a damn spot somewhere."

Charlie looked at his watch.

Double-checked it with the car clock.

8:50 am.

"Ten minutes. Shit on a stick!"

Charlie tore around the corner, finally spotting an open space.

"'Bout fucking time."

He slammed the car in park and jumped out, racing to the building.

Halfway there, he had to turn back. He forgot his summons."

"Shit shit shit shit shit," he said with every step.

He tried it again, nearly sprinting across the parking lot.

Vincent Hobbes Presents

Charlie's little legs churned as fast as they could on the hot asphalt.

He reached the building and pulled at the door.

8:52 am.

Charlie was out of breath when he entered. He hair was tussled, so he combed it back hastily with his fingers. He pulled the door and stepped inside, sighing a breath of relief he had not stopped to use the restroom along the way.

"Without a moment to spare," he mumbled.

This was an important day for Charlie. He had received his summons two weeks earlier in the mail. He had made sure to call the confirmation number, doing so twice just to make sure. The last thing he wanted was to miss his appointment. *This* appointment.

There were severe penalties for missing a summons, *and* for being late.

But he was finally here. He trotted to the front desk. Luck was on his side, and no one else was in line. Charlie hurried to the nearest counter.

A glass partition divided them. Charlie was surprised to see a woman behind the counter. An actual human! Normally, a robot would have sufficed, but Charlie figured a place like this would want to use a human.

It made sense.

Despite our flaws, humans were still proven to be more accurate than an automated service machine.

A robot was fine for taking orders at a fast food restaurant, but this was much too important.

The most important day of his life.

"H . . . hello," said Charlie, out of breath.

The woman looked at him, her eyes vacant.

"Is this your hour?" she asked.

"Yes it is," said Charlie, beaming.

"Name?" she asked without emotion.

"Charlie Hoag."

"Spell it."

"H-o-a-g."

"Ident number?"

"Six-two-oh-seven-two-eight-one."

"District?"

"Fourteen."

"Do you have your summons?"

Charlie reached deep into his pocket. For an instant, he couldn't find it. He nearly panicked, then realized it was in his front pocket. He sighed heavily, pulling it out and handing it through the small opening at the bottom of the plexiglass.

Clickity-click of the keyboard.

Tickity-tock of the clock.

Charlie waited anxiously as the woman verified his identity and entered his information.

He looked at his watch again.

8:55 am.

Charlie paced in place, nervously shifting his hands in front of him. He cracked his knuckles twice and brushed his hair back again. He was worried he had missed his time. He was worried, because Charlie had heard the penalties were harsh. He hated that he wasn't early. He knew better than that. Charlie hated being late. He was always early.

"I woulda arrived sooner, but the 12 was busy," he said

nervously to the woman. "I'm sure you know what I mean."

She said nothing, still typing.

Charlie looked at his watch again.

8:56 am.

"I'm never late," he added. "I always like being early. Especially to something as important as this." Charlie smiled.

She did not return the gesture.

He looked up at the clock behind her.

It clicked.

8:57 am.

"I just want to confirm that I'll get recorded as being *on time*. Technically, I'm three minutes early," he added with a fake, nervous chuckle.

The woman pushed a button and printed a slip of paper. She handed it, along with his ID card, back to Charlie.

"Be sure to have your ID ready again. They'll take it from you for final processing. Don't forget to pick it up after you're done."

"You mean I made it on time?"

"Yes."

"Great. That's juuust great. Whew! I thought I was late."

"Down the hall," she said, her voice uncaring.

"Oh, of course. Yes ma'am," he replied, nodding his head. Before turning, Charlie looked down at his ticket. He added, "Does it say anywhere about the time? I just want to make sure I don't get penalized for being late. I was three minutes early," he repeated. "I just want to make a note of it. I hear the penalties are—"

"The time is printed on your ticket," she said dryly.

"Oh, I see it. Good, it says 8:57 am. Usually, I'm always

early, but today—"

"Down the hall," interrupted the woman, her voice flat and monotone. "Last door on the right."

Charlie passed down the corridor. It seemed to take forever, even though he walked fast.

The walls were white, and the floor was shiny. Waxed daily, no doubt.

The hallways smelled of disinfectant—a clinical feel to the whole thing.

Overhead were fluorescent lights illuminating the hallway. They were bright and hurt Charlie's eyes.

He heard a soft tune overhead. No words, but the jingle was familiar.

Charlie walked the stretch, wondering why the need for such a long hallway. He noticed there were no doors.

Now that didn't make sense.

Only one room at the end of the hall.

Nothing hung on the walls, but that didn't matter to Charlie. The lack of color, the lack of life didn't bother Charlie. He was a product of the future—the new society; his own apartment was a simple mix of cinderblock and steel. Nothing fancy. Nothing special. Thus, the emptiness of the hall paled in comparison to the emptiness in Charlie's life.

It actually made him feel welcomed.

Still, he wondered—why the long walk?

His footsteps pattered.

On and on. Charlie checked his watch a dozen times. A hundred times. A thousand times.

It didn't matter, though. His ticket was stamped. He was

technically on time.

    Charlie hated being late.

    —And he heard the penalty was harsh.

He finally reached the door at the end of the hall. He jiggled the handle, and let himself in.

    Another counter.

    Another clerk.

    This time, it was a man.

    Charlie was still worried he might get in trouble for being late, but the man said nothing of it. He took Charlie's ticket and scanned it, finally handing it back.

    "Name?"

    "Charlie Hoag."

    "Spell it."

    And the process repeated itself, because repetition is part of the future.

Charlie finally entered. The room was massive, a wide auditorium. Hundreds waited.

    Hundreds like him.

    The lucky ones.

    They clustered in small groups.

    Others remained alone.

    Some sat, some stood.

    Charlie walked the outskirts, finally leaning against the back wall.

    He watched as some people laughed.

    While others sang.

    A few even cried.

He didn't understand that.

Charlie remained alone. He was always alone. Servitude meant sacrifice, and Charlie was most happy to be here. He had thought of this day for many years. He had hoped for it. The day he received his summons in the mail, Charlie knew it was the best day of his life.

Then again, Charlie had never known a woman.

"Ah, hello," he said to a teenager next to him. He was nervous, and hoped to make conversation.

"Hey," muttered the kid, his head looking down.

"My name's Charlie."

"Okay," the kid replied, uninterested.

"How long you been waiting?"

The youth turned his head, looking up at Charlie.

"I dunno. Awhile, I guess."

Charlie nodded his head. "I just got here."

A voice chimed overhead.

"Six-two-five-five-seven-eight-six."

The teenager looked at his ticket.

"What's that mean?"

"They're ident numbers," said the kid with a sigh.

"Oh, of course." Charlie mumbled the numbers under his breath. "Not me."

"Hm," replied the teenager.

"There's a lot of people here."

"Yup."

"I hope I get called soon."

The teenager tilted his head up, looking at Charlie strangely.

"I hope I do. I want to do my part, ya know?"

Vincent Hobbes Presents

"Okay," was the response. The kid looked back to the ground.

"I thought I was going to be late," added Charlie, as if the kid cared at all. "I took the 12. I knew I shouldn't have, especially this time of day."

And on and on, Charlie blabbed.

"Six-four-nine-five-six-two-six."

"... he nearly sideswiped me, I tell ya."

"Six-four-seven-six-two-six-one."

"... I swear, there's never a cop around when you need one," Charlie looked at his ticket, then continued, "So anyways, he cut across two lanes..."

The teenager shifted.

Another number was called out. A synthetic voice. An uncaring voice.

The teenager shifted, looking at his ticket.

"That you?" Charlie asked.

"Nah," said the kid. Before Charlie could speak once more, the teenager jammed his earphones in his ears, turned, and walked away.

Charlie didn't protest. He was accustomed to such things.

A few minutes passed.

A few minutes more.

In a room packed full of people, Charlie was alone.

As he waited, he thought of his apartment, wondering if he had turned off all the lights.

Did I feed the cat?

Did I lock the front door?

A woman neared him, leaning her back against the wall. She

looked pale, as if she might faint. She was clutching her ticket tight in her hand, staring ahead at the other people waiting. She was solemn, and didn't want to talk.

"Hello," said Charlie, his voice friendly.

"Hi," she mumbled.

"Are you late? I think it's past nine."

She looked at her ticket. "I'm 9:30."

"Oh," he replied. Not a few minutes passed before he began chattering again.

". . . I don't know why a cop is never around when you see one. Anyway, that's why I was late. I just hate being late."

More numbers called overhead.

People came.

People went.

"Seven-nine-seven-one-six-two-one"

The woman turned to Charlie. She hadn't spoken the entire time.

"That's me," she mumbled. "It's my time."

He tried to fake a smile, but this pissed him off. This woman—this 9:30, was called ahead of him.

"I just don't understand. Technically, I wasn't late. My ticket even proves that."

"It's my time," repeated the woman. She seemed sad, but Charlie took no notice. She crunched her ticket, shook her head twice, and disappeared into the crowd of people, toward the front of the room.

"Did they skip me?"

"Perhaps I should ask."

"Can they skip people?"

Charlie saw a middle-aged man nearby. He casually

walked to the man's side, and stood next to him for a minute, before asking, "Excuse me, sir. Can someone *not* be picked?"

"Huh?"

"Everyone's supposed to be picked, right?"

"I guess."

"It's just . . . they haven't called my number yet. That woman—the 9:30—she was called before me."

"Okay," the man muttered.

"I was supposed to be here at 9:00. I was running a bit late, but I was on time. Three minutes early, actually."

"No clue, buddy," the man said. "I'm sure you'll get called soon."

"I really hope so," said Charlie, excited. "This is a special day for me. For all of us," he added, proudly.

But the man said nothing. A few minutes later and his number was called.

Tick tock of the clock.

The synthetic voice kept a steady pace.

Some came. More went.

10:01 am.

"Something isn't right," said Charlie to the woman. She was older, looked like someone's grandmother. "I've been here an hour. That last guy—he was only here for fifteen minutes."

"I see, dear. My, I don't know what to tell you," she said, attempting to calm Charlie's incessant chatter.

"I don't mean to create a fuss, I'm just wondering if I should ask someone. Maybe they skipped me. Maybe they thought I was late. Aren't there penalties for that?"

"Oh, I really don't know."

"I always heard there were. I was on time, so I shouldn't have any penalties. See," he said, holding up his ticket.

"Yes. It says 8:57 am."

"Three minutes early," Charlie nodded.

The old woman was polite. She listened to Charlie intently. She answered his questions. She calmed him.

Finally, he asked, "Where do we go when they call us?"

"I think there's a door. Up there," she said, pointing. "They seem to be going there."

Charlie stood on his tip-toes, but he was a little guy, and couldn't really see.

"When they call my number, I need to know where to go. How come they didn't explain this to us?"

"I don't know, dear. Hush now, don't worry about such things."

"I can't help myself. I want to do right. I want to be early. I'd hate to not know where to go when they call my number."

"I'm sure you'll do fine," she answered with a smile.

10:39 am.

The old woman was called. She did not hesitate, she did not stall. The woman disappeared into the crowd and Charlie hardly noticed.

"There has to be some mistake. There has to be."

10:44 am.

"*Six-two-oh-seven-two-eight-one.*"

"That's me!" Charlie exclaimed. "That's my number."

Nobody around him took notice.

Vincent Hobbes Presents

Charlie mumbled the same identity number he had since childhood, just to make sure. He didn't want to be wrong, so he checked it twice. More so, Charlie definitely didn't want to be late. He pulled from the wall and entered the crowd. He headed to where he thought he was supposed to go. He had a hard time seeing, because he was so short, but Charlie pushed through regardless.

"Excuse me."
"Pardon. I have to get through."
"They called my number."
"They picked me."
He walked through groups of people.
Some standing, some sitting.
A few laughed.
Others sang.
Some cried.
He didn't understand that.
This was an important day.
"Excuse me."
"Pardon. I have to get through."
The most important day of his life.
"They called my number."
"They picked me."

There *was* a door. Another clerk stood at a counter, but no partition separated them. Not this time. Another woman, this one attractive. A beaming smile appeared on her face as he pushed through the last line of waiting people.

"Hello," said Charlie.
"Six-two-oh-seven-two-eight-one?" she asked.

"That's me," beamed Charlie. "Did I make it on time?"

"You sure did," said the woman. Her eyes were wide, focused on him. Her smile radiated her face. Her voice was soft—sensual.

"Do you have your ticket?" she asked.

"I do," he said, flirting slightly. He dug in his pocket, and couldn't find it.

"What the hell?"

"Excuse me, sir?" She pointed to his front pocket.

"Oh, of course," he said with a laugh. He handed it to her. The woman scanned it, and placed it in a bin.

"ID?"

He handed it over.

She placed it in another bin.

"The woman—"

"Yes?" asked the woman, tilting her head. This time, her smile seemed different.

Fake.

Plastic.

"The woman at the entrance said I'd get my ID back after. I was just making sure that's right."

"Oh, yes," said the woman, holding the same smile. This time it seemed different.

Deformed.

"We're finished," she said in a pleasant voice. "Just go into that room and take a seat."

"In there?" he pointed.

"In there," she repeated.

"Wow, I finally made it," he stammered. "I was hoping I wasn't late . . ."

Vincent Hobbes Presents

"You are right on time," she interrupted.

The room was circular. Cold and empty.
A chair was in the middle of the room.
His footsteps echoed.
Charlie sat down, making himself comfortable.
He tried to relax.
"At least I was on time," he whispered.
A blissful look crept across his face.
Charlie Hoag *had* been on time.
And he looked at his watch one more.
And at 10:59 am, the door shut and the gas entered the room.
At 11:03 am, Charlie's lungs filled.
Three minutes later, his heart stopped.
And at 11:05 am, Charlie Hoag's last thought flashed in his mind.
At least I was on time.

Thanksgiving

By
Jairus Reddy

A low hum was the only sound that spewed from Phil Carpenter's concealed position as he nervously recorded the events unfolding before him. He grasped his video camera tightly in his right hand, the heat from his overworked battery threatening to ruin it. The ensuing carnage was occurring only one hundred yards in front of him. *This moment, these pictures, this video footage will change the world*, Phil thought to himself.

Every man has that moment of clarity when he finally realizes all his hard work and persistence has finally been repaid, either by chance or by God. When one realizes this, death is the only aspect of life to look forward to.

This was Phil's moment.

Finally, after years of menial interviews with the citizens of Washington DC, after hours of boredom speaking on politics, after useless reporting of robberies and murder, Phil had a story that was his and only his. Phil smiled, thinking of the moment these tapes would be released to the fickle public eye. America, and the rest of the world for that matter, would watch in sheer terror at the events Phil was secretly taping. This was the biggest event the world would ever witness.

Vincent Hobbes Presents

Phil would never need to work again. Every producer, publisher, magazine, and major newspaper would pay millions of dollars for this story—this carnage.

As Phil continued to gloat in the glory that would soon follow, his mind never allowed him to contemplate one simple fact; he might not survive the encounter that would shatter the foundation of the United States, and the world, forever.

Phil was just a regular blue-collared journalist who happened to write for one of the biggest newspapers in the country. Also in the worst city in the country for a journalist with any imagination. Washington, DC. Everything was politics, politics, politics.

Phil despised the routine. He was often quoted as saying, "There's only so many political scandals you can write about before it feels like you've written the same one before." Deep down he felt like he could copy and paste previous articles and change the politician's name and no one would be the wiser.

Of course, this was before he was given the assignment he always dreamed of, the one that would grab headlines. Not because of made up scandals, or political bullshit, but a story that would burst the bubble of comfort that Americans had been living in since World War II.

No more talking heads. No more Republicans versus Democrats. *All* politicians would be thrown under the bus when this story reached the news.

Phil's boss of twenty-four years, Henry Rosenberg, had a lead about a secret gathering of the elite held every year, deep in the woods of the Appalachian Mountains. Every important world leader attended to discuss policy for the upcoming years, but a strong military force always secured the meeting. Rumor had it that no civilians were allowed entry, and no one in attendance was allowed to talk about the meeting.

It was his job to infiltrate the gathering, collect information, and escape; then give his footage to the newspaper upon completing the assignment. It was no small task considering the intel stated it was a good five mile trek to reach the supposed meeting place.

Phil wondered why, after working thirty years with the paper, they would decide to send someone to cover this story. Henry said the informant told him the main purpose of the meeting was to introduce the first human clones to the leaders of the world, as Bill C-23 was passed by legislators just over three months prior. This explained the urgency to cover the story.

America was the first country in the world to clone humans, but with the population continually expanding, and organ donations at an all time low, it seemed reasonable that cloning could save millions of lives every year. Bill C-23 took five years to pass through the government, and to be deemed constitutional by the Supreme Court, but it *did* pass. The selling point to Americans was that the clones would provide organs to those in need, at a price that was no more than pulling a tooth.

While he was excited about the prospect of being the first to reveal this story to the public, and to take a picture of the first human clone, he doubted the accuracy of the leads.

Vincent Hobbes Presents

How could we already have cloned a human barely three months after passing Bill C-23? Phil wondered.

Phil was a very pessimistic person who rarely believed the truthfulness of leads, rumors or scandals. But, he knew the mantra to which most newspapers adhered: It is not about the accuracy of the story, but the impact the story will have. He had accounted for the demise of many politicians; most stories were fabricated or just plain lies. But Phil didn't really have much of a conscience about this; he just did his job and followed his leads without question. He was not a vindictive person, like so many in the industry; he simply left his emotions and feelings at home and drummed to the beat of Corporate America.

Even so, he walked out of this meeting with a sense of pride he had never known before. After all the years of feeling like his job—his passion—was worthless due to restrictions placed on him by the paper, he now had meaning. Maybe he *could* unravel the truth.

He heard rumors like everybody else about this 'meeting'. Stories that countries agreed to war with each other to stimulate the global economy. Some were just plain hilarious. One told of human sacrifices made by the elite. Another that politicians simply arm wrestled each other and the winner of the match would get his way with which policies and laws would be passed.

The funny part about this assignment is that no one could be positive if these meetings even happened. The myth had been around since Phil started working for the paper in his twenties.

Like most in the USA, Phil doubted the truthfulness

of the rumors. Research had been done to see if any of the world leaders flew into any of the major airports during the supposed meeting, and all information gathered was always a resounding 'no'. Also, no motorcades or police escorts were ever seen near the Appalachian Mountains, which would be expected if an event like this really did occur.

Many, though, believed the meeting to be fact. These theorists had viable reasons on why these stories were true, but nothing solid to give support to such accusations. No pictures. No video footage. Not even a report from someone claiming to have seen or attended the meeting. The question still remained: Where did these stories come from if they weren't true?

Nevertheless, Phil finally received the assignment he always dreamed of writing. He was determined to find out what, if anything, occurred at what conspiracy theorists dubbed *The Meeting of Murkall*—his last hurrah before his looming retirement scheduled for July 31st.

The date was July 17th, 2022. Phil kissed his wife, Maggie, gently on the cheek, hoping not to wake her from her slumber. It was five AM and he knew better than to wake her at this hour. A woman's wrath is like a tsunami, knocking down anything in its path of terror, and at five in the morning, he didn't want to test the waters. Before he closed the bedroom door he heard her stir.

"Honey, what're you doing up so early?" asked Maggie.

Whew, at least she's not mad, Phil thought to himself.

"Remember—the assignment I received on the Appalachian Mountains. I have to be at the office by six o'clock to

Vincent Hobbes Presents

get a head start."

"I still don't understand why they're sending you to write a story about the Appalachian Trail. Seems like a miniscule assignment to give someone for their last story before retirement. Shouldn't that be a job for an intern?" stated Maggie, bluntly.

"I know what you're trying to do," Phil retorted. "You aren't getting any information about why I'm really going down there. God, after thirty years you still try to get me in trouble by asking me about my assignments. Don't worry, you can read about it on the front page in a couple days." He was obviously annoyed by the questions.

"Buzz kill. Probably not that interesting anyway, if I know your boring columns. Love you, babe. Please be careful. You have two weeks before your retirement and my beach house needs that pension check every month."

"Wow! Always knew you were a gold digger, but damn, you could be a little discreet about it," laughed Phil. "And boring columns? I write in DC. I can't make coal into gold, you know. I will be careful. And I love you, too."

With that, Phil kissed his wife before leaving the house, and headed on his final assignment—his final adventure.

Phil reached his drop off point, an unmarked trailhead in the Appalachians, around noon that day. The plan was simple enough: He would hike about five miles to the meeting location, and take as many pictures and as much video footage as his equipment would allow, then leave. A van would be waiting for him at the same point he was dropped off.

Sounded simple, but while Phil was in relatively good

shape, he was still pushing sixty and hiking ten miles in one day was no small feat. Not to mention, the terrain in the area was not forgiving in the least. Hills and valleys made the trek that much more difficult.

If that's what it took to finally get Phil his great story, he was ready to do it. Nothing could get in his way right now. Not a damn hill, not a valley, and definitely not the chance of going to jail, which was feasible if he was caught. He still did not have high expectations about the accuracy of the assignment, but Phil would complete it no matter the cost.

Only a little way into the hike, Phil was already feeling the effects of the heat, and realized his legs weren't as strong as they used to be. "I better have something to write when I reach the meeting site or I'm going to kick Henry's ass," Phil mumbled to himself. "How many more goddamn hills are there in this God forsaken place?"

He figured it was a few more hours before he reached the spot where the Meeting of Murkall was supposedly occurring. Hill after hill, valley after valley, and finally Henry was within a half mile of his destination.

"Who the hell would ever be able to gather intelligence out here? I haven't seen a road or even a house since I started the hike. There isn't a goddamn thing out..."

Before the words were out of his mouth, he saw the statue in the clearing. It wasn't anything he recognized or could wrap his mind around. It had human features, but the face was rather elongated, with sharp beady eyes, and an irregularly large mouth. Its hands had a long set of claws, one of which was holding a giant scepter. Worn from corrosion, it looked like a cross between a human and some other beast, and was completely out of place in the middle of the woods.

Phil started rattling off pictures with his Samsung. He made sure to keep cover so nobody came creeping around, catching his position.

"Goddamn, this is way too easy," Phil mumbled to himself. "Maybe there is some credence behind this lead after all. Or it could be some hillbillies who got bored of cow tipping."

Phil could easily see the statue was carved from stone. He couldn't get past the overwhelming metallic smell radiating from it, and how old it appeared to be.

As Phil was changing his film, three men in suits came strolling down the trail, stopping in front of the statue.

By their dress, he could tell they weren't guards. Plus, they were much too frail. They looked to be about seventy years old, and he recognized one of the men as Senator Palsey from DC. The men presented gifts at the base of the statue, bowed at its feet, and turned to leave.

Phil followed the men from a distance, taking pictures to prove that they were in fact in attendance at the conference. "That's some of the weirdest shit I've ever seen," Phil spoke to himself. "I can't believe this is for real."

About ten minutes later they reached what Phil thought must be the main base of the camp. A gravel road led up to rows of cabins. A smaller statue, resembling the one in the forest, stood in the center of the camp, surrounded by a massive fire pit. The three men strolled into one of the cabins as Phil hid amongst the foliage, concealing himself so no one could possibly spot him.

While he was excited at the possibility of the rumors being true, the camp was rather dead, with only a handful of elitists walking around, conversing with each other. Though Phil could not hear what was being said, it appeared to only be small talk—nothing out of the ordinary. There definitely wasn't anybody from another country.

Some had gathered around a table eating sandwiches and laughing amongst themselves. Others had wandered down the trail carrying gifts, presumably to the statue Phil had found an hour before. With no new material or real action, he decided to stop taking pictures until later in the evening, unless something presented itself.

The sun was setting and Phil guessed it was probably around seven. No one had been outside of his or her cabin for about an hour, and he was getting restless. *Henry, I can't wait to cuss your ass out when I get back. These goddamn mosquitoes are eating me alive while I sit here staring at nothing but cabins. Great last assignment, I got pictures of a statue,* Phil thought to himself.

Just as the sun disappeared behind the trees, five school busses pulled into the drive and the camp came alive. All the cabin doors opened, and out stepped man after man dressed in matching red robes with a black headdress. Phil wielded his camera as fifty of these men walked single file and took a seat directly in front of the smaller statue. The bus doors opened and around two hundred individuals walked listlessly to a section of the campsite, and stood there motionless.

Phil was snapping pictures of everything, but being conservative enough to not waste the film. He noticed all the people escorted from the bus looked identical, and all held an eerily emotionless expression.

They were bald, and their skin was as fair as any Phil had ever seen, like they had never been exposed to sunlight. They walked with a wide gait, looking very uncomfortable walking on two feet. Phil could see through his lens that they all had brown eyes and the same body structure. He figured they were of normal height and weight, roughly two hundred pounds. The only differences he could see were the outlines of breasts on the women in the group.

"Well, I'll be damned. That has to be the clones. I have the first pictures ever of a human clone," Phil boasted to himself, rapidly snapping his Samsung.

Using up the last of his film, Phil pulled out his camcorder to record the rest of the footage just as one of the robed figures stepped up to the podium. The man removed his hood and the face shocked Phil to his core.

President Brendan Hanley.

"My friends, my family, we are gathered here tonight to celebrate the great harvest. From today forward we will never have to worry about dying from thirst or hunger again. Our youth will remain with us forever," stated the President.

Amazed, Phil continued taping.

"With the passing of Bill C-23, human cloning will allow our kind to prosper for eternity, without our loyal subjects ever knowing our true identity or our intentions of a single-race world. Today marks the start of a new generation, a time when the harvest is plenty and our kind will finally make its claim as the most powerful ever. Hail our god, Murkall!"

With this the crowd went into a frenzy, screaming from their knees, hands raised to the sky, many crying on each other.

    The chanting began.

    "*Murkall, Murkall, Murkall,*" they cried in unison.

    The President put his hand up for silence.

    Phil was in awe of the events occurring before him. When the crowd became silent, all attendees removed their hoods. Phil looked at each person and noticed they were different than before. They resembled the statues, but had human features. Their skin was now pasty white, and their faces were more elongated than round. All had beards and long, flowing white hair. The wrinkles on the older men's faces were now smooth, and sets of claws extended from their hands. The President smiled, revealing a full set of incisors meant only for tearing. In five minutes, the men had changed into something not human, more like a beast—a demon.

    Phil could still recognize many of these creatures as some of the elite in the United States government. Fifteen were Senators, twelve were in the House of Representatives, two sat on the Supreme Court, and the other was the President. He couldn't recognize any of the others. *This isn't a meeting of the elite,* Phil thought to himself. *It's a meeting place for madness, or demons, or God knows what.*

    "What the hell is going on? These people aren't humans. I don't know what the fuck they are," Phil mumbled to himself. "I'm getting the hell out of here."

    As Phil said this, the moonlit sky suddenly went pitch black. Phil looked up and the once full moon was hidden behind something in the sky. What looked like a flock of geese blocked the moon, but Phil had never witnessed a flock of birds this thick before.

Vincent Hobbes Presents

Then, one by one, they fell out of the sky, landing by the campfire. Phil realized what he was witnessing. "No wonder there weren't any plane records. These goddamn creatures can fly." Hundreds of the creatures landed around the camp. Finally, the last landed and the moon shone bright once again.

As much as Phil's instincts screamed for him to run, he had to appease his curiosity, and finish the assignment. His body trembled with fear.

"Now that the rest have joined, the feast will begin," hissed the President. His voice had changed. "Bring forth the first treat."

One of the clones was thrown to the feet of President Hanley. "My friends, our survival, which has been questionable for hundreds of years, is now secure. These clones will provide us with the necessary nourishment we need to retain youth.

"We have fought long and hard for this. Sacrificing our dignity by taking the roles of politicians, bankers, and military officials, awaiting the day of our emancipation. Murkall has heard our cries and our suffering will soon cease. The battle against these disgusting beasts will start as is prophesied in the holy book of *The Kurball*. Then, and only then, will we be assured of the endless resource of human flesh on Earth.

"Murkall is pleased with the human hearts that have been presented at the base of his most holy statue. Now lift your hands, extend your claws, and bow your heads. Let us pray.

"Thank you, Murkall, for providing us this harvest of humans to ensure dominance of our race—forever. Without your guidance we would have died years ago, but through faith we have secured our future on earth. Let your supremacy and wickedness spread throughout our kingdom on Earth as we live according to your most holy standards. Accept the sacrifices of human hearts and the sacrifice of the virgin female as a symbol of our everlasting faith to you."

Amen.

"Bring out my daughter," said the President.

One of the robed creatures brought out his daughter, bound at the wrists and ankles, duct tape covering her mouth.

"You are the perfect sacrifice, my daughter. You have pleased me well, but your time on Earth is done. Join Murkall in the depths of hell." He tore the duct tape from her mouth and opened a door at the base of the figure. He placed her upright in the statue, closing the door and securing it with a metal harness. He grabbed a torch and lit the wood around the effigy.

The fire shot up rapidly and began to heat up the statue. The screams of President Hanley's daughter penetrated the night as she was cooked alive. The screams sounded more like a demonic moan, her voice echoing inside the stone statue. Soon the moaning ceased.

Phil, mouth agape from the sheer horror of what he was witnessing, continued to record everything. *My God, what on Earth have I gotten myself into?*

"Let the feast begin," hissed the President.

President Hanley sliced through the jugular artery of the clone, still standing obediently before him, and began to tear it to shreds. Phil watched in disgust as the feeding fren-

Vincent Hobbes Presents

zy ensued. The creatures struck down on every clone with a vengeance, ripping off flesh, drinking and bathing in their blood—gnawing on their bones. The screams were terrifying, yet none tried to run. Each accepted death as freely as he accepted life.

The creatures were indulging in the overabundance of human flesh. This was their Thanksgiving and no one would walk away without a full belly. Even when there was no meat left on the bones the creatures were licking the blood off the ground. Some even resorted to eating the cartilage off the bones.

"They are like piranha attacking fresh meat," Phil blurted out in amazement. "Except they're eating humans."

Phil dry heaved several times at this realization.

It was over within minutes. There were hardly any remnants of the clones by the time the feast ended. Just carnage. Phil was shaking from excitement and pure horror as he continued recording the terror surrounding him. It was then he realized he needed to leave—fast.

He collected his equipment, quietly but swiftly, and exited the scene. He turned around for one more glimpse before leaving to make sure his eyes weren't lying to him. When he turned he noticed some of the creatures sniffing the air. Immediately they turned towards him, eyes glowing red from excitement, and the chase was on.

Phil ran like he never had before.

How the hell can I outrun a creature that can fly? Phil thought to himself.

Up hills, down valleys, they chased Phil. The creatures remained about a hundred yards behind, but they slowly closed the distance, none taking flight.

Phil crashed through trees, trying to keep his balance. Branches ripped open his skin. The darkness shielded his vision. He was determined not to die.

They were only fifty yards behind him with a half-mile to go.

Keep running! That goddamn van better be waiting for me!

Now, they were only twenty yards behind him, but Phil could see the van waiting for him. They were gaining fast as Phil ran around the van and jumped into the passenger seat.

"Punch it! Now!" he yelled to the driver—it was Henry.

He pressed the accelerator hard just as four of the creatures hit the van, nearly tipping it over. "Henry, what the hell are you doing here?" yelled Phil as they sped away, sending a creature sprawling from the top of the van.

"I said someone would pick you up and that someone is me. What the hell was that?" asked Henry, calmly driving down the road.

"Henry, we're millionaires! The rumors are true! I recorded the politicians killing—get this—human clones! We can sell this shit for millions to anybody!"

"Well, I'll be damned," stated Henry. "Killing clones? That's hard to believe. You aren't screwing around with me are you?"

"Hell no! I was almost killed in the process. I don't think they're human. They looked like vampires. They ate the damn clones."

"Vampires eating human clones." Henry grumbled out loud. "I gotta see the tape to believe this. I've heard plenty of stories over my time, but this takes the cake."

Vincent Hobbes Presents

"I swear I'm not lying, Henry. Wait until you see the tape." Phil's heart was pounding and he couldn't understand what he'd witnessed, but the footage was all there.

Oddly, Henry didn't seem to care. "Why are you not terrified, Henry? This is an amazing, and frightening, discovery. They could take over the world. Henry, what's wrong?"

"I just don't really believe you, Phil."

"But you have to! It's all here," Phil motioned, holding up his camcorder.

Shaking his head, Henry answered, "I'll believe it when I see it."

Phil tried to convince him, but Henry just wouldn't have it. Realizing it was a lost cause, the two rode in silence.

Fifteen minutes later, Henry slowed down and pulled onto the shoulder of the road.

"Henry, what are you doing?" Phil questioned. "They're probably still chasing us."

"Look, we've been driving for almost twenty minutes. There's no way these *clone-eating vampires* could have stayed with us that long," Henry mocked. "I need a smoke, and I can't smoke in the van."

Phil gave in. Henry would do what he wanted; after all, he was the boss.

"Please, for me Henry, be quick."

Henry nodded his head and dipped out of the van, taking a long pull from his cigarette.

While Henry was smoking, Phil was watching the video footage on his camcorder. "The picture quality is perfect and unmistakable. The world will change forever." Still mesmerized by his recording, Phil heard Henry talking. "Henry, I can't hear you dumbass. The door's closed."

Phil looked up from his camcorder to see Henry talking at the front of the van. Phil froze, petrified in fear when he saw President Hanley and ten other men staring right at him through the window.

He jumped in the driver's seat to start the car when he realized the keys were with Henry.

Henry walked slowly to the van and opened the door.

"Henry, I was so excited about the story I didn't tell you that the President is one of *them*. Hurry up and get in the car or we have no chance," Phil whispered.

"Vampires," Henry laughed.

"Shut up and get in the car. This is not a joke," pleaded Phil.

"Hell yeah it is. You think we're vampires? No, we're more like a better adapted species who feed on humans to survive," Henry hissed. "You probably wondered why they didn't fly after you, didn't you? Well, their stomachs were too gorged with food. You didn't fail me, though. I knew you could do it."

Phil was frozen with fear. "You son of a bitch. You're one of *them*! Those cannibals. Why would you do this to me after twenty-four years of dedication?" pleaded Phil.

"You always bitched about not writing a meaningful story. Now you have the biggest secret known to man. The biggest story any journalist could ever ask for. I gave this to you as a present. It's a damn shame it will never make it to print."

The passenger door opened, the silhouette of a creature was all he could see. It hissed, fangs dripping with the thought of dessert.

Vincent Hobbes Presents

* * *

July 20, 2022

Headlines News:

Phil Carpenter's remains were found in the Appalachian Mountains this morning after an apparent attack by a black bear. He is survived by his wife Maggie and was retiring from The Post *at the end of this month. No funeral arrangements have been made at this point.*

INTO THE SMALL HOURS

BY
PATRICK GREENE

Richard Booth sat up so fast his head throbbed. Staring into the near perfect dark, he determined he was not in his bed at his spacious home back in Irvine. Something had reached into his sleep and snatched him into the waking world, apparently depositing him in a strange room. Another scream sounded, weaker, but in the same voice as the one he just heard... that was it; he had been awakened by a scream, and was in a hotel room somewhere in New Hampshire.

Richard jumped out of bed, nearly stumbling face forward as the heavy covers snared him tightly. Recovering, he stood listening in the blackness for several seconds.

The bedside clock read 3:33. A strong gust assaulted the building, reminding Richard of just how boldly the winter asserted itself upon this remote part of the country.

Though it had just happened, he couldn't be sure that the scream was not only a piece of dream that had followed him to the edge of wakefulness. Still, real or not, it had been enough to jar him from a peaceful slumber to a heart-hammering, wide-eyed lucidity in a flash.

An investigation was in order.

On edge and disoriented, Richard made his way to his door, groping about in the unfamiliar surroundings. Open-

Vincent Hobbes Presents

ing the door enough to lean his head out, Richard had a sudden image of decapitation—his own. He jerked back inside, and then chided himself for being childish and paranoid. Too many E.C. Comics as a kid. The scream, real or not, had regressed him to that ten year old who hid under his covers, imagining all sorts of leering, lumbering entities in the dark just out of sight. He took a breath and stepped out, scanning the right side of the hall, and finding only an endless line of doors, like rigid soldiers assembled for duty.

All was quiet. No parties or night owls on this floor.

On the other side, seven rooms down, a door stood ajar about two inches.

Through the crack, there was only darkness.

Richard pulled the privacy latch over to keep the door propped open and stepped out into the hall, intending only to walk close to the room, only to see if he could detect any sound.

An idea prompted Richard back to his room, where he grabbed his ice bucket. If someone caught him, he could make like he was merely going to get ice. Sure it was after 3:30, but it was his business if he needed ice at this hour, wasn't it?

Richard returned to the hallway, the bucket tucked under his arm nonchalantly, and took several slow steps.

The door creaked open a hair, stopping Richard cold.

He stared at the door, trying to decide whether to just walk on, or stay there a moment and watch for ... well, what? Richard became aware of his own heavy breathing and tried to bring it under control. The darkness of the room, number 442 on the door tag, was impenetrable.

Richard wished he had donned his glasses before making this venture.

The door was only seven or eight feet away. Richard took one more step forward, watched a moment, and then felt compelled by some sense alien to him to move on.

Parallel with the door, Richard couldn't resist a sideways glance.

No movement. But, there did seem to be a slight *shooshing* sound.

Richard went on past the door and down the hall tempted, but afraid to look back and see if someone had stepped out to watch him. At the end of the hall, he opened the exit door and shot a quick glance back. No strange faces stared back.

Richard filled the ice bucket, somewhat ashamed that he had been so immature and nosey, and now had to continue with the pretense just to make it back to his room. The hallway made an open rectangle, so that one could walk the hall endlessly without having to turn around. He could simply take the long way around, and avoid the mysterious open door.

But he felt the need to prove he wasn't snooping. He would walk by, making the ice bucket obvious, and return to his room. End of story.

The scream. Could it have been playful, sexual even?

He considered the still-fresh mental echo. It seemed desperate, frightened, not pleasurable. But why hadn't anyone else been disturbed? Maybe he would call the front desk when he got back to his room.

Back in the hallway, Richard ambled to his room, still

mildly curious. Passing the open door to room 442, he managed to avoid actively listening or watching. He carried the bucket on the side closest to the door, just in case he was being watched through the peephole. He even rattled the ice a little.

Yep, just a guy on his way back to his room with some ice. No big ordeal.

When Richard had made five or so steps past the door, it suddenly slammed shut.

Richard quivered with a wave of sudden fright, stepping up his pace, feeling his legs preparing to run.

He forced himself to stop, and glanced back toward 442.

Just the door.

Closed now.

Like all the rest.

Richard went in his room and turned the bolt. Dumped the ice in the sink. Turned on the bedside light, and stared at the phone for several moments.

"Yeah, I heard a noise from . . . this is Richard Booth on the fourth floor, I . . . excuse me, have you had any complaints about noise from . . . ?"

Richard rehearsed these and several other versions, realizing just how silly and paranoid he would sound. He decided against making the call, and turned out the light, settling back into bed.

After fifteen minutes, he realized he wasn't about to nod off anytime soon. He sat up and turned on the television. Infomercials, news, and talk shows were the only fare available on no less than twenty-four channels.

An extended testimonial about getting rich through real

estate investments managed to catch his attention. The insincere droning soon began to work its magic, and Richard felt his eyelids drooping.

He was reaching for the light switch, when he saw shadowy movement at the crack under his door.

Something seemed to linger there. As if listening.

Richard felt his heart beat increase.

He considered his options, and made a decision. He turned up the volume on the television, stopping every few increments so as not to make his strategy obvious. Easing out of bed, he treaded over to the door. Just as he peered into the peephole, the shadow under the door moved back toward the left end of the hall. Toward room 442. Richard caught only a glimpse of a moving black shape through the tiny lens.

There was no sound to accompany the movement. Richard had a sudden image of a skulking ninja, hunkering low with a deadly hooked blade in one hand, and some esoteric lock-picking device in the other.

He would have laughed at himself, if he weren't on the verge of panic. He clutched the door handle, determined to frighten his would-be stalker, as he had been frightened earlier when the door to room 442 slammed just behind him. But his hand, which he now noticed was shaking, would not obey. Instead, he went to the phone and dialed the front desk.

After nine rings, Richard hung up. He looked at the door, thankful that the shadow was not there. The real estate moguls continued their pitch on the television, oblivious that

Vincent Hobbes Presents

many months from the time they were taping, a potential recruit would find meager comfort in their images while playing cat and mouse with an unseen opponent.

Richard watched for twenty minutes, glancing often at the bottom of the door. With a long day of driving ahead, he knew he would have to get some sleep. Tomorrow, he and whoever was on the other side of room 442 would be far away from each other, and this would seem like nothing more than a mildly disturbing dream.

Richard turned off the light and the TV, and buried himself in the safety of the covers. After a moment, he turned himself on his side, facing away from the door, so that he would not be tempted to engage in any more silliness.

As another massive blast of wind jarred the windows, Richard burrowed into his pillow. Soon, sleep found him.

The phone, so much louder than his phone at home, startled Richard out of his sleep even more forcefully than the scream had earlier.

He fumbled with the handset, playing hot potato before finally bringing it to rest against his ear.

"Hello?"

There was no discernible sound on the other end.

Richard listened intently, hearing only his own strained breathing for several seconds. The clock read a flashing 12:00, indicating the power had gone out at some point. Perhaps this power outage had triggered the phone?

A busy signal soon replaced the silence, accompanied by the sound of another strong gust. Richard peeked out the window at the sodium-lit parking lot four floors down. No sign of the morning or anything living, even on the highway past the strip mall next door. Richard turned on his light and pushed down the hook, then dialed the front desk.

It rang repeatedly. At least nothing was wrong with the lines, but the lack of customer service was annoying. Huffing, Richard slipped into his robe and started for the door, prepared to find someone and complain.

He stopped in his tracks, as he spotted the shadow silently gliding to a stop in front of his door again.

Richard's mind and heart raced.

It was too much like a setup. Richard, the packaging designer for a produce company, had no experience with stakeouts, ambushes, showdowns, or any other such dangerous and overtly masculine business. But he had a survival instinct, and it was telling him something was most egregiously wrong here.

He took several halting steps forward, unable to force himself to look out the peephole, for fear of . . . perhaps an ice pick, jammed with deadly force into the tiny aperture.

The shadow/figure remained still, as though waiting for Richard to open the door.

Just as Richard summoned the courage and lunged toward the peephole, the shadow moved. Not back toward room 442, but to the opposite side, the side on which Richard's door opened.

Waiting for him to open the door, so he, or it, could force its way in and punish Richard properly for having stuck his nose where it didn't belong.

He stood back from the door, staring at the sliver of light. He searched within himself for courage, but found none.

Nerves singing, he lunged for the light switch by the

door, recoiling immediately as light flooded the room.
The sliver of light did not change.
Richard felt so different with the light on. The ten-year old Richie who used to frighten himself into nightmare-filled slumber had returned from the past, leaving behind the rational and settled adult Richard. He wasn't even so sure that the shadow under the door had been any more real than the scream at this point. Richard pulled the belt of his robe taut, and reached out to the door. He froze for only a second as he clasped the handle, then he turned it and stepped forward into the hallway.
He immediately looked to the right side, and was pleased to see no one and nothing unusual.
But a look to the other side revealed that the door to room 442 was opened a crack, as before, with only darkness emanating from within.
Little Richie returned, bringing the old school, E.C.-style terror with him in abundance.
The owner of the shadow under the door could have circled around, could now be heading back the other way. Or waiting around the corner.
Richard thought of banging on the door next to his. Looking back at room 442, he realized he had pitifully little evidence of any wrongdoing, and would likely be dismissed as pathetically paranoid. It also occurred to him that such an assessment might not be too far off the mark.
He would simply take the elevator down to the front desk, make his complaint about the phone call, and leave it at that.
Nearing the angle at the end of the wing, he stayed close

to the outside edge and slowed his pace, still imagining some assailant waiting with an ice pick, or fire axe, or ...

Richard sighed with relief as he rounded the corner and spotted the elevator halfway down the hall, with no obstacle between. The uneasy feeling was still with him, but he was home free if he made the elevator.

He heard the wind essaying another volley against the building outside, and longed for his huge bed and his warm wife and the more agreeable climate back in Irvine.

He stepped in front of the elevator, regarding his tired and disheveled reflection in the mirrored tiles that covered the wall there, as he pressed the down arrow.

From the other wing, where his room, and room 442 were, there came the sound of determined strides.

No door had been opened or closed, yet someone approached. It could only be the occupant of room 442.

Shit, Richard thought, as cold sweat broke on his forehead.

The as-yet unseen entity was making a move to finish this game. It could only be that.

He punched the down button again, and another time. The footsteps drew closer, accompanied by the *shooshing* sound he had heard when he passed 442 during his investigation.

Daring to look toward the corner, he saw the shadow that preceded the source of his now agonizing fear.

Unable to face the sight of his angel of death, he snapped his head back toward the elevator just as the doors began to slide apart, trying to ignore the particularly strong gust that wailed outside.

Vincent Hobbes Presents

That was when the power died again, and darkness took hold forever.

The Dragon of Delinar

BY
Vincent Hobbes

The royal court was massive, and hosted many. Tall pillars held high ceilings. Ornate tapestries hung from the walls. Paintings of old kings lined the room, and giant marble statutes of great warriors kept a careful watch over the king's men as they dined.

Servants poured wine.
Jesters made jokes.
Everyone feasted.

At the great table sat members of the king's royal court. Knights and political advisors, along with a few clergymen. These men were of renown, having served the king for decades. They trusted him, and all had become friends over the years. Much like the king, these men were also in their later years. Yet, they were young at heart, and dined as youthful warriors this night. They told jokes and laughed; they were in good spirits, for spring was upon them once more, and the sun's rays warmed the kingdom, melting the winter snow, filling the wide rivers, promising another plentiful season.

The men ate gluttonously. They were not bashful, stuffing their mouths full of food and smacking their lips in satisfaction. They ate with their hands. Delinar was a kingdom where it was considered rude not to go back for a second helping, and the volume of the belch meant the greater the compliment.

So, these two dozen nobles sat around the king's table, discussing various affairs of the kingdom. Some official. Some not. Either way, the great hall echoed with laughter, and the men's voices were pleasant, and all was hopeful in Delinar.

King Roland was a man of seventy years, having lived fifty of it seated on the throne. Although his body was slowly failing, his mind was still sharp. He was a wise king, and ruled his lands with mercy and compassion.

Peace had been achieved long ago, by both agreement and force. Delinar was powerful, and the kingdom had not warred with anyone in over a decade. Despite the monetary gain in war, the economy of Delinar flourished, and the people were quite content.

The king was also content. Roland sat back in his chair, sipping wine, and spoke in slow syllables. His closest friends surrounded him, and they listened intently as Roland told a story only the elders could remember. Everyone was enthralled, for Roland had a knack for storytelling, and they leaned forward in their seats.

Midway through his words, the doors to the great hall burst open.

Roland's words faded as he casually looked up, seeing two men enter the room. They moved with great urgency. Something curious was going on. Taking notice of the approaching men, everyone at the table focused their attention on the two.

Both were knights of Delinar, respected and well known to all. Gar, a captain in his king's army, walked ahead of the other. He took a few more steps, stopping shy of Roland. Gar was a beast of a man, and towered over the seated king. He had long hair and a trimmed black beard, bruises and cuts marred his face.

Despite his rugged appearance, Roland had no fear. He was king, and it was Gar who was in fear. Roland tilted his head, looking up at the warrior. He noticed the warrior's reluctant eyes, and knew something was wrong.

Gar's chest heaved, out of breath, and he took a few gulps of air before speaking. "My King, pardon the intrusion," he said. "There is something which requires your immediate attention."

The king tilted in his chair, his feathered white hair swishing as he did so. Unlike the warrior before him, Roland's own eyes gave no clue to his mood. Roland looked up at Gar without expression, studying the knight's face. He did not respond immediately, instead allowing an awkward silence to fill the room. Everyone turned his attention back to Roland, waiting for his reply.

This was something Roland had worked on for many years—the presence of divine royalty. When a king is silent, none dare interrupt, and Roland's court held their tongues, as did Gar. Finally, Roland nodded his head, allowing the man to continue. He said nothing and did not have to; the king's command was clear.

"Sire . . ." Gar sputtered his words. "You may consider hearing this with your own ears first."

Vincent Hobbes Presents

Roland's gaze did not leave Gar. The king was well acquainted with him, the knight being old enough to have seen many battles. Roland knew him to be valiant and loyal, and most of all—brave. If Gar's eyes spoke any truth, something was very wrong indeed.

"I trust your interruption is important," began Roland. "But do remember, good knight—this council has no secrets. You know this, for you sit at the same table. Now, speak your words," Roland finished, crossing his arms.

The knight nodded and began.

"My King, we were in the woods, north of the farmlands—where the river merges into three parts." Gar paused.

Roland nodded, knowing of the place. He had hunted those lands with his own father as a youth, and with his sons in recent years.

"There were seven of us," the knight continued. "We were hunting deer. And then . . . and then . . ." But Gar could not continue. His face was white, his lips quivering.

Roland had never seen such fear. "Speak up," he urged. "You are among friends, and have nothing to fear."

Gar's lip continued to quiver, but no words came out.

"By the gods, what happened?" demanded Roland.

"My King—" blurted out Gar. "There is a dragon in the forest!"

The entire congregation fell silent. They were shocked, each staring at the knight as they listened to his words. Everyone's jaws dropped and eyes widened; all except for the king, who showed no such reaction.

"Impossible," Roland replied calmly. "Dragons no longer exist."

The Endlands

Gar stood patiently, not knowing what to say.

Roland continued to stare at the knight. He could tell Gar was not lying, nor confused—only afraid. This worried the king, though he was careful not to show it. Roland looked to the man standing behind the captain. His name was Nup. He was young, having only been in the army for two years.

"And you swear to this?" asked the king.

Nup nodded enthusiastically. He was beyond nervous, and his voice echoed with unease. He had never met the king before, and was terrified having to stand in front of him. He responded quickly, "'Tis true, my great King. There is a dragon in the forest. I witnessed it with mine own eyes."

Whispers and murmurs filled the banquet room. All began speaking at once, careful to keep their voices low so as not to offend the king. They could not believe such words were coming from Gar, a trusted knight of Roland's army—a rational man, not known to tell tales.

This was beyond all comprehension.

Roland waited a moment, allowing the men their time. Finally, he raised his hand, and instantly the room quieted again.

Roland looked back to Gar and said, "Captain, tell us what happened, no matter how strange it may sound."

Gar began his story, focusing only on the highlights, for the king's time was more important than his own. "Sire—my men and I were hunting in the north woods. We were in deep, a half-day ride. We found a quiet spot and began hunting. A few hours must have passed, although I cannot be sure. We killed five deer, and were in the process of cleaning them when we heard a terrible noise."

Vincent Hobbes Presents

"A dragon?" questioned the king skeptically.

"Yes, Sire. But we did not know what it was at first. How could we possibly imagine we would? A loud rumble came from the skies. It was in the distance, but we could tell it was headed toward us. It was louder than any storm I have ever heard, and raced overhead before we could get a good look at it."

"What did you do?" asked Roland.

"We drew our swords and ran to an open spot in the woods, chasing it. 'Tis only but a small patch of open land, but it was enough. We could see the sky clearly. The noise grew louder and louder. I had to cover my ears. We held our ground, though, and finally we saw it."

Roland tilted his head, saying nothing.

"The dragon, my King. It flew directly overhead. It was close . . . much too close for my comfort, I can assure you. I confess, I was terrified. I thought surely we would all die."

Roland nodded at this. "What happened next?"

"It didn't attack, or I wouldn't be here to tell you. Instead, it flew overhead and landed in the forest behind us. It made an awful noise, even louder than when flying. My ears hurt . . . still do. I remember dropping to the ground and watching as it passed over, thanking the gods it did not devour me!"

"This is madness," mumbled King Roland, shaking his head. "A dragon in Delinar? You claim it flew? That it landed within our borders?"

"Yes, my King," Gar said, nodding. He lowered his head, bearing the shame of having to tell his king such news. He would forever feel guilty.

Roland took a deep breath. He looked back at the young

soldier, Nup, and demanded, "You claim this account accurate?"

"Yes, my King."

"With your own eyes?"

Nup nodded furiously, again reaffirming, "Yes, my King. I claim such."

"Amazing," Roland said loudly.

"Sire," said Gar. "I must tell you one more thing. This dragon spat fire that filled the forest. I've never seen anything like it! The woods were filled with flames and smoke and dust. If we had been closer, we surely would have burned alive!"

The entire room turned their eyes to their king. Roland took a moment, and then spoke. "It has been many centuries since mankind has seen a dragon. They have long since ended their slaughter on humans. The last sighting was over eight hundred years ago."

The room began to chatter once more. They spoke in small groups, each in a panic. Roland allowed them another moment. He understood that his men needed time to comprehend such a surreal concept.

For centuries, the only threat to humans was other humans. Delinar was larger and more powerful than her neighbors, and had no true enemies. Their civilization was made of strong warriors, and most could hardly remember the last battle they lost. Yet, the matter of a dragon was much different than that of an invading army. Dragons were believed to no longer exist, and that belief was now shattered. If, of course, this knight's story was true. But Roland had no reason to doubt the captain. Everyone had heard stories of dragons from days long past, but most dismissed them as fables. This was a modern world, where mankind was in no need of fables. Yet, this wonderment of news proved that dragons were indeed real.

A beast from the unknown was upon the kingdom.

A fire-breathing dragon.

"You say fire filled the forest?" asked Roland.

"Yes, Sire," answered Gar.

"Do you suppose the dragon meant you and your men any harm?"

"I do not know. But I *do* know that if the beast wanted us dead, it could have done so with ease. It was massive, large enough to consume an army."

Roland nodded again, taking in the information. "Gar, you stay here, as other questions will no doubt arise. You," Roland said, looking at the young Nup. "Go back to your home. Do not speak of this until I say otherwise."

Nup nodded his head, affirming his orders. He turned, scurrying out of the great hall, relieved to no longer be in the presence of the king. It would take hours before he would stop shaking.

Roland turned back to his table of knights. "We must take this report seriously, for I have no doubt Gar is speaking the truth. This is a dangerous time for Delinar, and we must exercise caution. I am sure you all understand the severity of this situation."

His council did.

Roland looked to the man at his right. He was a brave soldier, and leader of his king's army. "Hagar, tonight we will remain watchful. Double—no, triple the guards on the walls and in the towers. Brace the main gate, too. Pull back the patrols. There is no use in making it easy for the beast. If it decides to attack tonight, we must be prepared."

"Yes, my King," answered Hagar. "The reserves, too?" he asked.

"The reserves, too. After that is done, I want you to prepare a detail of men," continued Roland. "Many men. On the morrow, you will ride to the north forest."

Roland was old and frail, and his cough had reappeared over the past few days. He was not able to make the ride himself, but trusted Hagar would go in his stead.

"Enter slowly and be careful," Roland commanded. "Gar will escort you to the location of the creature."

Gar gulped, but said nothing.

"Do not attempt to engage it, unless it attacks first," continued Roland. "Study it. Find as much information about it as possible. Most especially, find out if it can be killed. The survival of Delinar depends on this."

"Yes, my King," Hagar responded, bowing his head.

The morning was cool. Fog covered the open fields, hovering low under the rising sun. The knights of Delinar rode hard across the plains, nearing the forest. Each was heavily armored, and trusted the man to his side. They rode as one unit, for the protection of their kingdom. These veterans were no strangers to battle, and had no fear. Each could only assume today was the day they were all going to die.

Hagar was at the head of the group. He led the brave men

to certain doom, and held his head high doing so. He did not fear death. This ride was a spiritual time for the warrior, and he relished every moment of it.

They rode for hours, finally arriving at the location. They stopped their horses at the edge of the woods. Gar pointed out the five deer carcasses left behind in their hasty retreat.

"'Tis in *that* direction," he said. "We will have to travel on foot. The forest is too dense here."

Seventy men entered the forest. They held their giant broadswords, double-handed grips on the hilts. These men carried no shields and wore little armor, for these were ancient times, and modern weaponry was an invention yet to come. Thick animal hides with patches of hard wood were their only protection. It was not much, but it mattered not. The knights of Delinar trusted their abilities in combat.

They crept closer, keeping quiet. The sun was high in the sky, making it easy for the men to see their surroundings. They recognized the shapes of the forest; all was silent, and they heard nothing.

Careful step after careful step, the men spread out. They moved through the woods, closer to the dragon.

"Remember what the king said," Hagar spoke. "We are not to provoke the beast unless it poses a threat."

The men had little trouble remaining quiet. They were hunters, and knew how to make themselves unknown in the woods. They moved onward, hoping to approach the dragon off-guard—or better yet, sleeping.

Hagar held up a fist.

His men halted.

"Careful now," warned Hagar. "If this dragon can burn these trees, it will have no problem doing the same to us. Stay alert, men."

They crept on.

The blackened forest was eerie. Small fires were still scattered about. The forest was charred, a raging fire having burned all night. It smelled like ash, burnt flesh, and something else. Something they had never smelled before. No birds chirped and no squirrels chattered. The woods were silent, save the popping of timber. Black soot clung to everything. Tree limbs smoked and patches of grass smoldered. The smoke was heavy, yet was fortunately drifting in the opposite direction.

It had been against the men's instincts to approach with the wind to their backs, but they followed Hagar's orders without question. He was a respected warrior and there was no reason for them to doubt his decision. Now, it made sense. The smoke blew away from them. If otherwise, it would have been impossible to see, and perhaps even breathe. This was also to their advantage; the dragon might not see or smell their approach.

"Stop!" Hagar's eyes went wide. He scanned a cluster of snapped trees ahead. "I think I see something." Hagar pointed. Ahead of them, in a small cluster of trees, was an object—an odd shape.

They approached the toasted cluster of trees, working their way around in a semi-circle, surrounding the object. It protruded from the tree trunks, shining in the sunlight. The men could not make out its strange shape.

They mustered their courage and drew closer, spreading

out, surrounding the dragon.

Finally, Hagar reached out his sword, touching the tip to the object. It made a dull thump against it, and nothing more.

"*Hmm*," grunted Hagar. "I know not what this shape is, but it is not alive. Move on."

Closer and closer.

Then, they saw it.

The dragon.

It was enormous, larger than they ever imagined. Its shell gleamed in the afternoon light.

"'Tis the beast's wing," blurted out Gar. "Part of it anyway. See how thin it is, and the way it's shaped?"

Hagar was skeptical. "Are you sure?"

"Aye. 'Tis bigger than I remember, but 'tis surely the dragon's wing. The body must be over there." Hagar pointed along the outline of the wing.

Hagar looked in the direction, then focused back to the beast's ripped wing. "It appears hurt," he stated.

It was true, the dragon *was* injured. The creature's wing was twisted and deformed, and wedged between a variety of trees. A few sections were torn open, and a strange liquid substance dripped from it. The smell tingled the men's noses.

"Foul smell," observed Hagar. "Dragon's blood."

"What do you suppose happened?" asked Gar, looking to Hagar for answers.

"Perhaps it hurt itself while landing. We must be cautious. If this dragon is hurt, it will surely be aggressive."

"Sir, look. Over there!" shouted one of Hagar's men.

Hagar and the others rushed down the length of the

wing, ducking under it. On the other side they saw the massive body of the dragon. It, too, was a mangled mess. It appeared lifeless, but they were taking no chances.

They examined it carefully from afar. The dragon's body was just as shiny as the wing. After consideration, Hagar affirmed, "*Ah*. It was the beast's scale."

"Sir?"

"The first part we came across. A scale must have broken off. I never expected a dragon's hide to shine, and I figured it would be thicker. Either way, it looks like this beast is dead."

Without saying a word, another knight pointed to the dragon. It was broken into two large pieces, having snapped in half. Its belly was also split wide open around the midsection, spilling its contents.

"I can see it's insides," commented Hagar.

Another knight asked, "Is it dead?"

"I believe so," replied Hagar. "It must have wounded itself upon landing. See those trees sticking through its sides?" he pointed at the obvious. "They impaled it when it tried to land."

"*That* was the noise we heard," responded Gar, understanding. "When I saw it flying close, it was going too fast. I suppose the beast misjudged its landing, or was injured or …"

Hagar nodded, understanding they might not completely find out the truth. He was relieved, as well. Glad the beast was dead.

The men poked and prodded, remaining watchful. They, too, were relieved. There would be no misery upon Delinar. They felt fortunate, because it would have taken an army to fight such a beast.

The knights investigated closely. They walked up the length of the dragon, inspecting the nasty gash along its side.

And the men saw something that made their stomachs turn. The sight disgusted them. Inside the dragon's open belly were the remains of humans.

Hundreds of them.

"It is a man-killer," said Hagar grimly.

"How many has it devoured?" asked Gar.

"Over a lifetime? Maybe thousands," replied Hagar. "Perhaps more."

The bodies were mangled beyond recognition. They were strewn inside the beast, twisted in odd shapes. Others were burnt to a crisp.

The knights of Delinar had seen much battle in their lifetimes. Much death, too. But this display was too much.

What could be done against such a beast?

The gods truly spared their kingdom.

And each man prayed to them, hoping there were no more. Because if this was only the beginning . . .

"*Ack.*"

The men heard a noise. It came from the far end of the dragon, near its tail. Raising their swords, Hagar and his men raced forward.

"What was that?"

"Over there. Inside the beast."

Hagar stuck his mighty sword into the ground. He turned, and with both hands, carefully pulled away a section of the dragon's loose hide.

A man lay underneath.

The Endlands

"Is he alive?" asked Gar, wide-eyed.

"He is breathing," answered Hagar.

Hagar turned to the man inside the beast. He leaned close and asked, "Are you alright?"

The man did not say anything. He was obviously in shock. His skin was burnt in places, and the pain was nearly unbearable. His arms and face and hair were melted away. Red splotches covered these areas. Infection was already settling in.

Hagar inspected him closer. The man had a deep gash above his eyebrow. Another across his chest, although the bleeding had stopped.

Hagar stared at the man's clothing a few moments. It was strange, not from these parts. The man's shirt was covered with debris, but Hagar could make out its color. It was blue—vibrant, and the knight thought it odd. The man wore his hair short.

"What is on his face?" asked Gar.

None knew the answer. The man had something attached to his face, covering his eyes, melted to his face. Perhaps a decoration of this man's kingdom.

The man moaned something. He opened his eyes briefly, shutting them fast; the sunlight hurt. He moaned again, and wiggled his body, struggling to free himself from the beast.

Hagar motioned to his men to help. They reached in, pushing away the dragon's organs, freeing the eaten man.

They placed him away from the body. A knight held up the back of the man's head, while another offered him water.

He drank heavily.

"Do you have a name?" asked Hagar.

Vincent Hobbes Presents

The man looked up. Another wave of fear crossed his face. He was in utter confusion, and began speaking rapidly, babbling.

The knights could not understand the language. It was definitely human tongue, but the words made no sense. Perhaps a different kingdom, far from these lands.

The man repeated his words.

"Were you eaten by this beast?" Hagar asked bluntly.

The man did not answer. The man had no doubt experienced the tragedy of being eaten, and living through it. His mind could not comprehend this fact. He was talkative, but kept muttering the same words, or so it sounded.

Hagar persisted with a few more questions, but it was in vain. They could not understand this man's language, therefore, he could tell them nothing of value concerning the dragon.

"We will take him back to King Roland. He is wise, and speaks many languages. Perhaps he can understand this man. There is not much else we can do. I will stay guard with half the men, and keep searching for answers. The other half will return to the castle, and present this man to the king."

The king waited. It was after dark when the men arrived. Roland was most anxious, but did not let on.

The knights carried in a man. Roland could tell immediately that he was severely injured. They set the man gently down.

"My King, the dragon is dead. It died upon landing," said one of the men.

"I see," said Roland, nodding. He was pleased with this news. But this stranger made him curious. "And who is this?" he questioned.

The men told their king everything. How the dragon's belly was split open. About the hundreds of dead bodies it had devoured. About how this one man seemed to be the only survivor.

"We tried speaking to him, but could not make his words," commented a knight.

"Hagar thought it best to bring him to you," said another.

Roland walked to the man. He crouched down to one knee, his eyes staring at the injured man.

He was definitely in shock. The man looked around the room, as if unaware of a royal hall. His eyes flickered back and forth, blinking rapidly as he looked into Roland's eyes.

Roland kept a soft look on his face while studying the man. He could tell the man was in pain, and most likely would not last the night. The king's men had done well tending to his wounds, but the man's injuries were beyond help. Roland could tell he was uncomfortable.

"What say you?" asked Roland. "What part of this world do you hail from?"

Finally, the man began chattering. He rambled, even interrupting the king.

Unfortunately, Roland did not understand the language, either.

And the man jabbered on, furiously trying to understand what had happened, and where he was. But despite his efforts, they could not understand his words.

Yet he said to them anyway, screaming at the top of his

Vincent Hobbes Presents

lungs—

"My name is Jackson Hunt. Our plane took off from Philadelphia this morning. Did we crash? Where is everyone? Who are you? My God, where am I?"

The Best BBQ on the Interstate

by Jennifer Chapman

The last five hours, and three hundred mile trek through Oklahoma and Arkansas, were causing Henry to yawn uncontrollably. He'd been up and down the I-40 corridor in the last twelve years so many times that the days ran into one another. Most of the time, he never really knew what day it was.

Two years ago, after his wife, Jodi, had finally left him, Henry went into business for himself. He bought himself a brand new '04 Kenworth; her shiny chrome went on forever, and he loved her straight nose. The green outside bore the name *Henry's Pride, Delivery With Excellence*. It was big enough to hold a fridge, and there was plenty of room for cooking.

The Kenworth hammered down the freeway, past the truck stops and off-ramps. The truck stop food had put on an extra fifty pounds in the last five years, and Henry knew that was mostly why Jodi had left him. She claimed it was loneliness, but it could've been both. It didn't matter, the truck was his home. Henry knew he had let himself go, it was hard to get exercise or even the motivation in his line of work. After awhile, showers weren't as important either. Henry had no family, they never had any kids. Jodi was unable. They tried doctors, but no one could help them and in

Vincent Hobbes Presents

his heart he knew that was the biggest part of her depression. So Jodi's family was about all he had and after she left she took them, too. He never really liked them too much anyway. Her mother always said, "You can't love a trucker, 'cause they're in love with the road."

Arkansas was always muggy, even in the fall and the winter. That's why it's so green all year. And as much as he loved the trees here, the one thing Henry always looked forward to was eating, especially down south. Anything from grits to BBQ; Henry loved it all. Some of the best BBQ had come from Arkansas. The small towns he drove through were usually full of diners, car lots, and churches. Mostly, they were people who had been out in the boondocks too long, obsessing over Jesus and holy salvation while they beat their god-fearing children.

When Henry was asked if he has been saved, his reply would always be yes. *Hallelujah!*

Now Henry was a religious man. He believed in God, gave at Christmas or when he saw fit, and was a believer. But he also knew the difference between himself and the fanatics.

1

Steve sat on a stump, eating something from a plastic container. He finished and put it in his backpack. Then, he poked his head out of the woods; the interstate had been very slow today. There was the normal truck traffic, but no one had wanted to pick him up. Sometimes they do, sometimes they

The Endlands

don't.

He climbed out of the bushes and walked up the embankment. His greasy, dark hair hung in his eyes, and his t-shirt was un-tucked from his tired blue jeans. Hitching had become a regular thing, once a week, whenever they needed him to go out. Steve was tired of hitching. They asked him all the time and he didn't want to do it anymore. *I'm gonna stop this soon*, he thought. He stuck his thumb out just about the time Henry came around the corner.

Henry's stomach had been growling for quite some time. It was near impossible to find any *good* BBQ on I-40. Maybe he would go to that shop off 89 after he got through Little Rock. That wasn't too far away. He saw the boy on the side of the road, looking pitiful, yet smiling. As a solo driver, and a divorcee, Henry didn't have many souls to talk to. He knew better than to stop. His gut told him no, but he was lonely, and it would be awhile until dinner. So, he stopped.

Steve hated the jake-brakes on these trucks. It irritated him immensely. It reminded him of his father, who was also a trucker. But, little Stevie was never allowed on the truck, or to ride with his daddy. Mom said Stevie couldn't be alone with daddy. His father would preach on and on about the goodness and forgiveness of the Lord, and then beat Stevie. Steve hated him. He hated him very much, but Stevie took care of his bad, bad daddy.

Henry put on his best grin and unlocked the door. "Well hello there." Henry said, as the hitchhiker stood up and peered inside.

Steve smiled back. "Hey, man, I've been out here all day. Feels like I'm being cooked alive."

Henry laughed. "So where're you headed?"

"Well, my folks live in Memphis, and it's a mighty long walk there from Amarillo." Steve grinned.

"Well, come on in boy. Name's Henry."

Steve jumped in the truck. "Good to meet ya, Henry. Name's Steve." The lanky boy put down his backpack and asked, "Where you headed, Henry?"

"I gotta be in Nashville tomorrow night, I've got plenty of time. The load is just toilet paper anyway," Henry said, laughing. "I can drop you at the Flyin' J outside Memphis. How's that for close?"

"That would be great," Steve smiled at Henry. "How long you been truckin'?" he asked.

Henry took a drink of his soda and said, "Well, forever. At least it feels that way. After my wife left, I bought this here beauty," Henry continued, rubbing the dashboard. "And away I went. A'int looked back since."

"What about your kids?" Steve asked. "Have any?"

"Oh no, never had any. Doc said she wasn't equipped for that. Kids are great, but not for this life. I might get lonely, but I wouldn't trade it for anything," Henry said.

Steve ran his hand through his hair. "Wow, it's kinda the same with me. I stick out my thumb, someone picks me up, and I get to meet all sorts of interesting people. It's a kind of weird freedom, ya know?"

Henry nodded. "You got a wife, Steve?"

The boy smiled. "Yeah, I got a girl. She don't like my parents, so she won't come with me. Our car won't make it, so here I am."

"Sounds like you got it figured out."

Steve looked out the passenger window, smiling. "Yeah, I like to think so."

Henry noticed something. "Hey, man, uh, ya got something in your teeth."

"Oh, yeah?" Steve pulled the visor down and grinned. He pulled a little piece of meat from between his teeth, and then wiped it on his pants. "Must've been from yesterday. I just love BBQ. It's the best!"

"I know what you mean," Henry said. "I love BBQ, too. I was actually gonna stop at this joint outside of Little Rock, off 89."

"You mean the Piggy Palace?" Steve asked.

"Yeah, that's the place." Henry said.

"Hell, my uncle owns that place," said Steve.

"No kidding? They have great BBQ."

Steve thought for a minute and said, "Ya know what? I know this place off 309. It's a friend of mine's place. I'd even say it's better than my uncle's."

Henry's eyebrows went up. "Well, hell, that's right up the road. After all that talk about 'Q, I'm starving. You hungry there, Steve?"

The boy smiled at Henry, "Hell yes, I am. Haven't eaten since yesterday."

Henry grinned, saying, "How 'bout I buy us some dinner, since you were kind enough to suggest your friend's restaurant?"

Steve raised his eyebrows at Henry. "I'll tell ya one thing; they marinate the meat for at least twenty-four hours before they cook it. It falls off the bone."

"Is there truck parking?" Henry asked.

"Plenty. Take a right off the ramp," Steve said, pointing. The hand painted sign for Dainsville, population two hundred-two, pointed to the right. As Henry turned the big rig south, he noticed the sun was beginning to set.

2

They passed a few houses, gas stations, and of course churches. The setting sun gave everything a reddish tone as if on fire. The windy four-lane highway started to narrow, turning into a two-lane road. Only an occasional truck would go by, and Henry would make sure to wave.

"How far down is this place?" Henry watched the horizon turn a brilliant reddish-orange.

"Not too much farther. Just gotta spot the fence. It's down a little dirt road. All the locals come out here for dinner, even the sheriff."

"Must be good. That dirt road a'int too bad now, is it?" Henry asked, slightly concerned.

"Ah, no, it a'int too hairy. No big potholes or nothing." Steve smiled again, big and toothy.

Henry nodded. "Okay. I've been in some pretty hairy places with big ol' potholes. I'd hate getting stuck."

Steve sat up, watching the road for the restaurant, ignoring Henry's concern. "This is totally gonna be worth it. Then, maybe next time you're runnin' through, you can stop by again."

Henry could hear his stomach growling. "Well, son, if it's as good as you say, I will."

Then, they came around a corner and Steve said, "There it is!"

The fence had a sign out front: The Lonely Pork Stop.

The sign was white, the letters painted black. It was attached to a fence that had become old and faded over time. The dirt road was more like a lane with wild flowers running down the sides; the surrounding forest was thick and lush.

Henry rolled down his window and breathed deep. "Oh, man, I can smell it from here."

Steve nodded, adding, "I'd say it's the best BBQ in Arkansas."

"My mouth is watering."

"Just wait 'til you taste it."

The road went up a mile, and in front of the pair was a little house. There was a doublewide off to the side, a barn in the back, and plenty of parking. Henry could see the cooker out back, the sweet smoke rising to the tops of the trees. The front window had The Lonely Pork Stop painted in big blue letters, along with a picture that was a bit disturbing. It was a picture of a pig on a skewer above a pit. However, the pig was still alive, and appeared to be screaming. Being cooked alive.

"What a weird picture," Henry said.

Steve wouldn't look at it, and responded, "Yeah, I try not to look at it. Kinda weirds me out. They cooked a pig alive once, it was terrible. I guess that picture is to remind them of it," Steve said. "The animal rights were called, almost got shut down, ended up just paying a fine."

Vincent Hobbes Presents

"Man, that's terrible." Henry finally parked his rig, opened the door, and got out.

Steve followed, saying, "Ya want me to lock it?"

"Nah, nobody's gonna mess with her, especially out here. People in the sticks don't usually walk up to trucks and try to get in. That only happens in the big city. In fact, I usually leave her unlocked, even at night. I figger no one is going to want to see what could possibly be in this sleeper, could be anything." Then, Henry patted his big belly, saying, "I'm hungry." As the pair walked, Henry noticed there were no cars in the parking lot, and only one pickup in front of the doublewide.

A little girl, who looked about six, sat on the front porch eating a rib. "Stevie!" she exclaimed, jumping up and throwing the rib down. She ran over, excited. "You're here! I'm gonna go tell everyone that you brought a friend."

Steve laughed. "Okay, honey, we'll be right behind you." As the little girl ran up the steps and into the restaurant, Steve turned to Henry, saying. "That's the owner's daughter."

"What a sweetheart," Henry said.

"Yeah, she's a good kid."

Steve opened the door and a bell chimed. A second later, a monster of a man walked out of the kitchen. He was huge, with bright orange hair and a matching beard that nearly hung down to his belly.

"Hey, Steve, long time. Where you been?" The man walked up and put his hand on Steve's shoulder. He had to have been at least six-three, maybe two-fifty. He looked Henry up and down and added, "And who have ya drug in with ya this time?"

"This is Henry. He picked me up on the interstate and he's givin' me a ride to Mom's," Steve replied.

"Isn't that nice," said the man. He put his paw of a hand out, and Henry took it. While in mid shake, the man's grip tightened. It hurt, and Henry tried to pull away. Turning to Steve, the man asked, "He ain't hit on you or anything funny like that, has he?"

"What?" Henry asked, dumbfounded.

"Hell, no!" said Steve.

"Are you nuts?" Henry asked, his hand still in the man's grip.

The big man finally let go. He laughed, a boisterous chuckle that made him shake all over. "Shoot, man, I'm just kidding ya, Henry."

Henry shook it off and returned the chuckle, saying, "That's one hell of a welcome." He was uneasy, but he let it slide. Henry figured the man was only being protective.

"So, what'll it be boys? I couldn't possibly guess why you're here," said the man.

"Steve said that ya'll got the best BBQ in Arkansas," replied Henry, rubbing his belly. "So, I said hell, let's just go there."

Steve piped up, and added, "Yeah, he was gonna stop by my uncle's place, but I told Henry the meat was better here."

The man grinned proudly. "I must say, it is." Then, he glanced over to Henry's Kenworth. "That's a nice Kenny you got there. What year is she?"

"'04," Henry replied proudly. "She and I go everywhere together. She never complains, and she never talks back. We've got the perfect relationship."

"Is that so?" the big man asked.

"Yup."

"Well, come on in and sit down. Name's Will, by the way. There's some brisket and ribs in the smoker. They'll be done in a bit. We also have fresh beans, corn, mashed potatoes, and all the fixins." Will showed them to a table.

"Nice to meet you, Will." As he sat down, Henry said, "I'm pretty hungry. I think I'll take one of everything."

"Would you like something to drink, Henry?" Will asked.

"Got any brew?" Henry asked.

"Yeah, we got Bud. That okay?"

"Bud is fine, my man," Henry answered.

Will opened three Budweisers, and sat down. He passed them out and took a sip from his own, saying, "It's gonna be another ten minutes or so. That'll give us enough time to bullshit before we stuff our faces."

"Sounds good," said Henry, taking a swig. "How long you been out here, Will?"

"Well, my brothers and I grew up in Louisiana. I met my wife there. We were happy, but we didn't have any room to stretch our legs, or our business. Then, we heard about this piece of property through a friend of ours. It sounded really great, so we came to have a look, fell in love with the place, and decided to stay. It was perfect, just what we had in mind. It has that small town feeling. Everything was included; the restaurant was already here. We bought the property, a doublewide, and here we are." He took a swig of his beer. "You ever been married?" asked Will, taking note of the fact there was no ring on Henry's finger.

"Yeah, I was married at one time," Henry said.

Will looked out the window, and said, "My wife passed a couple of years back; it was a heart attack, they said. Miss her every day. But, I'm thankful I still have my daughter. She keeps good company, and she looks just like her momma."

"Oh, I'm sorry." Henry sighed, "I think my wife just got tired of being alone, and you know, I really don't blame her. I was gone all but four days a month, and would call every day, but I think sometimes it didn't help." Henry played with the label on his beer.

"Well, what about kids?" Will asked.

"I don't have any. Doc said she wasn't equipped for it, so we were never able."

Will nodded, "Well I guess with your job, you really wouldn't be there for 'em anyway, huh?"

Henry took a drink, "No, probably not. So, did your brothers move with ya?" Henry asked, changing the subject.

"Oh yeah. They went into town, and should be back soon. They do most of the slaughtering, and I'm the cook. They earn their keep around here. They're both younger than me, so someday this place will be theirs, or maybe yours," he nudged Steve, "if ya keep coming around."

They all sat there for a minute enjoying the beer. Henry looked at Steve, "You know, Will, we could smell that 'Q from back on the road. Ah, that heavenly aroma."

Will smiled, "Well, Henry, lots of regulars come in for my BBQ, so either its good, or they're too lazy to drive anywhere else." He laughed. "I bet those ribs are done. Steve, can you help me out?"

Steve reluctantly got up, looked at Henry and said, "Look at this, I come for a visit and they always seem to put me to work." He laughed.

Henry sat alone now, able to take in the surroundings. The restaurant had a very homey feel. There was a brick fireplace in the corner, and all the tables and chairs were made of oak. The whole place was dark, the only lighting being small lamps hanging over the tables and above the mahogany bar. Big bay windows went all around the room, and old pictures of loggers and trees decorated the walls. There were old tools hanging up, giving it a rustic look, and on each table Will had placed a vase with plastic flowers. Alongside was a condiment tray with an endless supply of BBQ sauce and napkins.

A few minutes later the two came out of the kitchen with the biggest plates of food Henry had ever seen. One had just meat: ribs and slabs of brisket. Another held mashed potatoes and gravy. The other two were biscuits and corn.

"Sorry, we're out of beans," Will said.

Henry just stared and said, "I'm so happy, I think I'm gonna cry." They chuckled.

"Well, Henry, I figure you're the last customer of the day, so we may as well finish what's in the back. Oh, and no charge, I figure you're takin' Steve to Memphis and all," Will said as he set down the plates.

"Oh no, I couldn't; besides it's on my way. If anything, it's nice to have the company. Let me pay for something," said Henry.

"Okay. How 'bout three shots to celebrate a great meal and great company?" Will replied.

"Oh yeah, great idea," Henry said. Will got up and went to the bar. Henry rose from the table, asking, "So, where's the men's?"

Steve said, "Go around the bar and all the way to the back. It's the first door on the right."

When Henry passed the bar, Will asked, "Jack okay?"

"Jack's great man, and the food looks incredible."

Will took a little vile from his pocket, looked at Steve and smiled. He unscrewed the top and poured a little bit of white powder in the bottom of one of the glasses. Then, he filled the three with whiskey. Steve ran up to the bar and said, "Will, this is the last time. I don't wanna do this anymore. I hate this shit man, this guy's nice, ya know. I feel kinda bad. I've paid my debt," he finished, taking a glass.

Will said, "Hey, business is business, but fine. After ten years they've quit looking for your father anyway, Steve. Your debt is paid in full for my services." He grabbed the other glass.

On his way to the bathroom Henry could've sworn he heard muffled cries, but he wasn't sure from where. When he came back out there was no noise. *Must be the beer,* he thought. He walked back into the bar and they were waiting with glasses held up. Henry took the last on the counter and said, "Hey, is it okay if I crash in my rig until morning?"

"Of course, no problem," Will grinned. They all gave cheers and swallowed the sweet burning liquid down.

"That hit the spot," Henry said.

"Well, if you'd like another, there's more here," Will said.

"Well, thanks a lot . . ." Henry sat down, taking only a moment to admire the food, then dug in.

"We make everything from scratch; we raise our own pigs, the corn, potatoes. It's the life."

"I'll bet you get a lot of truckers in here, huh?" asked

Henry.

"Oh, occasionally they get sent down this road, but most don't stop. I think the sign confuses them and it doesn't look like there will be parking. But that's okay; we get plenty of regulars," said Will.

"I'll bet," said Henry.

Henry bit into a rib and the meat just fell off the bone, melting in his mouth. "Okay, okay, I give; this is the best BBQ I've ever had," Henry said as he swallowed. Will and Steve just smiled at each other.

Will noticed Steve was staring at the window outside. "See something out there, Steve?"

"Oh, that damned stupid sign with the pig gives me and Henry the willies," Steve said.

Will turned and looked at Henry, "So, Henry, don't like my sign, huh? You come on another man's turf and insult his home?"

In mid-chew Henry stopped, not knowing what to say. "No, I, uh . . ."

Will stared at him, and clenched his jaw, then relaxed. "Man, you're way too nervous. I'm just giving you guff," he laughed. "It is kinda creepy, but you should've heard that piggy squeal, sounded almost human."

Will and Steve burst out laughing, but Henry didn't think it was that funny. "I'm telling ya boys, this BBQ is to kill for, it's gotta be the best."

Will piped up, "Well, how 'bout another round there, Henry?"

"Oh, I suppose. Can't have too much, gotta get up in the morning and head out." He smiled at Steve. "Oh, Steve, by the way, I got an extra bunk in my trunk if ya need a place to crash."

Steve looked up from his food, "Yeah, I think I will take you up on that offer, Mr. Henry." Henry was a trucker, and he never had much of a chance to have a drink, so he was really starting to notice the floating sensation from the liquor making him a little sleepy.

Steve got up, "One more round boys?" He confirmed.

"Hell yeah, bring it on!" said a buzzed Henry. Will poured the shots; they repeated the toast, and once again the sweet burning sensation seared down his gullet. They finished the meal and Henry yawned, "Oh man, I'm gonna sleep good tonight." He got up from the table and said, "Well, gentlemen, I think I'm ready to pass out. Steve, I'll put the bunk down and leave the truck unlocked for ya. And thanks again, Will, for the dinner, it was delicious." By now the powder that Will had put in his shot was kicking in and he was getting lightheaded. "I've got to go to bed now." And with that they watched him stumble to his rig, almost not making it inside.

3

They waited an hour and went out to the rig. It didn't take them long to get Henry out of the truck and into the basement. Henry wasn't a small man so they had waited until both brothers got back to help. Henry never stirred.

Will said, "Good, I figure, he'll be wakin' up just in time to watch you boys do your work. What a surprise that will be."

Vincent Hobbes Presents

Tommy grinned, "Yeah, bro, for him," he said, laughing.

Matt spoke up, "No shit, dumbass, who else?" They all stood around Henry as he lay on the floor passed out. "Man, it's a wonder we got him in here."

"He'll be out for a while. Let's get him in it," Will said. Steve and Will headed up the stairs; Will looked back and said, "You better start getting the other one ready."

"Yeah, we know, we're on it," said Matt.

Everything was blurry when Henry opened his eyes and realized he couldn't move. His head was cloudy and the place smelled like . . . *what was that, BBQ sauce?* He looked down and realized he was in a barrel. A big oak one filled with liquid. The substance was thicker than water and his whole body was submerged, except for his neck and head. He started to panic, *No stop, breathe, don't freak out,* he told himself. He looked around and saw six other barrels. There was a man, who appeared to be sleeping, in the one on Henry's left. He glanced at his surroundings and spotted a big hand-painted sign, which looked the same as the one out on the road, reading **ALL MEAT MUST MARINATE FOR AT LEAST 24 HOURS.**

Oh my God, he thought, *no it can't be, him, me, no, it can't. What kind of people would do this? I'm sitting in BBQ sauce . . . ARE THEY MARINATING ME? I gotta get out of here, they're gonna cook me.* Henry found it convenient that he had no wife or kids or anyone to look for him. Squirming, he tried to move the barrel and the lid jiggled a bit, but it was one of those heavy duty old oak ones that people used to ferment alcohol and was way too heavy.

Henry looked over at the man next to him. *This must be*

who I heard last night, God why didn't I do something? "Hey pssst, man, are you awake?" He didn't stir. "Hey, man, wake the hell up."

The man slowly opened his eyes like he had also been drugged, "What the hell!" he screamed. "I thought this was a dream! I woke up earlier, and I was in here by myself, I guess I must have passed out again after that. That little shit! It was that hitcher Steve, he tricked me."

"Yeah, he got me, too."

"We gotta get out of here," the man said. "I don't really know how long I've been in here." He kept looking around in a panic.

"Hey, man, let's try to get out of here together. Do you know how many people there are in this place?" Henry asked.

The man looked at Henry, "No, not sure. I know that guy Will and that little bastard Steve. I think there are two others also; they must have stuck us in here. Hey, just in case I don't get out of here, my name's Jim Thompson. I live in Dallas. Could you maybe look up my wife and kids and let them know that I love them and I'm sorry I couldn't make it back home?" Jim started to cry.

"Hey, man, don't worry, we're gonna get out of here alive," Henry said.

"Man, I can't feel my fingers, or legs, or anything. I'm all numb. I don't know if I could fight them right now anyway. They're gonna cook us man! Oh, man, I ate that brisket, I think I'm gonna be sick." He turned away sobbing.

A few feet from the men sat a metal table, and next to it a tray on wheels. The tray was covered in knives and syringes. He noticed some shelves behind the table they contained

Vincent Hobbes Presents

several bottles of different medicines. One of which was labeled **Novocain**. A mop and bucket sat in the corner. Next to that was a chart numbered one through six with number two circled. Henry hoped he was in number three.

The doorknob turned and he heard two men talking. "Yeah doggie! I hope they're both awake, I want the other to watch." The men were twins, but not identical. One stood a little bit taller, and one was a little bit bigger. "Well lookie here, the little piggies are awake. We've been waiting on you. Gotta get started on tomorrow's dinner special: all you can eat." Tommy, the bigger of the two but shorter than his brother, snorted and clapped his hands together.

"Shut up, Opie," Matt said.

"Hey, don't call me Opie, stupid."

Matt looked at Tommy and said, "Yeah, yeah. Remember, we can't get them all riled up, too much endorphin in the meat makes it tough."

"Yeah, okay, whatever," Tommy said.

"YOU GUYS ARE SICK MAN!" Henry yelled.

"No, only him. He'll eat ya raw." Matt motioned to his brother, grinning at Henry.

"Oh, no, no, no, no!" Jim cried. They removed the open lock on top of the barrel and took off the lid.

"Leave him alone, you bastards!"

"Cannibals more like it," Tommy said. Matt slapped Tommy upside the head. "Ow," Tommy whined, rubbing the spot.

Jim started screaming, "NO, LET ME GO! I GOT A FAMILY!!!"

Jim struggled as they laid him on the table, strapping

him down, taping his eyes open and his mouth closed. Matt grabbed a bottle of Novocain, and handed it to Tommy who was holding a very large syringe. They pumped up Jim's vein in his arm and injected the needle. Jim's muffled cries made Henry cringe. After a few minutes, Jim stopped fighting and relaxed.

"Now, Mr. Henry, you need to watch this so you know what's going to happen to you next," Tommy said.

Matt looked angrily at Tommy, "Dude, shut up. If you can't control yourself then go upstairs."

Tommy sulked and helped his brother with Jim, occasionally flashing Henry a big grin. It was as if to say, "*I can't wait to taste you, big boy.*" Henry realized screaming wasn't going to help, no one would hear, just like last night when he went to the john.

"Go to hell! I'm not gonna watch this shit!" Henry yelled at them.

Matt looked at him and said, "I'm sorry, my friend, but you're going to have to."

Tommy came over with some tape. Henry tried to struggle, but was unable. Tommy taped his eyes open and mouth shut. "Oh, this won't take long. We do this all the time, and we really don't like to break tradition." All Henry could do was watch as these inhuman acts took place. And knowing Jim was still alive! "Let's make sure he's numb."

And with that, they made an incision in his left thigh. He didn't make any movements so they started sawing off his feet, and even though he couldn't feel it, the sound of the bones was maddening. Henry thought Jim passed out from shock, his mind shutting down. Henry swore he would go to

Jim's wife and kids to deliver the message.

"We gotta bleed 'em," said Matt. They took his arms and slit his wrists, then his throat, blood spraying across the room and on to the concrete. A thick stream hit Henry square on the chin, making a fine red line across his mouth. Henry could smell it emanating in the room, filling his nostrils, driving him mad. He started to cry, the tears wetting his open eyes. Soon the gurgling from Jim's throat stopped, his body spasmed, and he passed on.

They stuck Jim on a meat hook in the corner and started skinning him. Tommy walked over and took the tape off Henry's eyes and mouth. The stinging was excruciating. "Okay, give us a blink now." Henry blinked, and just stared at Tommy.

He smiled at Henry and said, "I wonder what you taste like. You see, they all have different flavors. Depends on what they been eatin.'" Tommy walked over and cut a chunk out of Jim's leg. He popped the stringy meat into his mouth. "Well, hell! I think this one's Irish, he been eatin' cabbage and onions." He smiled at Henry. Henry felt his stomach turn, and vomited. The milky white flew across the room, some hitting Tommy, the rest lying under his nose.

Tommy looked at Henry disgusted, "Man, that's so gross!" Matt walked over with a rag and cleaned up Henry's face, looking irritated. Tommy was chewing with his mouth open.

Matt glared at his brother, "Tom, that's so gross. What's wrong with you? Wait 'til he's cooked."

Tommy shrugged, "Come on Matt. You know I love 'em raw."

"I know but there's no time for snacking. We gotta carve and cool the meat before it spoils."

"Yeah, okay." He taped Henry's eyes back open and walked over to Jim. As they carved the meat off Jim, Matt was whistling. Tommy had his tongue hanging out the side of his mouth. Jim's body jerked as they cut off pieces of red stringy meat. "Mmmmm, look at that rump roast. That's gonna feed at least six to ten people," said Matt. The raw citrus flavor of the vomit filled his mouth and Henry's stomach turned again, but he was able to hold it back this time.

By the time they were done, they had removed all meat from the torso and placed it on another rolling tray. All that was left was the skeletal structure and a few strips of meat here and there. Jim's head lolled to the right, eyes still taped open. They opened a big steel door and wheeled the cart into a fridge for cooling. They came out and looked at Henry.

"Well, I say man, you must have been in here for at least thirteen hours, and you still got nine to go." They took the tape off his eyes and tears swarmed in. Henry saw the plastic they had laid down before they started was covered in blood.

"Man, he squirted everywhere." Tommy said. They cleaned up the mess and turned to Henry. "Now if you're hungry, you just scream. We'll bring ya some BBQ. We gotta go to town, but we'll be back in a few hours." They laughed as they walked up the stairs.

"Man, he's gonna make some great burgers. He'll grind up real fine," said Matt.

Henry sighed and looked over at what was left of Jim, they had put him in the shadows of the corner, but Henry could see his eyes, staring blankly into nothingness.

Vincent Hobbes Presents

Okay, I gotta get out of here, he thought. *How can I get out?* He sat and thought for a long time, trying to see a way out of this. He looked around the room and saw a pair of axes in the corner, but how could he get to them? Then he thought about the lid of his barrel and how loose it was when he was moving around. He noticed the latches on the side keeping it in place, but they were loose and a little bit rusty. Henry started squirming around inside the barrel; his mass of a body was in a crouched position, making his legs go numb. *One good jar, and with the pressure of me and the sauce, the top might come off, but how?*

4

After what seemed like an eternity, the doorknob upstairs turned and he froze. He heard the door squeak open and then, "He-wo? Matt, Steve, Tommy, Daddy? Are you down here?"

"Hello? Who's there?" Henry called.

He could see the little feet at the top of the stairs. "Who are you, Mister?" the little voice asked.

"I came with Steve earlier, do you remember?" Henry asked.

"I want to come down there, but they don't let me. I'm not supposed to, Daddy says. Have you seen my daddy?" she asked.

"No, honey, I haven't. But, I could kind of use your help down here," Henry said.

"Well, I guess. My daddy says to help people when I

can, you know. I could come down and help you." She came down the stairs and stopped, laughing at Henry. "Hey, Mister, whatcha doin' in the piggy barrel?"

Hope filled his mind as Henry smiled at her, "Well, honey, I was playin' a game with your friends."

"They're my uncles," she said.

"Sorry, your uncles. We were playin' hide and seek, only thing is, this here latch got stuck on and now I can't get out."

She laughed, "You're in the piggy barrel. That's funny!" She looked at the ground, kicking around a pebble. "You know, no one really plays with me around here. Too much to do, and they leave me alone all the time."

Henry smiled at her, "I'm so sorry, but, I'll tell ya something. I sure would be glad to play with you if you can help me out of here."

Her eyes brightened, "Really? Swear on it?"

"Yes, I swear," Henry said.

"Okay." She walked over to the barrel and removed the open lock. "There you go, Mister." Henry stood up, his legs pins and needles, and carefully climbed out of his wooden prison. She was laughing hysterically, "Mister, you got sauce all over you."

He grinned at her, "Yeah, it was dark when I came down here and hid in the barrel. Thank you for helping me out. So, what do you want to play, sweetheart?"

She thought for a moment and said, "Hide and seek!" then started to giggle again. "Mister, all you got on is your undies and piggy sauce!"

Realizing he was only in his briefs, Henry blushed and said, "Yeah, I gotta find some clothes. By the way, what's your name, sweetheart?"

She smiled and said, "Cindy Marie."

"Okay, Cindy, I think I need some pants and a shirt or I won't be able to hide anywhere, 'cause you'll smell me from a mile away." He was very cold, and looked frantically for anything to cover himself. He finally spotted some clothes lying in a pile in the corner. "Are there any adults here now?" he asked, wiping himself off with someone else's shirt. He shuffled through the pile until he came across his clothes.

"Oh, I don't know, that's why I came down here."

Henry kept thinking about the fact that when he saw her before, *Cindy had been eating a rib*. It made him sick to his stomach, then angry that someone would do this to a child. "Now, you go hide and I'll count to a hundred," he told Cindy, "I'm gonna go change and then I'll come and get ya." She squealed with delight and ran up the stairs. He looked around, grabbing a syringe and the axe from the corner. He made his way up the stairs to the door. He could feel his heart pounding as he gripped the handle.

He slowly turned it and just then he heard in the distance, "Hi guys! Hey, I found that man you were playing with in the basement and let him out. He was in one of those piggy barrels, can you believe it? He's gonna come and get me, we're playing hide and seek. I better go before he finds me!" she finished, running to hide.

Henry heard Matt say, "We better finish the game, huh, guys?" Tommy and Steve laughed. "I'm gonna go look in the restaurant. You guys go out back and check the barn. Since his rig's still out front, he's gotta be around here somewhere."

Peeking out the door, Henry could see the front of the

The Endlands

restaurant. Tommy and Steve were heading out back, and Matt was walking in the front door. *I'm surrounded*, thought Henry. He ran behind the bar and in to the kitchen.

He could hear voices calling, "Come out, come out wherever you are. We wanna play, too, Henry." There was just enough space for hiding under a table by the stove. It would have a fairly good view of both front and back doors. Henry knew it was too late to run; besides those trucks weren't made to accelerate, so he waited.

The kitchen door opened and in walked Matt. "Henry, come on out buddy. Don't worry, we've decided to let you go." He had a baseball bat in his hands. Matt wandered around the kitchen, looking in all the cupboards. He was moving very slowly and Henry was sitting as still as he could, waiting for the right moment. He could hear his heart pounding in his chest; his breathing filled his ears like static. His hands had become very sweaty and he was unable to wipe them off for fear of making noise. He picked up the syringe in his left hand and waited. He could see Matt's feet as he walked around the kitchen, finally stopping in front of Henry's hiding spot. And in one motion, as Matt crouched down, Henry took his shot. He plunged the syringe in Matt's eye, injecting the contents, which ran straight to his brain. Matt dropped the bat, screaming and jerked the needle out of his eye. "Oh shit! My eye ... MY EYE ... !"

But he didn't have time to say much else. Henry scrambled out from under the table and grabbed the bat, then proceeded to hit Matt as hard as he could on the side of his head, knocking him to the ground. Blood poured out of Matt's eye and head; he just laid there like a wet noodle. Henry took the axe and, grabbing one of Matt's legs, pulled him in to the basement. He laid him on the floor in the corner next to Jim's body. Henry kicked him in the side. Matt stirred a little, opening his one good eye, but was unable to move. *Well, looks like it was Novocain in that needle,* Henry thought, *that's great.* He heard the back door slam open, and hid under the stairs in the shadows.

"Matt, are you in here?" Tommy shouted as he and Steve came in the back door. They saw the blood on the floor, but no one was around. "I bet Matt's got him in the basement," Tommy laughed. Steve followed him through the other room to the basement. Tommy opened the door, "Hey, Matt! You down here?" Matt moaned, only semi-unconscious. Tommy cautiously came down the stairs, "Matt?" he hollered his brother's name again. Starting to get nervous, he instructed Steve, "You stay up there, somethin's not right." Halfway down the stairs Henry came out of the shadows, axe gleaming in the light.

"What the . . ." Tommy said, as Henry drove the axe into his shin. Thinking of survival, of the little girl, as he did it. Bone and blood flew everywhere.

"YOU SICK BASTARDS! You're done for!"

Tommy fell down the stairs, arms flailing. He fell on his face, breaking his nose, blood spraying the concrete. "AHH, God! Steve, help me!"

Steve came down the stairs slowly and saw Henry standing above Tommy with the axe. Tommy kept screaming, so Henry taped his mouth closed. He looked at Steve, "So, aren't ya gonna run Steve? I mean, hell man, you're the one who tricked me into this mess! Go run and get Will, you coward." Henry was ready for anything at this point.

"Kill me, Henry," Steve said.

"What?" Henry said.

"Please kill me." Steve closed the door and came down the steps.

Henry raised his axe. "Don't come any closer, Steve. I don't want to hurt you. I just want to get out of here alive."

Steve stood on the stairs, hands up. "Henry, I've been doing this for so long. I've helped them kill so many people, and I can't live with myself anymore."

Henry didn't believe him. "Steve, I don't want to kill you, but I will do what I need to do to get out of here alive."

Just then the door flew open. Will came down the stairs, his eyes gleaming with rage. "What the hell is going on here?" Will paused behind Steve when he saw what was happening. "Steve, get the axe!" he shouted.

Henry was out of his mind with rage, "Barbeque, huh? You prick! You feed that to your little girl! I can't believe it! Don't come any closer, or I will kill you both!"

Will looked at Steve, "Get down there," he commanded.

Will gave Steve a small push towards the body, and Henry holding the axe. Steve struggled, so Will pushed him aside, "Fine, I'll get him." Will's steps were like thunder on the stairs.

As he passed by, Steve pushed Will as hard as he could. "Kill him, Henry! I can't stand this anymore." Will fell, stumbling down the stairs. He hit his head and landed next to Tommy, who had passed out. Henry grabbed the other axe, now holding two.

"Come on, Steve, you want him dead, you do it." Henry

proclaimed.

Steve came down the stairs towards Henry. As he neared the bodies, Will grabbed Steve's leg. "You . . . traitor." Will was starting to get up, blood pouring from his ear and nose. Steve looked at Henry, and Henry tossed him the other axe.

Steve raised it above his head and said, "God forgive me for my sins," then lowered the axe through the middle of Will's head. There was a crunching noise, blood and pieces of brain sprayed out of the crack in his skull.

Steve fell to his knees crying, "Henry, get out of here! I have to finish this while I have the strength. Call the police, you did nothing wrong! It was all us, this whole time, we tried to kill you. We killed all those poor people and I brought them here, all of them. I knew it was wrong, but I didn't care. Will killed my dad Henry, and I not only asked Will to do it, but I ate him after he was cooked! I'm sick Henry, ill, and I don't want to do this anymore. Tell them I went crazy with an axe, started chasing people around. You split and heard screaming as you were leaving. Tell them you're worried about the little girl you saw and aren't sure if she's okay. Henry, I have to pay for my sins. I can't live like this anymore. Now go!"

Henry wiped down the axe and walked up the steps, not looking back. The door to the basement slammed behind him as he left the restaurant.

Cindy was in his sleeper when he opened the door to his rig. "BOO!" she yelled as she jumped out.

"AHHHH!" screamed Henry. "You scared me, Cindy."

"Where were you?" Cindy asked. "You finally found me,

Henry."

He looked at her apologetically, "I'm sorry, sweetie. I was talking with your family. Look, I gotta get out of here, but you go and play in the yard. Your daddy and uncles are busy now, don't bother them. I'm so sorry, but I gotta go back to work." Henry rambled, looking over his shoulder.

"Well, okay, Henry. Maybe you'll stop by again sometime and play with me," she said.

"I will, sweetheart, if I come through again, for sure." He helped her out of the truck. His keys were still in the ignition. Looking in his rearview, finally feeling safe, Henry saw her waving as he drove away. As he got on the interstate, he dialed the police, telling them the story the way Steve wanted it told.

That night, Henry locked his doors for the first time.

Glass Prison

by
Christina Estabrook

"Wake up! Wake up, honey," Jack softly whispers. He runs his hand down his wife's arm, which is still shaking from her nightmare. In the distance, lightning brightens the night sky, revealing the scene outside their bedroom window. Thunder crashes in the expanse, a soft rumbling call.

Once his wife awakes, Jack quickly falls back to sleep. But for Sarah, there is no more sleep tonight.

She sits up quietly, looking for her red slippers in the dark. She is nearly in tears as she slides them on, not from fear, but because the nightmare has returned every night for two weeks now. She has slept next to none.

Sarah walks slowly down the hall to the open living room. *It's always the same, just louder and more vivid each time. What does it mean?* she wonders.

She walks over to her large French windows. Throwing back the tan, satin curtains, she watches the rain start to fall on her flowers outside. The smell of rain in the air is somewhat calming, but alone in the dark she can only dwell on her own fear. The sounds of the river in her back yard reminds her of how alone she and Jack really are out here in the middle of Rolling River Forest.

The dream, she thinks, *is always the same. I'm asleep in bed* and, for some reason, Jack is not next to me. I can hear him in the distance, just barely calling for me. It's cold and I see shadows moving all around the room, laughing and speaking all at once. I can see my breath, and when I exhale I see a face. I see Jack's face, but it's not really Jack.

There is blood all over his face and chunks of skin missing. And his eyes . . . Sarah thinks, his eyes are black as coal. There's no life, no sign of Jack. It's something else. I run and I can feel my flesh being ripped open all over, but I can't see what's doing it. I make it out the door and into the yard. The voices grow louder and they are coming for me—taunting me. The moonlight is always so bright, casting an eerie yellow-orange glow. The trees all seem to be moving and rearranging their paths. They're reaching out, slowly coming for me. I see faces or impressions of faces. It's as if they're peering out from within the trees themselves.*

Sarah walks up to her window. She places her hand and forehead on the cold pane of glass, feeling her warm breath bounce back on her face. She watches the steam rise up from her flower garden as the rain cools the earth. The movement of a small toad bouncing in the garden catches her eye. She stares wide-eyed at the toad as he moves absentmindedly through her flowers, enjoying the refreshing rain.

"I need some coffee," Sarah says. She turns away from the window and begins walking to the kitchen. Not wanting to awaken her husband again before the alarm goes off, she decides only to turn on the light above the range. The soft light illuminates the counter and stove, but not much more. Sarah opens the cabinet and finds her coffee. She walks over to the stove to be sure she didn't grab her husband's decaf. Satisfied with her choice, she scoops two big servings into the filter and fills the pot with water. She stands by the counter, watching the coffee brew. Sarah can see out the window, the sky outside just starting to turn purple and pink as the sun begins to rise.

She looks at the clock on her microwave—it's 5:45 a.m. Sarah smiles, not because she is happy, but because that's all she can do. She reaches for her favorite coffee cup. It's chipped and stained, but the pink mug was a present from Jack, and she loves it despite its flaws. Rubbing the rim of the cup, she remembers the Valentine's Day she received it, filled with chocolate kisses and a reservation to Serendipity Day Spa in town. Sarah smiles and pours her first of many cups she will drink today to keep going.

The rain has nearly finished pouring as the sun starts to creep up with beautiful pinks, oranges, and purples peering out over the treetops. The nightmare is still rerunning in her mind: images of Jack's face, his eyes tormented, lifeless and full of hate. A shiver crawls up her spine, causing an all-over shudder.

The memory of Jack laughing at her as she begs for help makes her heart jump. She takes a quick sip of coffee to clear the thought from her mind. "Jack would never hurt me," Sarah says aloud.

The forest around her home starts to slowly come alive. The sounds of birds, crickets and frogs fill the air. Sarah watches as her garden lights up from the morning sun. Her roses and orchids are glistening with raindrops. The red mulch around her stone pathway is somehow beckoning her to come sit and relax. The white, stone cherub birdbath in the middle of the garden is now full with water. It has wel-

Vincent Hobbes Presents

comed two small sparrows, which flutter around, gently washing their feathers.

Surrounded by so much beauty, Sarah wonders how she can be plagued with such horrible nightmares that now have her too frightened to venture outside her door after sundown. She also wonders how she can allow silly nightmares to put such horrid thoughts about her husband in her mind.

The alarm goes off down the hall and Sarah can hear the first signs of Jack emerging from his slumber. The oaken, hardwood floors creak under his feet as he walks to the bathroom. She can hear Jack whispering but cannot make out what he is saying. It is the same routine he follows every morning before leaving for work.

A few minutes later Jack appears in the kitchen. He is a well-dressed, handsome man. His black hair is kept neat and there's no sign of gray, though he will be thirty-five in a few weeks.

His lovely, marble-blue eyes and soft features make him appear much younger than he really is. Jack walks up behind Sarah, placing his arms around her waist, and gently holds her. "The sunrise out here is always so beautiful," Jack says. "I take it you were unable to fall back asleep?"

Sarah nods her head. She turns slowly to face her husband, handing him a cup of steaming coffee. "It's my coffee, but it's already made," she tells him.

"That's fine," Jack says, and smiles softly. "I'm starting to worry about you, Sarah. You're barely sleeping at all anymore. You also stopped going out for walks in your garden at night. This isn't like you at all."

"I'll be fine. I'm not the only person in the world who has

reoccurring nightmares," she claims.

"No, you're not, but you need to sleep, honey. Maybe if you told me about your nightmares," he suggests, "perhaps they would go away."

"Jack, don't be silly. They are just dreams, and I really can't remember what they are about once I wake up. It's fine, really."

Jack smiles before placing a kiss on Sarah's cheek. "I have to go," he says. "Do you need me to stop by the store or anything on my way home tonight?"

"No. I think we're all good for now," she replies. "Now go on before you're late."

Sarah watches from the living room window as Jack climbs into his green Ford Explorer. *I just can't bring myself to tell him about my dreams*, she thinks. *I don't want him to know how I see him, or what I hear. I don't want him to think I'm going crazy.*

The Explorer backs down the long, dirt driveway. Jack is careful to wait until he is alone, looking in the rearview mirror at the dark shadow in the back. "Keep it up. I'll have her soon," he says. "She already thinks she's going nuts." The shadow moves around the truck, whispering back to him.

It's a long way to town, an hour alone on Rockport Road—the dirt road they live on—and another twenty minutes through Main Street, in town, to Jack's office. Jack works on the Committee for Forest Preservation.

It is sometimes long hours, but the rewards are great, in Jack's opinion. They get to see all the treasures from ancient civilizations that were once the tenants of the beautiful area.

Sometimes they even get to keep a few old relics, like the mirror in the hall. The goal is to try to leave as much in the woods as possible, to show how people once lived.

Sarah turns and walks down the hall. "May as well get dressed," she tells herself. There are no windows in the hallway, but it stays dimly lit from the light shining in from the two bedrooms.

Sarah stops and turns on the hall light to get a better look at the pictures hanging on the wall. The memories that line the walls always put a smile on her face—her wedding pictures, where she and Jack said their vows, the beautiful Rolling River Falls in the background.

Their midsummer picnic in the garden, the flowers in full bloom, is portrayed in another frame. Then, of course, just past the huge, oval mirror is Jack's favorite picture. It's a picture of Sarah taken by the lake at the end of the street from their home. The first snowflakes of winter were falling and the last of the oak leaves litter the ground. *It's a beautiful picture*, she thinks. *The lake is so clean and clear, and the lily pads are still there. There are no flowers, but they are still beautiful on the water's edge.*

As she turns to finish going down the hall to her bedroom, a flash of light catches her eye. In the mirror, for one second, she sees Jack's face. Sarah turns to look but the face is gone as quickly as it appeared. "I must be going crazy," she says.

Sarah stands and looks in the doorway to her room. She knows deep down there will be nothing there, but she has to look just the same. Sarah walks into the bedroom and proceeds to make the bed; her silk sheets first, then the Egyptian cotton comforter. She fluffs the pillows, looking around. The room is quite nice, with large cathedral ceilings and the same beautiful hardwood floors as the living room. The bedrooms are equipped with huge French windows, allowing Sarah and Jack to take in all of nature's beauty year-round. Sarah walks around to the closet and grabs faded jeans and a light blue t-shirt. She gets dressed, thinking that today feels different. Everything seems darker somehow; colder than usual.

In her spare time, Sarah likes to work in her garden and write a little poetry. Today there is a poem in her head she feels is somehow related to her nightmares, but she is not sure how. There is a nagging feeling to get it all out. She turns to leave her bedroom, a bit more leery of her hallway and pictures than before.

For some reason I get the feeling I am supposed to look at the pictures again.

The mirror stares blankly out at the hallway, reflecting nothing now except the empty wall that sits across from it. Still, there is something terrifying about the mirror, and the words in Sarah's head are just as scary as what she thought she saw in the mirror. Sarah proceeds down the hall a little farther, carefully looking at the photos again.

This time she notices something. In each photo there seem to be shadows; shadows she never noticed before. Sarah leans closer to the pictures and notices that each shape has what appear to be faces, each containing blank stares and hollow eyes, standing in the dark.

"Oh my God, why didn't I ever notice those before? I have looked at these pictures every day since we took them."

Standing even closer now, Sarah looks at her wedding picture, and sure enough there are the shadows and the faces. Even Jack's eyes appear hollow—distant, as though looking through her and not at her. A chill fills the air around her and she begins to hear voices.

There are too many voices at once to make out any particular words, just mumbles and laughter. Sarah turns to run down the hall, terror filling her head and body—goose bumps everywhere. Then, the voices are gone.

Crying now, Sarah spins around in the hallway, looking for shadows, faces, anything—but there is nothing. It's only Sarah, alone in the hall with the mirror staring back at her—the reflection of her pale face and huge green eyes looks horrified, as though quietly waiting for something else to happen. Sarah holds up her hands, looks at the palms, and then turns them over to examine the back, looking timidly at her wedding band. It sits on her hand, but somehow the diamonds seem dull, as if faded or foggy, and her hands seem older now, wrinkled slightly.

Sarah walks with her head down like a scolded child returning to his or her room. *It's a bright and sunny day*, she thinks. *I will go for a walk, maybe down to the lake and back.* Sarah opens the front door and heads down the path through the yard.

A poem she heard as a kid keeps running through her mind the entire way to the lake:

> "A mirror hangs upon a wall, where cobwebs or
> secrets or lives may fall,
> Where shattered dreams will litter the ground, the

blood splatter eye catching from all around,
Dead leaves pile up as the wind blows them in, and
whispering stories of evil within,
A sorrowful smile that no one can see, coldness
taints the air with death as it breathes."

Sarah keeps repeating the poem over and over. *What does this have to do with me?* she asks herself. Just ahead of her is the beautiful lake. Lily pads with lush pink and white flowers float along the surface. All the way around, duck moss covers the clay edges of the lake. The evergreens and oak trees provide shade and make the lake so inviting this time of year.

The sounds of the wildlife are the only noises to be heard. Usually these are relaxing sounds, but today nothing relaxes Sarah. The sounds of locusts and crows swirl around her head. Small fish in the lake cause ripples to spread out, and tadpoles swim away from Sarah's approaching shadow.

She sits down on the bank, throwing small pebbles into the clear water, watching them fall slowly down to the bottom. *It's so easy to lose track of time here. The air around the lake is surprisingly cooler today than yesterday.*

"Must be from the rain last night," she tells herself. Sarah sits, looking around at the trees and the shadows, but sees nothing out of the ordinary. For some reason, after the incident at the house that scared her half to death, everything appears tranquil. She studies the trees themselves, looking for faces she really hopes will not be there, and they aren't. She listens intently to the sounds around her, listening for voices of any kind, but there are none. *It is the same now as it was yesterday.*

Vincent Hobbes Presents

After a long time of sitting and watching the sun slowly move across the sky, Sarah starts to wonder. *Should I tell Jack what I saw today? I was awake when it happened. That was not a dream. It was something else. But what else could it be?* she wonders. *How do you explain something like that? How can you tell someone your mirror had the face of your husband covered in blood with flesh missing? How do you tell your husband that you heard voices without him wanting to admit you to the closest mental hospital?* Sarah thinks. She gets up from her lakeside seat and begins the short walk back home. *Time waits for no one.*

She tries to think about something else the entire walk home, anything other than the fact she saw her husband clearly dead, or something like it, in the mirror. Sarah tries telling herself it was just a hallucination brought on by lack of sleep. But even though she keeps repeating, "It wasn't real," to herself, the goose bumps are still there, and the closer she gets to her house the more the feeling of fear washes over her like a wave.

Was it the actual mirror? We found it for crying out loud. It was in the ruins here, like everything else we find. Could it have some sort of power? Was it just as I thought? Is it bad dreams bringing all of this on? Am I going crazy? Why do I see Jack's face like that? What does my husband have to do with this? Sarah asks herself these questions over and over but no answer presents itself.

When Sarah reaches the front yard she suddenly stops, as if a wall has been put in front of her face without her seeing it. The shadows are in the window. They look like people staring at her. *Jack's car is not in the driveway, so it isn't Jack,* she thinks. There's no cell phone reception out here, so they never bothered to get one. And the nearest house is over twenty minutes away. Sarah stands there in the yard, moving closer to the window a step at a time.

She stares as hard as she can, straining her eyes, but nothing is there. Sarah can see everything in the room. The shadows are definitely moving around her living room, in front of the windows, yet she cannot see through the dark images. *But what is causing them? There is no one in the house,* she thinks.

Sarah approaches the front door. The handle begins to turn back and forth, over and over, as if someone is trying to open the door. It's as if someone cannot turn the knob enough in any direction in order to open it. Sarah reaches out just as Jack begins to pull in the driveway. The knob goes still and the shadows disappear. Sarah grabs the doorknob and it's as cold as ice, frosted even. She opens the door and walks inside to see that everything is exactly as when she had left.

Jack walks up the small path from the driveway to the door as Sarah waits there for him. "Honey, are you alright?" he asks her. "You're pale as a ghost, and shaking all over."

"Yeah, I'm fine, now that you're home," she replies.

"Why—what's wrong?" he asks.

"I . . . I just thought I saw someone in our house," she responds.

"What? Are you sure?"

"No, Jack, I'm not. It was just a shadow or something. There's no one here," she contends.

"Just the same, maybe you should wait here and let me

go in and look . . . just to be sure." Jack states, kissing her on his way in.

Sarah watches from the open doorway, feeling flushed and slightly embarrassed.

She waits at the door, watching as Jack walks into the living room and kitchen. He then proceeds to the hall entrance. When he reaches the hall, the shadows come back. Fear wells up as Sarah stands speechless, observing her husband walk slowly down the hall, turning to look at the mirror. She notices his reflection. It is just like the one from earlier.

The shadows follow Jack down the hallway to the bedroom and inside. All the while Jack never seems to notice them. He walks through to the bathroom, strange voices and howls coming from the room, and she hears Jack say something. Finally, he calls out for her to come inside.

Sarah enters the house feeling terrified at what she just saw and heard, not wanting to tell Jack about it; this time out of fear. *Jack is somehow involved in something he shouldn't be messing with, or he's out to get me. I know he saw it. He looked right into the mirror. He must have felt the shadows, noticed it was darker than usual—colder, too. He must have,* she thought to herself. *He was speaking to them. I know it.* Sarah steps over to the sofa and sits down, looking for the TV remote, anything not to give away what she saw and what she's thinking. *Was I supposed to see that? He knew I was watching him, listening for him.*

"Jack, I'm going to start dinner. What would you like?" she calls out to her husband.

"Whatever is quick and easy. Maybe I should cook dinner tonight," he replies.

"No, no, that's okay, really. I'm fine," Sarah tells him as she gets up from the couch. She points the remote at the television and turns it on, leaving it on the Discovery Channel. She walks behind the sofa and into the kitchen. It's not dark in the house yet, even though the sun is starting to move behind the treetops. Sarah wants to take no chances. She turns on the kitchen light, illuminating every corner.

Sarah opens the freezer, taking out a frozen lasagna. She lays it on the counter and turns the oven on to 350°. She then returns to the lasagna and takes off the cardboard covering, tossing it in the trash. "Hey, Jack, does lasagna sound okay to you?" she asks.

"Sounds good to me," he replies.

Sarah leaves the kitchen and makes her way to the hall, turning the light on as soon as she reaches it. As she starts to walk down the hall, she can hear Jack in the bedroom changing his clothes. Sarah stops and looks at the pictures on the wall. The shadows in the pictures are still there. She decides to keep that little secret to herself.

By the time Sarah turns to look at the mirror, Jack appears behind her. She jumps in response to his touch. "Dammit, Jack, don't do that!" she yells.

"I'm sorry, I didn't mean to scare you," he says.

Sarah snaps back, "Yeah, well you did. Jack, I want to go lay down for a little while, okay?"

"Yeah, go ahead," he tells her.

She then says to him, "Put the lasagna in the oven in about five minutes. It will need to stay in for about an hour."

"Okay, no problem. I'll wake you up when dinner is ready," Jack replies.

Sarah turns into the doorway to the bedroom, but not before looking back to see Jack's reflection in the mirror. She just has to know if she will see it again. She does, this time from the back—large places where hair and skin are missing, blood clots making the hair stick out in some spots, and blood dripping down the back of his neck. Sarah hurries into the bedroom, not wanting to alert Jack to what she sees or to what she is now looking for.

She walks over to the bed and lies down, shoes and all. She doesn't really expect to fall asleep, rather just stay away from her husband and the mirror, and hopefully the shadows, or whatever they are. However, sleeping next to nothing the past two weeks has taken a toll, and no matter how much coffee she drinks throughout the day, she can't escape the plain and simple fact that she is exhausted.

Sarah falls asleep rather quickly, and before she knows what is happening, she is out like a light.

She falls into a deep sleep, a much needed one. She starts out dreaming about nothing more than sleeping, but that is short lived. The next moment, Sarah is at the lake, watching herself sitting by the bank and relaxing. The sun is shining through the tree line and she is warm. A few leaves have fallen in the lake, lazily floating on the surface, causing tiny ripples as they begin to slowly take on water, one side at a time, and then sink.

Sarah stares blankly, her mind focusing on nothing but the image of the leaf and how serenely it makes her feel. She sits there, a slight smile on her pale but sweet face, her light brown hair moving ever so gently in the breeze. She leans over the edge of the lake, taking in the beauty of the clear, cool water when her reflection starts to come into view. A sad looking figure with sunken eyes stares back at her, the brown barely noticeable from the dark circles around them—her pale, soft skin looking more like a gray balloon half out of air, dark lines framing her once beautiful features.

Slowly, she lifts up her hands. She sees her hand is the same pale, gray shade, withered and wrinkled, and wants to cry. Her hair is now more reminiscent of an old mop, tangles and tufts sticking out from every direction, dirty dreadlocks of straw-colored hair hanging down too heavy to move on the breeze. The person in front of her is a walking corpse.

Sarah stands up to run; yet, before she can take a step she is at home in bed. Her husband is calling her name from the foot.

"Sarah, dinner's almost ready. Are you coming or would you rather sleep?" he asks.

"I'm awake now, I'll be right there," she answers, thankful this dream is different from the other one she's been having, but it is just as disturbing. *Surely this one ties in with the other one somehow*, she thinks to herself.

Sarah stands up to walk to the hall, noticing she has fallen asleep with her shoes on. She walks slowly to the door, stopping to look back at her bed. She thinks she would have felt better waking up from a nap, but somehow she feels worse, more tired and frightened than before she actually laid down. Shaking her head as she leaves the room, remembering the dream in vivid detail, she steps in front of the mirror. *I have to look now. I have to see.* Her hands appear normal—pale—but still that of a young and beautiful woman—no wrinkles, no gray skin. She can't see her bones protruding through thin, withered skin.

Looking into the mirror, she is pleased to see her face looking as normal as usual. There are no sunken eyes. She can see her brown eyes clear as day, her lips pursed tightly from concentrating on every feature. Satisfied she is not a corpse, Sarah puts a smirk on her face and shakes her head as she walks the rest of the way down the hall.

The lasagna smells good and she will force herself to eat, even though she is not overly hungry. Sarah is not surprised to see that Jack has dished up plates for the both of them, and is already sitting at the table, waiting for her.

"That small nap seems to have helped you a little," he tells her. "You look a little more rested than you have lately, is what I mean."

"Oh, I do feel a little better, still tired, but I needed the nap," Sarah replies with a forced smile. She pulls out the simple wood chair from the matching table and sits across from Jack in her usual place. She picks and moves her food around, creating the illusion that she is eating.

Sipping slowly on the iced tea Jack thought to pour for her, Sarah briefly looks up at her husband, but only when she is sure he won't notice.

"Not much for talking tonight, huh?" says Jack, looking up from across the table, a fork full of lasagna in hand.

"I'm sorry, I guess I'm more tired than I thought," she replies.

"Well, do you want to tell me about these dreams you're having? I mean, it can't hurt and you may be able to sleep better by getting them out in the open," he tells her.

"It's not that easy. I told you I don't remember them after

I wake up. I only remember feeling terrified."

"Okay, well maybe you ought to go to town and see the doctor, like I said."

"Jack, I told you I don't like doctors, and besides all he would do is prescribe me some pills that would make me sleep and I wouldn't be able to wake up 'til morning no matter what I was dreaming. No thanks, I'd rather wake up."

She gets up from the table and Jack can clearly see how agitated his wife is. He knows better than to push the subject any further if he wants to keep his spot in bed tonight. Sarah walks into the living room and sits down on the couch, knees pulled up to her chest. The television is on, but surprisingly Jack has not changed the channel. She knows she left it on the Discovery Channel when they walked in the house earlier. *Surely, Jack would want to see the news, or something other than 'How It's Made'.*

The noises and voices she heard are fresh in her mind again, and getting louder. She is sure she can hear Jack whispering, too. There is a cold chill in the room, and the windows appear to fog up slightly from the difference in the temperature. Sarah can hear voices all around her, whispering and giggling, but cannot completely make out what they are saying. With every voice, she concentrates on looking for one that could be Jack's, but none are.

Sarah watches Jack's reflection in the living room window as he finishes his plate and gets up from the table, beginning to make his way to the living room. His mouth is not moving and he appears normal, but still Sarah cannot shake the feeling of hurt and fear, knowing that Jack has something to do with all the voices she is listening to. *My dreams are a warning, they have to be,* she thinks. Her slender body curls up tight on the couch, trying to make herself stop shaking. She slowly digs her fingernails into her knees, hoping to make her body and mind concentrate on the pain she is feeling, rather than the fear and the cold.

She watches the window more intently, noticing the closer Jack gets to the window, and the clearer his face appears in his reflection, the more the outside wind seems to pick up. The wind is throwing the bushes, tree limbs and plastic garden statues everywhere. They land with thuds on the narrow deck just outside of view. The voices are in her ears, getting steadily louder. They are high-pitched and in languages Sarah is sure she has never heard before.

Jack slowly picks up the remote and sits down beside his wife. He looks as relaxed as possible, flipping through the channels. A smile comes across his face as he sees his favorite commercial and stops to watch it. He laughs every time the people forget what side their gas tank is on.

Why? Sarah ponders. *It isn't that damn funny.*

He reaches over, placing a hand gently on her knee. Sarah looks over at him and once again she forces a smile.

It's dark out now, she thinks to herself. *I slept through the sunset today. Thank goodness I thought to turn on some lights earlier, and Jack, as usual, never thought to turn them off.* The coldness in the room doesn't seem to bother or affect Jack in any way, but Sarah is freezing from head to toe.

With her husband's warm hand on her leg, she concentrates on the voices. She is trying to decipher how many different voices she is actually hearing, praying to be able to comprehend just one. Sarah wants to desperately understand what is happening to her and around her, and why.

Just as she is getting completely lost in thought, she notices the shadows again; the windows inside showing outlines of people where there are none. Jack seems not to notice once again, yet they are right in front of him.

Sarah sits up a little higher on the couch and Jack pulls his hand away as she moves. He never looks in her direction or acknowledges her other than that. Sarah is hearing more than whispers in her head now; *these* are all-out talking, even yelling at times. The shadows seem to move across the room, hovering on the ceiling and circling the couch around them.

Still, Jack sits quietly watching TV, and even seems to be smiling.

He knows what they are; he has to see them. I'm not crazy. I'm not hearing things or seeing things.

All at once, each voice seems to melt together and converts from yelling to a high-pitched, ear-shattering screech. She drops from the couch, clutching her ears, and rolls around on the floor. Sarah can hear Jack laughing at her, echoing in her head, somehow louder than the screeching itself.

A moment later the screeching is gone. Sarah lies motionless on the floor with Jack beside her, his hand on her back and calling her name, a concerned tone to his voice. When Sarah removes her hands and rolls over to look around. The shadows are gone, too. Tears fill her eyes and she can only cry as her husband scoops her up in his arms, holding her.

"Sarah, please tell me what to do," he begs her.

Jack moves the hair out of Sarah's face and kisses her forehead, rocking her on his lap. Sarah just cries, staring into

Vincent Hobbes Presents

nothing. She looks back to the window at her reflection. It is normal, streaked with tears, but there is still the image of Jack—his flesh missing in spots, blood stained and matted hair, just as she saw in her dream and in the mirror.

This is not my husband.

Sarah never answers Jack. She just sits there awhile, for what feels like an eternity, staring at the reflection in the window.

Jack's voice sounds like he is trying not to laugh.

Sarah pushes off Jack and slowly stands up, every part of her body sore from being in a tight, fetal position; not to mention being scared to death and a headache to match. She only wants to take a bubble bath and not come out.

"Sarah, what the hell was that? What happened to you? One minute you were just sitting there, the next you were having some sort of fit on the floor," he says.

Sarah turns back to look at him, her shoulders slumped—her face tear-streaked and tired looking. "I really don't know. I don't know anything anymore," she answers. She turns, heading for the hall.

She walks down the passage, eyes to the floor, trying to sort out what is happening. Hearing Jack laughing at her, and then holding her like that. The confusion and fear consumes her every thought. She never bothers to look at the mirror as she passes by—she doesn't see the woman in the reflection, the spitting image of her, pounding on the mirror. Sarah never notices the screaming as she walks into her bedroom, continuing to the bathroom.

Sarah turns on the light in her large bathroom. As she leans over the tub and turns it on, the wall-sized mirror reflects the beach-like décor, and her tired pale face. The rising steam has an instant, calming effect. Sarah gets undressed, grabs her bath salts and bubbles, and pours a generous helping into the water. The green tea aroma fills the air and milky, white foam begins to circle the tub. She swirls the water around before stepping in for a long soak.

Sarah sits down, first just splashing the water on her, then sliding down to wash her hair. She sits back up against the tub and tries to let the liquid relax her, but every time she touches her skin, she sees in her mind the reflection from the lake. And she cannot shake the horrible screeching. She closes her eyes and places a wet washcloth on her forehead and sits back.

Jack stays in the living room. He smiles slowly as he climbs to his feet, taking his place back on the couch. He looks over to the window, smiling the whole time, before waving his hand at the shadows to go. He points the remote back to the TV and flips through the channels. "There's never anything interesting on TV," he says.

The voices start up again but this time Jack speaks back. "Good, you did very well today," Jack acknowledges to them. "It won't be long now and the mirror will trap her soul, setting you free in her body." The smile on Jack's face widens and he resembles more of the half-dead man from the mirror, rather than the loving husband he used to be.

As Sarah remains soaking in the warm bath water, the woman in the mirror screams and yells louder and louder, but her glass prison reveals no sound. Pounding with her fists, cracks appear on her side of the mirror and trickles of blood flow down her wrists, dripping on the mirror then disappearing as soon as they touch the glass. Her tearful shrieking and warnings go unnoticed by Sarah, but not by the shadows.

The voices start up softly in the hallway and the woman in the mirror can hear them coming for her, getting louder with every second. She vanishes from the mirror, the shadows filling the glass with swirling blackness, tormenting her. The shadows are angry at her for trying to warn what was left of *her* on the other side of the glass.

Jack follows them and the mirror fogs over like frost on the windows.

Sarah sits up in the tub. She can feel something is wrong but cannot tell what. The water is still warm, but only warm. She doesn't quite feel the relaxing sensation she is accustomed to at bath times. The feeling that she isn't going to be around much longer keeps her from any form of relaxation.

As she stands, preparing to get out of the tub, the voices from the mirror begin to fill her ears and, once more, Sarah freezes in place. The mirror in the bathroom, fogged from the warm bath, clears in the cold air that fills the bathroom. Sarah stands there with her towel wrapped partially around her waist. As the mirror clears she begins to see her reflection, but doubled.

Her reflection begins to separate. Looking at her from inside the mirror is an eerie vision of a bloody-looking Sarah holding a towel, tear-streaked face, blood dripping from her wrists. Also looking from the other side is a different Sarah. The reflection from the lake: gray, wrinkled and withered skin, blood-matted hair. But a big smile lines her face as she stares blankly with her sunken eyes.

The images of good and evil stand before her in a last effort to warn her. Sarah closes her eyes chanting, "I'm normal," over and over. Her body shivers with cold and fear, and she tells herself she isn't crazy. When she opens her eyes, the bath water turns red and begins swirling around the tub at her feet. She tightly closes her eyes again and covers her ears, tears running down her face.

The shadows surround the Sarah standing inside the mirror, ripping at her face and swiping her towel. The Sarah in the mirror cannot fight back or run anywhere. The shadows keep her in her glass prison. She stands there, begging for the other part of her, the one still cupping her hands over her ears with her eyes closed before her, to look up and notice her warning, and run.

Jack is there also, on the other side of the mirror, half of his face normal as usual. He turns to face her, the mangled mess showing Sarah what awaits her.

Just as the last drops of bathwater go down the drain, the mirror turns back to normal. Sarah steps out of the tub and picks up her towel. The tub is clean—no blood, no cuts on her, and she is still herself, at least for now. She is alone in the bathroom.

She begins to get dressed, wrapping her hair in the towel. She looks at the clock on the counter. She has been in the tub for over an hour. Her skin has wrinkled from the long soak, but at least it is skin-colored. Sarah turns toward the door and grabs the knob, her hand sticking to it from the cold. As the door opens, she can hear Jack laughing from the other room.

She walks through the bedroom toward the hallway, creeping slowly, as quietly as possible, wanting to know what Jack is laughing at. She listens, but he stops just as she hits the doorway. She walks out into the hall and attempts to make her way to the living room. She hears the voices again, coming from the mirror in the hall.

She stops in front of the mirror, expecting to see the same horrid visions she has been seeing, but she sees nothing. She continues down the hall to the living room where Jack is waiting for her. The television is off. "What were you laughing at? I could hear you all the way down the hall." Sarah asks him.

"Oh, sorry about that, I didn't realize I was so loud. It was just a funny commercial," he replies.

"Why is the TV off?" Sarah questions.

"Other than commercials, there was really nothing on to watch," he says. Jack stares intently at Sarah until she becomes increasingly nervous.

"What?" Sarah asks.

"I guess I'm just wondering if you're really alright or not."

"Look, Jack, I think I may need to get away from here for a few days, you know, try to get my head together."

"Oh, I don't know about that. I think you need to rest and maybe see a doctor about your dreams, but I do not believe you need to leave. This is your home," Jack tells her with uncomforting assurance.

"I know this is my home, but something is not right here," she tells him. "Jack, look at me. I feel like I am going crazy, I see things and hear things. I can't sleep," she cries.

"I noticed. But, Sarah, I really think you need to see a doctor. This is just a house, nothing more, nothing less."

Sarah looks toward the windows, but now everything with a reflective surface has that same image, like a story laid out in front of her.

"Maybe you should try to lie down and sleep. You had a long bath and maybe you will sleep a little easier tonight," Jack suggests.

Sarah gets up without a word and makes her way down the hall to her bedroom, taking the towel off and leaving it on the floor at the foot of the bed. With her hair still wet and tangled from the bath, she sits on her bed with her head in her hands and cries, every inch of her thin body shivering as her tears soak her hands. She lies there, feeling that she is going to die. She can't leave and can tell by the expression on Jack's face that he will not let her. She looks through the crack between her fingers and sees shadows all over the room, even though the lights are on.

She is being watched now, around the clock; somehow she knows this is true. Her every move and every mumble will be reported to Jack and to the beings in the mirror. It no longer matters if she leaves the lights on or not, there is no safe place for her to hide. Sarah curls up in a ball on her bed, watching and waiting, wondering what is going to happen to her tonight. She knows she has to stay awake. *The key is not to sleep, that's when I'm in constant shadows,* she thinks.

Sarah rocks back and forth, humming anything that comes to her mind, thinking about pictures she wants to draw and the places she would like to visit. She remembers how happy she was when she met Jack, how she fell in love with the beauty of this house and the land around it. She thinks about all the places she walked in the surrounding woods, carving out her own little paths. Fear sweeps over her once again. She recalls how many times she thinks she has heard voices following her or something moving behind a tree or bush.

Sarah thinks about how many times she thought she saw something out of the corner of her eye, even asking Jack if he saw that. *How long has this been happening to me?*

"What is happening to me?" she whispers.

Once again, sleep comes for her. She drifts off, leaning up against the headboard. The dreams immediately take her. She is standing inside the mirror looking out, and her house is gone. The mirror is not in the hallway. She can see trees and lily pads; she is staring up from the bottom of the lake.

Light bends and moves with the water and the waves. There is no way out. No one will be able to hear her, or see her. Sarah drifts between sleep and consciousness, catching glimpses of what is supposed to be her husband standing over her. She cannot keep her eyes open; she cannot stay awake. The entire room is dark and she can hear Jack whispering, but not to her. It is too dark now to see where the shadows are, but the breeze they create can be felt all over.

In the dream, she sees herself once again standing in front of the mirror, staring at her reflection. But now she is the one inside the mirror. She pounds her fists on the glass, screaming. Blood once again runs from her wrists, and the mirror shatters. Sarah falls to the floor in pieces, looking out from a broken piece. The withered and grey Sarah, her worse half, stands above her, smiling. She begins picking up the mirror's pieces.

The sleeping, dreaming Sarah can see Jack holding onto a piece of his skin, tearing it from his face, his eyes blackened and his smile dead. He picks up a piece of the shattered mirror and tosses it into the lake, water pouring in. Sarah begins to cry, and all at once the remaining pieces of the mirror are tossed into the air and fall into the lake, the water pouring faster now, turning red with blood.

Sarah will not wake up from this dream. Instead she now remains forever trapped inside her glass prison.

THEY

BY
VINCENT HOBBES

The storm ravaged the four as they traveled the dark, curvy roads of the Rocky Mountains. It was night—late. The storm reached for them, entangling the two couples on the crystal white road. The snow fell briskly, swirling across the road in a maddening fury, threatening to overtake them.

Mike steered his orange, late-model Chevy Blazer cautiously on the ice-coated mountain road. The truck drifted and Mike tugged at the wheel, maintaining its place on the slippery path. His attention ahead, Mike was also trying to collect himself as he drove into the unknown—an unsettling fear awakening within him. *Maybe I made a mistake.* The headlights pierced only a few feet into the dark Colorado night as flurries of falling snow swirled around the creeping vehicle.

"Hey, Mike," spoke his younger brother, Brian, who was seated in the passenger seat beside him. "Maybe we should turn around," he suggested. Brian was three years younger, and his tone was cautious, careful as he questioned his older brother. He held a tiny flashlight, and an unfolded map rested on his lap. "I think . . . I'm not sure, but I think we took the wrong exit back at Silver Springs," he added, his voice lingering.

Vincent Hobbes Presents

Their wives sat in the back seat, behind the two brothers. Both of their eyes were wide with anticipation. They sat quietly, worried and confused. Kelly and Taylor struggled to calm themselves, but they were still shaky. Kelly's blue eyes had long since lost the gleam that usually resided in them. They were hollow and scared. Upon hearing her husband's hesitant words, Kelly tilted her head towards Brian, glad to hear he wanted to turn around as well.

We're all thinking it, Kelly thought to herself. *Mike is so damn stubborn, but he should be thinking it, too.*

Mike finally spoke. His attention was on driving, and in a raspy, almost sullen voice he replied, "Maybe we should. Maybe we shouldn't."

Kelly was growing angry with her brother-in-law. *Typical Mike.*

Mike took one hand and pushed back his brown hair, then placed it quickly back on the steering wheel as they rounded another shoulder. "I think we should continue on. We've been on this road for almost three hours. Why turn back now?" Mike asked.

Kelly was struggling not to shout out loud. She held her breath, trying to relax. *He is so arrogant. Always have to be the bold, older brother, don't you Mike?*

Mike continued talking, taking a moment to look back in his rearview mirror at his wife, Taylor. She was seated directly behind him, smiling as he gazed at her. Her small smile gave him a boost of confidence. Mike then said, "No, we'll find a place soon enough. It's just slow going is all."

"Yeah," Brian agreed reluctantly. "All I'm saying is I think maybe we're on the wrong road."

"And maybe we're not," retorted Mike. "Besides, this road has to eventually end up somewhere."

Brian thumbed the road map nervously. It sounded like popping June bugs under foot as he handled it. "Well, we could always turn around and head back to Silver Springs. We could stay overnight until this storm blows through." Brian was not doing a good job at acting brave, and knew he should not be challenging his brother. He could not help it though, he was scared.

Kelly did not care if her husband was being a coward or not. *We're all thinking it. Mike has to be thinking the same thing, too. Follow your brother's advice and TURN AROUND,* she thought.

Mike waited a moment, the same conflict rolling around in his head. "We could turn around. Yes, we could. And provided we don't slide off the road or get broadsided by another car, there is always the issue of . . . gas. Or, lack of it," he finished in a quiet voice, peering at the dashboard.

The three passengers instantly leaned over Mike, seeing for themselves the steadily dwindling gas gauge.

Mike knew Brian was worried, as were their wives. However, the constant questioning had begun to take Mike's concentration off the road. "At a quarter tank of gas, we wouldn't get very far. So, what we need to do," Mike paused, "is keep going. We should find a gas station or hotel soon enough." Although he attempted to maintain control, Brian could hear desperation creeping into his brother's voice.

Their attention changed focus, and the possibility of being lost, *and* spending the night in the middle of the mountains, made the women chatter loudly.

Vincent Hobbes Presents

"Are we going to run out of gas?"
"I knew it. I just knew it."
"We never should have driven this late at night."
"Yeah, we should have stayed in that town."
"Are we going to have to spend the night out here?"
"We'll freeze to death."
"I knew it. I just knew it."

The women's rippling burst of panic unnerved both Mike and Brian, who always seemed to maintain a certain calm collectiveness in the face of trouble. However, their wives had gotten them riled, and they were beginning to lose their patience.

"Now that's enough!" commanded Mike, his voice authoritative. "There's nothing we can do. We'll just push forward and hope for the best."

Brian, realizing his brother was creating dissent, chimed in, "Mike is right. We'll just keep going. There has to be a town or something in the next thirty miles." He slowly folded the map, realizing it was of no use anymore. He had to have faith they would make it. Brian let out a loud, exhausted sigh and looked forward. He knew the trip was supposed to be relaxing, a long awaited vacation, yet he did not feel relaxed. Not one bit. Brian slowly reached back, grasping Kelly's hand. It was cold and clammy. He held her hand firmly, sighed again, and shifting in his seat. Brian then looked ahead once more, staring intently into the dark, swirling snowstorm that drifted silently down from the dismal skies.

The storm was growing steadily more intense. The Colorado winter winds jabbed and stabbed at the Blazer, as if desiring to push the four-wheeled vehicle off the road and into the powdery snow banks. Feathers of snow blasted at the windshield, obscuring Mike's vision as he slowly pushed forward. The flakes fell from the midnight sky like powdered sugar, adding nearly three inches of snow in the past half-hour.

The minutes went by and became an hour. None had spoken in that time, yet the tension in the car was almost visible. It was dreamlike—an unbearable mimicking of how eager life is to be cruel. The gas tank now rested comfortably on the red dash, teetering on empty.

Past empty.

Mike thought to himself, *This night . . . this storm . . . why me?* The oldest of the four, the man in charge, was drained of all that was plentiful and merry. Usually in high spirits, Mike was frustrated, and a bit scared, although he was careful not to reveal his fears.

Taylor sat behind him, trying to maintain her dignity by not freaking out. Mike looked at his wife in the rear view mirror once more, making brief eye contact. The quick glance betrayed his muddled thoughts. His wife knew him too well.

Amongst the screaming and howling winds outside, and the chugging of the large engine, the four sat silent, frozen. Occasionally, one would take a brief glance at the falling gas gauge, which balanced as if on crooked stilts on the empty mark.

Taylor tried to relax. *Not much farther now,* she thought. *Not much farther until we meet this night, face-to-face.* Her attempts at calm were in vain.

She was past afraid.

VINCENT HOBBES PRESENTS

* * *

The orange Blazer pushed a few more slow miles into the shadowy depths of the storm.

The sputtering began.

The truck began to lurch at slow, steady intervals, finally stalling at the top of a hill. Mike struggled with the steering wheel, fighting it, pulling at it, finally stopping the Blazer gently on the side of the road. The tires were only inches from the depths of a deep ditch.

The four sat in desolate silence, an eternity of hell. Only the sounds of their breathing were audible. The silence placated their fears, although this was only temporary. They knew they faced the open arms of insanity outside the warmth of the truck.

Kelly was the most distraught. Tears welled up in her eyes, pouring down her flushed cheeks. A nostalgic glaze coated them as she silently wished—hoped—prayed to wake up from this horrific dream. Yet, the night answered with a gust of wind, spitting forth its vengeance, and reminding her that this situation was the furthest thing from a dream.

Kelly was a city girl. She had been the only one not enthusiastic to go on this trip in the first place. Now, she was stuck in a blizzard. The simple thought of being stranded at night in nature's powerful grip paralyzed her with fear. Kelly felt as if she would crack at any moment.

It was Taylor who broke the silence. "What the hell are we going to do? I mean, seriously—what do we do?" she asked. Taylor was trying to control her own panic, but she wanted answers. The unknown grew inside her like a constant ridicule to her sanity. "Are we going to have to spend the night out here? If so, we'll freeze to death, won't we?"

Her husband was not blind to that simple and possible destined fate. The prospect of dying within the shadows of a cold, mountain road churned in his mind. He was both angry and scared. Nonetheless, Mike's survival mode was beginning to take charge. He squinted his eyes and looked through the windshield of their tomb. He stared for some time, into the night, and the night stared back. This time, however, it seemed Mike won the contest.

"Look," he exclaimed, pointing into the distance, a twinge of hope in his voice.

The other passengers stared forward in unison, straining their eyes into the floating darkness of the storm.

"What? What do you see?" asked Brian eagerly.

The stretch of time that passed before his answer was maddening. Mike finally said, "Well, I think . . . I might be mistaken, but I think I see lights."

At that mention, all four leaned further in their seats and strained their eyes, looking past the puzzle of snow flurries and searching for what could be their salvation.

Kelly responded, desperation in her voice. "I don't see anything. Are you sure you see something, Mike? Are you sure?" She was nearly pleading with her brother-in-law.

"Yeah, I don't see anything, either. Maybe it's just—" Brian stopped his words as his older brother opened the driver's side door and stepped out into the frozen night. A cold blast of chilly air entered the truck before he closed the door.

Brian immediately looked back towards the women and said, "Don't worry." His instincts were tossed mercilessly out of control, and the women could tell by the look in his eyes.

Yet, through his personal troubles, the man did maintain an ambience of control. Brian nodded his head in approval of his brother's actions, however strange they were, and for the moment, the two women were convinced of his countenance. *Yeah, as if this stuff happens all the time to Mike and me*, he thought to himself with bitter sarcasm. Brian oddly felt a stab of resentment, although he did not know towards whom.

Minutes passed.

The three drew in breaths simultaneously.

They exhaled in unison.

Minutes more.

Then, as they all secretly felt that in some demented, idiotic way the earth itself had swallowed Mike whole, the driver's door opened abruptly. There was Mike, covered in a blanket of snow, cold and shivering, yet not dissuaded by his bizarre actions.

"Well, d... did you s... see anything," Brian questioned, oddly his childhood stutter slipped out—it had been many years.

Mike looked at him oddly and then replied, "Well, it's colder than our mama's freezer, but I walked, oh, I'd say about a hundred feet up the road." He paused for a moment. It was not intentional, for he knew the rest were in limbo, but he felt oddly like laughing. It was like having a joke stuck in your head and it not rearing its ugly duckling head until old Aunt Martha's funeral. He grinned and gritted his teeth to control the laughter.

Mike snapped back to his senses and continued, even though he was bewildered as to why he would think any of this nonsense was funny. "So, the snow is pretty much blinding, but I did see it. I knew it." *La de dah. I knew I was right.* "I saw lights. Looks like a gas station, and definitely lights on at the home front."

Everyone in the Blazer was smiling now. Everyone that is, except for Kelly. She gazed through the windshield, which was solid white, and stared ahead skeptically.

Within minutes, the group had formed a plan. The two brothers were to bundle up tightly and make what Mike estimated to be a thirty-minute trek to the gas station, serve themselves up a gallon or two of gasoline into their red gas can, and maybe grab a thermos of hot joe for the ladies. They would be back in about an hour. *Back in no time at all.* With a little luck, the attendant might be nice enough to drive them back, lowering their estimated travel time to less than forty minutes. The women would be fine, even without a heater, having a pair of wool blankets in which to bundle themselves.

With that, the brothers kissed their wives, stepped from the Blazer, locking the doors tight behind them, and began moving briskly into the depths of darkness—towards the light of the gas station. It was indeed cold, but their spirits remained settled, yet cautious and wary. They walked on.

An hour passed. The women kept constant check of the time, and both Kelly and Taylor began to fidget. They had kept relatively warm; each was draped in a scratchy, yet warm, wool blanket. They shivered more from fright than from the cold. Kelly finally leaned forward in her seat, looking into the abyss, then sat back again. Finally, the two busied themselves in gabbing conversation that the two men would have rolled their eyes at had they sat and listened. Nothing like a little 'girl talk' to keep their minds from wandering and roaming. Nothing better to push away the nightmare.

They remained constant in their conversation until over an hour and forty minutes had passed, and then, like their innermost nature prescribed, they worried.

"They said an hour at the most," Kelly mumbled. She flicked her eyes to meet Taylor's, and then back again to her watch. She acted as if time was an element that she might be able to grasp in her clutches and manipulate. Kelly rocked back and forth. "An hour at the most," she repeated. "An hour . . . an hour . . . an hour."

"Listen, Mike could have misjudged the distance. It probably took them longer at the gas station than he thought," said Taylor in a comforting voice. She, too, was worried, but she also realized that something such as this could not be dependent upon a deadline. Taylor knew that if Mike could see the gas station lights from the Blazer, they would not have any problems reaching it. Both men were in good shape and spent time in the outdoors. The roads would be slick walking, but not impossible. *But still.* "They're probably just taking it slow, having to carry the gas and coffee back," she said, almost as an afterthought.

Taylor managed a smile, trying to relax her sister-in-law. Unfortunately, it was not working. Kelly was simply the type of woman who could not keep rationality intact. Her mind raced for perverted and disastrous reasons as to why her Brian was not back yet. *One hour. One hour. At the most.* "Well, what if—?"

However, Taylor headed her off. "No, we're not playing *that* game Kelly!" She spoke to her as a parent would a child. She had to. Being a schoolteacher, Taylor went back to her roots. Her voice became stern. "There is no reason to get worked up when probably in just a few minutes the boys will be walking up." Noticing the tears beginning to swell in Kelly's eyes, she added, "Do you really want Brian to think you're a baby? Because he will if you don't stop acting like that. He'll think you have no faith in him whatsoever." Taylor then lowered her voice and said calmly, "Don't worry. They're alright, and will be here soon. Just relax."

Kelly nodded her head, wiping away the few tears that had gone astray, and wrapped the itchy, tattered wool blanket tight around her shoulders. Her eyes shifted in constant motion. Back and forth and back and forth, trying feverishly to see signs of life outside the Blazer. Snow coated the windows, as if freshly painted, and obscured her vision to the outside world.

Twenty more minutes passed and Taylor also grew increasingly worried. The winds outside howled ravenously, worse as time passed. It would blow through the pass in powerful bursts that rocked the off-road vehicle side to side. Taylor gazed at Kelly, trying her hardest to assure her that everything would be all right. Kelly sat silent and numb, focusing on the silver watch that cuffed her left wrist. Panic had now entirely set in for Kelly and she simply knew that everything was wrong. *One hour. He said one hour. Damn you, Mike, damn you and your one hour.*

Suddenly, the two women felt a thud against the driver's door, causing both to nearly leap out of their skin. They maybe would have if they had not immediately seen the figure outside wearing a yellow ski jacket. It was Brian, pounding on the window. Kelly anxiously reached over Taylor, pushed the driver's seat forward, and unlocked the door, opening it wide. The rush of wind instantly pounded at their eardrums. The wind screamed an eternity of anguish, like a small child who wanders past the racks of blouses and suddenly realizes that mommy is no longer around. The wind whined, piercing the air as if afraid.

Afraid of what? Taylor thought.

Kelly's face brightened immensely, a great weight dropping from her shoulders. Brian stepped closer, his head leaning into the Blazer, and Kelly's arm shot forward and grabbed him, pulling and hugging her husband at the same time. Taylor slid to the right as Kelly took her spot, helping Brian inside. She giggled loudly.

It was then that Taylor noticed something was not right. *Not right at all.*

Kelly pulled Brian firmly towards her. Then she noticed the blood. He had some cuts on his face and a gash on his hand. *But there's a lot of blood.* Taylor leaned to help and noticed Brian's face had gone stark white, pale with shock. He was expressionless as they grabbed him. With uncanny strength, the girls pulled him halfway into the backseat of the Blazer.

Kelly didn't see it.

Taylor did.

Then, Kelly looked at her crumpled husband and screamed bloody murder.

She grabbed at Brian, who grunted, yet otherwise remained silent. Kelly pulled her hands back and looked at them. They were covered in a crimson liquid. She looked at the seat where Brian lay and saw the pool of blood forming. Kelly began crying loudly as she stared in horror at the man she loved.

Brian began convulsing. His body shook, and white froth formed at his lips. Kelly screamed even more. "Oh my God! Oh, no. No no no no!"

Taylor sat dumbfounded, unable to help. Her eyes were wide as she stared at her brother-in-law.

Brian's right arm had been ripped from his shoulder and the stump was leaking profusely, pouring all over his wife. Kelly, still grabbing hold of Brian, afraid to let go, kept screaming and screaming and screaming. The blood pumped from the pulpy stock where once Brian's arm had been. Fibrous tissues and torn muscles hung from the gaping hole. Protruding outward were a few inches of jagged bone, slanted due to whatever pressure might have done such a thing.

"Oh my God," screamed Kelly again. "No, Brian, no!"

Brian was losing consciousness. His eyes rolled back, and his face was as white as the snow outside. Blood dripped from the corner of his lip. He breathed heavily as Kelly held him. Brian reached his left hand to his other side, trying to grasp at his missing right arm. He kept looking down, not understanding the cold sensation he felt. It was like a pestering itch that he could not scratch. His head bobbed front to back like a newborn baby.

Brian began to cry.

Kelly was completely hysterical at this point, screaming so loudly that her voice penetrated the howling wind and seemed to ripple through the metal of the Blazer. Taylor could tell Brian was trying to whisper something, and she leaned over Kelly, listening. Brian kept reaching for his missing arm. Taylor grabbed his chin and faced him towards her. Kelly could only sit helplessly, still sobbing, holding her husband.

"Go," he quietly told her.

"What about Mike? Brian, where's Mike?" Taylor asked, trying to stay calm, but not succeeding. "Answer me! Where is your brother?"

"Just go!" he managed to say in a rough whisper. Finally, Brian's head fell back and he passed out.

Taylor did not understand what was happening, but she did understand the severity of the situation. She needed to get Brian help. She tried not to think about her own husband as she jumped into the driver's seat. Once again, she repeated, "Brian, where the hell is Mike?"

Brian awoke for a moment from his stupor and stared forward, looking past Taylor and into the night. His eyes were wide as he managed one last word, "GO!" Then, Brian lowered his head for the last time, his eyes closing.

Taylor had seen the fear in his eyes. She did not understand it, but this was not the time for her to question. She reached at the ignition and turned the key. "Please God, just let it start," she whimpered softly. The engine clanked once, but to no avail. She cried. She panicked.

Again, she turned the key.

Nothing. And again. Nothing.

Kelly's screams from the backseat drowned out the big

engine's attempts at life. "Baby. Oh no, baby! Where is your arm?" Kelly was completely hysterical as she violently shook Brian in a vain attempt to understand the madness. She could not fully realize that her husband was dead.

Taylor turned the key again and the Blazer sputtered twice, then caught. *We have a chance. A little one, but we do have a chance.*

Without thought, Taylor slammed it into low gear and mashed the accelerator for all that it was worth; the swollen tires spat ice and rock as the truck lurched forward. Taylor realized she could not see and fumbled with the windshield wipers as she pushed crazily forward. Behind her, Brian was still as his wife held him. Kelly was looking at him in her arms, absolute terror on her face. *Where is your arm, baby? Where is your arm? Please don't leave me!*

The Blazer bolted down the mountain hill, gaining speed while it once again began to shudder and lurch. Taylor knew she did not have much time. She was lucky to even get the piece of junk started, but now it was only running on vapors. The Blazer grabbed up another short hill and as it reached the top, Taylor's eyes widened as she saw *them*.

The Blazer's engine coughed twice, then went silent.

Kelly violently vomited in the backseat.

Ahead of them was indeed a gas station, well-lit and open for business. The Blazer rolled towards it as Taylor sat transfixed in her seat, staring at *them*. The truck was rolling quickly and Taylor held the wheel, her knuckles white. She looked again at the gas station ahead of her. It was bright and three cars were at the pumps, four more in parking spaces. She felt a tingle of relief as she saw movement inside the building.

They were there, in the darkness, but Taylor felt they would make it to the gas station in time. They were in the distance, but the gas station was close. *We'll make it. Someone here can help.* Her relief was short lived.

Terror hit Taylor. As they rolled into the parking lot, she realized things were not right. *No, not right at all.* Shattered glass littered the ground. The hood of one of the cars was mangled, windows shattered. The pumps, under the ominous flickering fluorescent lights, had been destroyed. Trashcans were turned over. She looked inside the store as she coasted the large truck to a halt. Slamming it in park, Taylor undid her seatbelt, but did not exit the vehicle. Inside the store, she saw more of *them*. If Taylor had been able to look back, in hindsight, she would have welcomed the shock. The shock protected her. Her mind was racing unevenly, dancing from one parallel universe of horror to another, yet the shock numbed it.

The boogeyman is real. Don't believe me? Take a look outside . . . ha ha ho ho he he—take me to the funny farm—

As Taylor sat dumbfounded, it was Kelly who reacted. Still not aware that there was no help left for her husband, she understandably wanted to find aid. She rested Brian's head back and climbed into the front seat, opened the passenger door and stepped from the truck.

Taylor reached for her. Her mouth was dry and the words were only in her head. *No . . . don't go . . . they* are *here!* Her hand barely missed catching hold of Kelly's sweater. Kelly, in her haste, left the door open as she sprinted towards the store. Taylor could only watch, unable to comprehend.

Kelly reached the door of the convenience store. The chingle changle of the bell rang as she rushed through the entrance. Immediately, she began shouting for help. "Somebody help! Call 911 . . . something . . . my husband needs help!" She was bawling hysterically. Kelly was in utter panic, completely without composure. She shouted and pleaded to the patrons for help.

It took a moment, but Kelly finally stopped yelling. She became silent.

Taylor watched from the Blazer, horrified, as the *patrons* inside stared back at her. She blasted the horn of the truck twice.

Kelly stood in the store, trembling as *they* looked upon her. Slowly, she stepped back. One step. Another.

Taylor twisted the key, attempting to start the Blazer again. *How insane is this? Only twenty feet from a gas pump. Only twenty feet.*

Kelly's back bumped the front door of the service station. The bells jingled as the door opened. Instantly, *they* were upon her.

Taylor watched as *they* mutilated her sister-in-law's body. *They* shred it to pieces. Then, *they* scrambled through the door, racing towards her. It took her a moment, but she realized the passenger door was still open. She reached for it.

One of *them* reached it first. It snarled and slashed at her. Screaming, Taylor opened the driver's side door and leapt out, her feet hitting the cement hard. She sprinted.

Another scrambled inside the Blazer. *They* began devouring Brian's dead body.

Taylor ran as fast as she could. She passed a stalled car; a

Vincent Hobbes Presents

half-eaten body slumped at the wheel. She then passed the pumps, jumped over a trashcan, and headed out of the parking lot. Then, she saw Mike. Her beloved Mike. Her husband of four years. The love of her life, lying dead and mutilated next to the green dumpster.

She kept running. Taylor bounded across the slick street, running for her life. She ran toward the trees, toward the darkness.

Her feet shuffled and her heart pounded. Behind her, she heard *them*. Taylor gained some distance, but her breath was becoming short. She crashed into the tree line as the fierce howls bellowed from behind. The wind roared in her ears and the branches cut at her face.

Still, she ran.

Farther and farther into the woods she raced. She fell down, got back up and kept moving. On and on, Taylor made her way into the depths of the forest. Into the great Rocky Mountains. In the distance now, she could hear their chaos. She could hear *their* noises. *Their* grunts. *Their* howls.

Finally, Taylor stopped. She could not go on. She clung desperately to a nearby tree, holding herself up as she tried to catch her breath. The forest was dark around her. It was silent. She could no longer hear *them*.

My God. I made it. What do I do now?

Taylor panted. She wiped her sweaty brow.

I think . . . I think I lost them. What do I . . . what do I do?

Taylor began catching her breath.

What do I do—?

Then, a noise—a snarl.

The Endlands

Rotten and rancid—a smell.

Foul and wicked, *THEY* appeared from behind the shadows.

About the Authors

Jordan Benoit ("King of the Jungle")

Jordan was born and still resides in the Dallas, TX area. He attended the University of North Texas, where he received a Bachelor's degree in Fine Art, and has provided his graphic art talents for several literary projects, including *The Endlands*, *Eldohr Adventures*, and *Legends in Time*, as well as produced artwork for other personal endeavors.

Jordan has been writing fiction since his adolescent years, and is one of the co-creators of *The Endlands* and the *Legends in Time* series. He is well versed in the fantasy realm and the majority of his writings fall into the genre. Jordan is also continuously working on his own science fiction universe, with another upcoming project, *The Makhaira Chronicles*.

Jennifer Chapman ("The Best BBQ on the Interstate")

Jennifer Chapman is a freelance writer and poet. She has published a poem for The International Library of Poetry in *Forever Spoken* as well as this short story, published with Hobbes End Publishing.

Jennifer is part of The Freelance Writers Association and is currently working on several short stories and her second novel.

Christina Estabrook ("Glass Prison")

Christina Estabrook is 30 years old and currently resides in New England with her husband and children. Christina has used her love of every genre to push her desire to write bone-chilling stories, using the very limits of imagination to create alluring tales in both short story and novel form.

With one horror novel already published, *Forest Of Souls: The Awakening*, she dove into short stories and created "Glass Prison", a gripping mental ride into the darkness within us all. She has six other short stories currently being looked at, and is in the final stages in the creation of her next full novel *Black Candle*.

Janelle Garcia ("Finders Keepers")

Janelle Garcia is currently working towards an MFA in creative writing at Florida Atlantic University. Her short stories have been featured in *Quiddity, Quality Women's Fiction*, and *The Binnacle*.

Janelle writes from South Florida, where she lives with her husband and two children.

Patrick Greene ("Room 422" and "Into the Small Hours")

Drawings from Patrick's early childhood display morbidity beyond those delicate years; childishly-rendered skulls, piles of dead bodies, and monsters of every variety occupy those early sketches, to be supplemented later by tales of madness and the macabre as he learned to write. But Greene maintains that the real defining moment of his lifetime obsession with horror began with a sneak viewing of the classic shower scene from *Psycho*.

Perhaps it's no surprise, then, that, along with weird fantasy and horror stories, Greene is also a part of the burgeoning horrotica movement, stories combining sexual thrills and scary chills in more or less equal measure.

Film, too, is a favorite medium for Greene's self-expression, allowing him the opportunity to portray usually less-than-sympathetic characters in *Sinkhole*, *A Dance for Bethany*, *Bell Witch: The Movie*, and other films. Currently, several of his original screenplays are in development, including the apocalyptic thriller *S.O.L.* at Chatsby Films, *The Mourning Portrait*, a period horror movie co-written with award-winning filmmaker Paul Schattel, and *Seraphim*, a violent supernatural slasher flick, with Saint/Sinner Entertainment.

All three are slated for 2011 shoots.

Vincent Hobbes

Vincent Hobbes is the co-creator of the *Legends in Time* series. He lives north of the DFW metroplex with his wife, two dogs, and two cats.

Cristin Martin ("A Night in Polidoria")

Cristin Martin was born in St. Louis, Missouri, but has lived in North Texas most of her life. She attended Texas Wesleyan University where she received a Bachelor's Degree in Art, her emphasis being two-dimensional art, primarily painting and drawing. She received a minor in English and focused mainly on British Literature. While at school, Cristin was a member of Gamma Sigma Sigma sorority. She graduated in May of 2007.

"Night in Polidoria" is her first published work. She is interested in writing children's books and hopes to be published in the future.

Nathan Palmer ("Propaganda")

Nathan is an active writer, producer, and co-creator of *The Endlands* and the *Legends in Time* series.

With a love for life, and the outdoors, Nathan enjoys exercising his passion for storytelling. He also finds solace in reading the works of Robert E. Howard, H.P. Lovecraft, and Edgar Allen Poe.

Jairus Reddy ("Thanksgiving")

Under pressure from several authors, Jairus Reddy is pleased to contribute to *The Endlands*, and hopes you enjoy the anthology.

David Stubblefield ("Flying Fish")

David Stubblefield has a history in communication, most of it oral. He served as a pastor for over two decades, and has also enjoyed teaching high school and graduate college classes. This experience gave him additional avenues for storytelling. He has a Ph.D. in history/archeology, which he says has also been good for his 30+ year marriage.

Remember: Agatha Christie was married to an archeologist. She said she liked it "because the older she got, the more interested he was."

David's favorite genre of reading is science fiction, and he loves a story that surprises and makes you think. David and his family live in Texas.

Craig Wessel ("Loose Ends")

Craig Wessel has been writing for over fourteen years. Most of that has been spent writing non-fiction titles in the computer game industry. He has over forty books published, in addition to numerous short articles and website pieces.

Among other works, he completed a choose-your-own-adventure series for Scholastic, wrote a parents' guide series for computer and video games, and was a regular contributor to Gamespy.com and other online game sites.

"Loose Ends", the short story included in this anthology, is his first published short story.

Tamara Wilhite ("Phases of Normal")

Tamara Wilhite is the author of *Humanity's Edge, Sirat: Through the Fires of Hell* and hundreds of technical articles.

She is an industrial engineer, mother of 2 (human) children, and a blogger for the Institute of Industrial Engineers.

For more information about

visit:
www.theendlands.com

For the latest news about our authors and events, or to learn more about upcoming releases and other projects from Hobbes End Publishing, visit:

www.hobbesendpublishing.com